THE ORCHARD

An Adventure of Murder, Betrayal, and Love

dlhayden

ISBN: 978-0-9829364-0-5

Printed in the United States of America

Published 2010 by AAMZ Publishing LLC

http://www.AAMZPublishing.com

This book is fiction,

except for the parts that aren't

Dedication

My wife, Sharon, was the driving force behind this novel. She had faith when convictions seemed to run out, and clarity when eloquence was not obvious. It was through her persistence this work was completed.

I offer a special Thank You to the people assisting me with the final draft; Cheryl, Skippy, Sharon and Lexi. Without their help this novel wouldn't be as rich or rewarding to the reader, or to me.

PROLOGUE

Those bastards! Those damn bastards. If they'd only left her alone, the man seethed. They've killed her. I hope they burn in hell.

The clock ticked, but time stood still as the innocuous and mundane world around scurried along. Isolated and in anguish, events leading to this moment raced by uncontrollably as if a leaf whipped to and fro.

Blurred were acknowledgments from well-wishers. Phony smiles were a façade to cover the anguish trapped beneath the surface begging for release. Condolences from the line of strangers were tokens of empathy, but cheap tributes for a soul vibrant, alive, and extolling warmth. The loss created a rip in humanity and was impossible to mend.

Remnants of the funeral Mass were evident as a processional was set in motion. The lengthy motorcade began its crawl while observers paused solemnly and lowered their eyes to pay homage to a fallen colleague.

Some she knew well, others in passing, although, each communicated respect for a life extinguished prematurely. Many from afar were familiar only with her deeds, yet compelled to reach out and acknowledge farewell.

"I've covered our tracks. That bitch is set to take the fall. She's screwed," the man recalled the exchange by the group that began the downward spiral.

Those touching parts of her life packed the church. Old and young alike, death stunned them with an awareness of mortality. Although the mature crowd recognizes the inevitable, the inexperienced wish to deny this certainty. Before a deadly adversary curbed her vitality, this was also her perception. Quenched unceremoniously was a flame, doused like a cheerful candle burning with vigor.

The Eulogy contained magnificent words to define her life, yet was a shallow portrayal devoid of admiration for an unbridled spirit. Chiseled on a tombstone are the years of birth and death. The space separating the dates depicts the richness and agony of the journey, and symbolizes events, character, and endeavors that personify a person. How we endure embodies who we are. Her path was full of misfortune, but through it all, she remained gentle, steadfast, preserved high ideals, and held to firm convictions.

"If you'd killed her like you were supposed to instead of smashing her into that damn wall, we'd already be out of here," a recollection escalated the man's anger.

We live to believe misfortune won't happen, and struggle to cheat death. However, the tolling bell will chime at the appropriate hour. Children torn from a mother split the world from a caring heart and a loving soul. There can be no human justification for a life concluded that meant so much to so many.

Slower, I wanted to scream. Why hurry the inevitable? Slow down. There's plenty of time.

The measured cadence of the processional wound through the countryside as the crowning farewell was fast approaching. For her final rest she chose a small knoll overlooking an orchard. It was here she became engrossed, absorbed in contemplation, and lost in another realm as the hours slipped away. This was hallowed ground, set apart by nature with abounding beauty.

Early spring brought blossoms that filled the air with a pungent aroma of something newly created and forged. Often she watched the wind whistle through the trees as it plucked petals and lifted them helter-skelter. There wasn't any wonder why she wanted to spend eternity alongside an orchard she treasured. This was home.

She chose a humble coffin, not overstated although crafted at the abbey. Burgundy was the shade, carefully selected and meticulously applied to oak as baby blue silk graced the interior. Draped in a navy satin dress, the contrasting fabrics celebrated her golden curls and she appeared angelic.

"What if she starts to remember? What do we do then, kill her?" a voice capturing the group's intention rang in the man's head.

Inching along, it was evident the overture was closing fast. A funeral tent flapped in the distance as the motorcade approached the corner of a narrow lane.

Can't someone slow these cars down? I wanted to shout. We're getting there much too fast.

The cortege turned into the narrow path to lead the stream of mourners to the selected spot. Farther up the drive, the hearse stopped as my heart skipped a beat when it became evident this moment had arrived. Just a few steps would place us beside a freshly dug rectangle cut deep in the earth. The box holding the body of a dear friend would soon roll across a silvery frame that spanned the hollow cavity, with the stage set for acquiescence to the closing bell. The last formality remaining was to lower the box and forever be ordained to the earth.

Sitting in the front row, furious with the bastards who murdered her, events came to mind that lead to this moment. While staring at the oak box and disconnecting from the sobs of those gathered round, a peace shrouded me as my attention drifted to the moment we met. Unremarkable when the event ensued, upon reflection I came to appreciate how special she was. And, as we became familiar it grew evident just how extraordinary.

ONE

A sign in the coffee emporium was emphatic the shop had been in the same location long before Starbucks or Seattle's Best became popular. The owner of the establishment bragged to customers that national chains had stolen his concept, and there could have been some truth in that statement.

The shop was in a central location, a common attraction and favorite hangout catering to workers in nearby offices as they stopped on the way to work for a beverage or a bagel. Coffee paraphernalia on display chronicled a history of the coffee bean. Pictures illustrated it was actually a seed called a coffee cherry found on a tropical evergreen.

Following a trail plastered on the walls, an illustration showed customers could find the plants in Africa, the Americas, and Southeast Asia. The pictorial illustrated coffee plantations thrive near the Equator, between the Tropic of Cancer and the Tropic of Capricorn, with the growing environment contributing to the flavor. Also shown was how the bean was roasted and ground before reaching the cup of the consumer.

It was in this coffee shop Helen Faulkner and I literally bumped into each other. The klutzy encounter changed my life, and for the better, I must add. At the moment of collision, Helen provided no external gesture to indicate she might have the least bit of interest in me as a friend, much less a boyfriend. She popped out of nowhere, and I later found this was her usual stop over before trudging to the office. For as long as I had been patronizing the shop, how I missed seeing her before is still a mystery.

She glowed. Her beauty caused her to stand out, like someone displayed on a pedestal and easy to notice among the bustling crowd. Later she confided that her curiosity peaked as her eyes fell on me and was as captivated as I had been. But people attracted, often act like there is little interest in the opposite sex fearing rejection.

"I'm sorry, I didn't mean to shove you," I said.

"No, no, it's my fault. I'm the one to be sorry, please forgive me. I'm in too big of a hurry this morning," remarked the woman. "Now look what I've done. You have coffee all down your coat. Here, let me help you wipe it off." In an instant, she grabbed a handful of paper napkins and began to swipe at the leather to eradicate the hot liquid.

"Thanks, but it's really not much. A little soap and water, and it'll clean up easily when I get home."

Neither of us could agree on who bumped into whom, but however it happened, we both spilled our coffee in the process.

"Do you work around here?" I asked. "I've never seen you in the shop before."

"Yes, down the block, at Beeson's."

"Really!" Seeing an opening, and interested to find out more without appearing forward, I said, "Would you like to have lunch? Maybe we can get through a meal without spilling something."

"No thanks," Helen replied. "Maybe we'll do it another time."

She was hesitant.

"It's just lunch," Matt remarked. "You do eat, don't you?"

"Sometimes. When I do I usually bring lunch," remarked Helen. "But, we just met, and I've never seen you before. I don't even know your name."

"How inconsiderate, I'm sorry, the name's Matt, Matthew Walker," I responded and held out my hand. "What better way to get acquainted? At least let me buy you a sandwich so I can make amends for spilling whatever was in your cup. I normally don't ask just anyone to lunch."

Looking at me quizzically, the woman must have been thinking, I wonder how many other women he uses this line of bull.

"No. I really shouldn't," said the woman.

Sensing a sinking sensation that I would never set eyes on her again, I declared, "It's not a lifetime commitment, just lunch."

Hesitating, she thought for a moment, then conceded, "Oh, alright. I'm Helen, by the way, Helen Faulkner. Where would you like to meet, Matthew Walker?"

"How about the deli on the corner?" he replied. "We can usually get served and be out in an hour if time is a problem."

"Lunch for me is eleven-thirty to twelve-thirty. Is that all right?"

"Great. I'll see you at eleven-thirty. Be sure to bring your appetite. I promise not to spill anything."

I admired her shapely figure as I watched her walk away, and felt as if I were floating up a flight of stairs and had finally reached the top step. It was at this moment I realized I had just met the most fantastic person, and she had agreed to have lunch with me. Secretly I hoped this awkward meeting could turn into something more, fantasizing this gorgeous female would be the future mother of our children.

TWO

There were no hitches to impede the initial luncheon and many followed as our psyches began to click. Converging in modest out of the way places, admiration for the woman increased bit by bit with each rendezvous. As our hearts entwined and exceeded anything believed possible, I began to think of her as a friend, not simply a future spouse.

During these interludes, she asked about my background and I told her, "I'm thirty-four and a business consultant that specializes in troubled companies, helping them get back on track."

Later I related living alone. And then I told her, "I'm from a large Catholic family and have three brothers and four sisters living. Two older brothers are deceased."

"I'm sorry about your brothers," she said.

"Dad died years ago, and Mother's in a nursing home. She has Alzheimer's."

"Does she still recognize you," Helen asked.

"It depends on the day of the week," I remarked.

With family upbringing out of the way, we moved on to other more pressing topics. Through failed relationships, I concluded love, marriage, and children were beyond my reach. I felt inept with the opposite sex, had given up on a companion, and settled for being single and living alone. The chance encounter with Helen had shattered all those notions.

Helen was of a small frame, modest in stature with fair hair.

"I'm thirty-two," she offered. "In my first marriage, my husband stumbled in front of a car while leaving a pub and was killed. We were married eleven years, although, he was drunk most of that time."

She related the drinking escalated the last couple of years before the accident. Nevertheless, two children resulted from the union, a boy, Michael, and a girl, Samantha.

Over the next months, we met haphazardly, first one place then another whenever we could steal away for a quick bite. Then out of the blue, Helen took a leap of faith and offered me the privilege of meeting her children. An introduction was something I had aspired, but didn't want to appear forward. The date was set, and I had an invitation to the Faulkner's for dinner.

Nervous? Hell no, I'm petrified, I thought.

I could only imagine how to approach her children after beginning to have feelings for their mother. Although, I wasn't quite sure at this intersection what those emotions entailed. Attraction, mutual respect, or the four-letter word I hadn't come to terms with and eluded me, love.

Oh, sure, plenty of first and second dates had been in the picture, and sometimes a third, but they never went anywhere.

There was no chemistry. But, when I encountered Helen Faulkner, everything changed in an instant.

The day of reckoning was set. Nervous and a little shaky, I knew that somehow I would get through this initial standoff, and perhaps by some miracle come away unscathed.

Helen told me that her son liked model trains, so I bought him a starter set of an HO gauge train set. It included an engine, a couple of boxcars, a caboose, and a fair amount of track, just enough to pique his interest. For Samantha, a Honey Pie Huggums doll, soft and easy to cuddle, carry around, and take to bed.

What? I couldn't do battle empty handed. I had to have something to bribe those little bairns.

Being clueless of the exact route to the Faulkner farm, work was left-behind early. How many minutes it took to arrive at the precise moment was also a mystery.

The journey through the countryside began soon enough, but with the Faulkner home tucked away in farm country, and after a couple of wrong turns, I went amiss. Flat out lost would be a better term. This caused me to backtrack, regain my bearings, and change directions several times.

And then out of nowhere the road appeared, and before long, the house was in sight. For me, navigation never happened to be a strong suit. Luck being on my side, my car stopped in front of the Faulkner home with a couple of minutes to spare. This eliminated my anxiety, as punctuality was a preference.

After this incident, I made a mental note to invest in a navigation system the following day. Something simple to use, and point a dummy like me in the right direction. Ashamed of being lost, I never told Helen about the hopelessly disoriented first trip.

The small farm was plopped on a back road from hell. Although, at first glance, it was a more beautiful layout than could be imagined for the locale.

The structures were humdrum, an older two-story residence configured with a small barn out back used for storage, both about the same age. But the acreage and trees surrounding the buildings provided ambiance to the estate.

With the grass and shrubbery neatly trimmed, the rear of the acreage embraced an orchard, a focal point, and 'twas the time of day the sun was lowering behind the trees. An ethereal glimmer provided a backdrop of sunlight as it passed through the foliage. The magnificent display was a vista of splendor unexpected in the Hoosier heartland. This sight alone made being lost worthwhile.

Carrying a sack filled with peace offerings, I pressed the doorbell. Heard resonating from the back of the house was the scanty sound of chimes, followed by a rustling movement. A little hand delicately tugged at the sheer curtains covering the window. At that instant, I knew it was too late to turn and run, so I froze. The dreaded encounter with little people holding my future in their hands was inevitable. If for some reason her kids didn't like me, this relationship, or whatever it was, would be over in a snap. So somehow, I had to dig up the resolve to stumble through the first encounter.

The door swung wide and Helen appeared radiant as always. The dress she wore was a simple garment, neat and freshly pressed. Regardless, she would look ravishing in anything. Pulled away from her face, her golden locks glistened. Her smile caused me to wilt, and dispelled all uncertainties about the visit. For some reason I always turn to Jell-O when around her.

Welded to her legs were two beautiful towheads, dead ringers for their mother. Michael was ten and tall for his age, while Samantha was eight. If these two got lost in a crowd, God forbid, finding them wouldn't be a problem. Glancing at their mother would provide an exact replica.

As I stood in the doorway petrified, Helen leaned over and kissed me on the cheek, and asserted, "Hello, Matt, welcome to our home. I'm glad you could come. Have any trouble finding us?"

"No, none whatsoever," I lied.

She looked at me quizzically, and remarked, "I want you to meet my children," and lovingly placed a hand on each child. She then pronounced, "This is Michael, and here's my daughter, Samantha."

Bending over to shake hands, I said, "Hi, Michael, I'm Matt. It's nice to meet you. Your mother has told me a lot of good things about you." To Samantha I said, "Samantha, what a pretty name. You wouldn't be able to wiggle your nose, would you?"

Baffled by the remark, it was apparent the child was too young to recall the old TV show about the good little witch with the same name. The children warily clung to their mother, unsure of an intruder invading their territory. Believe me; I understood exactly how they felt.

"Thanks for the invite, Helen. These are for you," I said, holding out a vase of long stemmed roses, yellow her favorite color.

"My goodness, flowers, I wasn't expecting these," replied Helen. "They're lovely. Thank you so much," she remarked appearing excited, and drew the bouquet to her face to inhale the aroma. "Let's not stand in the doorway, come inside. Let me take your jacket," she stated as I slipped out of my coat. "Would you care for something to drink? Tea? Coffee? Or a soft drink, perhaps? How about a glass of wine?"

"No, thanks, I'm fine, maybe later."

Kneeling, I opened the bags that I was carrying and said to the children, "Kids, I thought you might like a present, if it's alright with your mother."

Helen gave a nod of approval as I passed out the gifts. The eyes of both the kids lit up like a Christmas tree.

"Mom, look, it's a train set. Wow! It's electric and everything," shouted Michael.

Samantha had already torn open the box and had her arms wrapped around the doll, cuddling her newest friend.

"I think you made a hit," said the mother. "This should occupy them for a while. I'm going to the kitchen and put dinner on the table. Hey, kids, would you come and help, please. You can play with your new things later."

Without a word, the children left the new gifts behind and followed their mother into the kitchen.

"May I help?" asked Matt. "I can always do some heavy lifting."

"Michael and Samantha set the table," replied Helen. "I could use someone to carry bowls and platters to the table. You can help with that if you like."

The crew advanced to the kitchen and a steady line formed to carry dishes for the meal. While the table began to overflow, the children chitchatted about their newest temptations. Once the table was prepared and a blessing made over the food, the meal began. The adults took their fill, but the children didn't appear hungry. Preoccupied by the newest attractions, they took little on their plates so they could hurry to play, and before long disappeared.

"Your children are beautiful. They look exactly like you," I remarked. "And they're so well behaved. You've got to be proud of them."

"Yes, of course I am, but I'm prejudiced," replied Helen. "Had you known their father, you'd also see how much they resembled him."

"I would imagine bring up two children alone hasn't been easy."

"If it hadn't been for the house and the small acreage I inherited from mom and dad, and some life insurance when Jerry was killed," replied Helen, "life for the kids would be much different. The orchard provides a small income and helps pay the taxes and upkeep with the fruit it produces. Dad was so finicky with that darned orchard. If it wasn't for that, oh well . . . How about some dessert?"

"I'm always a sucker for good dessert. Oh, by the way, the meal was delicious. Thanks for inviting me. Living alone, I usually don't cook. I eat out most of the time."

"You're welcome. I'm glad I could keep a poor fellow from starving."

"Yeah, so am I."

When the dishwasher was loaded and leftovers sent to the refrigerator, popped was the cork on a bottle of Chablis as we sat on the sofa to relax and become more acquainted. A joy to be around, Helen was charming and articulate as always.

"Do you like living in the country?" Matt asked.

"Oh, when bad weather hits, there are times I wished we lived closer to town," Helen replied. "But growing up, I thought this place was heaven, especially the orchard. It seems like I spent most of my childhood under those trees, and had a good time crawling through the branches, just as the kids do now. At the time, I was just trying to figure out how life worked, which was a challenge. When I went off to college, I couldn't wait to come back and spent every available moment there."

"It sounds like you're leading your children down the same path," Matt replied.

"I believe they've grown to love the orchard as much as I do," offered Helen. "Being there never seemed to hurt me, so I think they'll turn out okay. What about your childhood?"

"Not a lot to tell. Our family wasn't wealthy, but we were comfortable," replied Matt. "I went to college on student loans and waiting tables, but that was a good thing, it helped me learn how to be frugal. Last spring I paid-off the loans and now I'm debt free."

"Good for you," Helen applauded. "Too much debt can be a killer."

"That's what I thought."

Holding back, I recognized a change in how I felt about this person. I wasn't ready for something permanent, in particular with someone I just met with a ready-made family. This wasn't my vision for the future. Brought up as a traditionalist, I expected love and marriage to arrive long before children. However, I realized this inimitable situation was a package deal. The children were an unalterable part of the equation, and a faction unable to sever. The arrangement would be a simple all or nothing.

"I've got to get the kids in bed or they won't move in the morning," said Helen. "School, you know."

"May I help?" Matt asked.

"That's a good idea. Afterwards we can visit a while longer," responded Helen. "I'll give you a tour of the house on the way to their rooms."

While strolling through the house, Helen pointed to the distinctive features of the home, the handcrafted woodwork, creaks on certain stair steps, and remodeling that brought the structure into the present century. When combined, these added charm to the old place.

After tucking the children in for the night, we returned to the den, poured another glass of wine, and picked up where we left-off.

"It's getting late and I can't sit here for long. I need to leave soon so I can get home before midnight. I have an early morning," Matt cautioned before the conversation became too engrossed. "How long have you been working for the construction company?"

"Oh the company is into far more than just construction. But I started working there a while before Jerry died. I met Howard Jenkins at a party Jerry and I attended, and sometime later, he called and asked if I wanted a job. He knew all about my education, said the company wanted to set up an inventory system, and needed someone to spearhead the project. He thought I could be the right person for the job. He also told me that whoever was hired would be in charge of the department, and the person would report directly to him."

"What did you think about that?"

"It sounded like a challenge. After I got the job, I've come to love it. So far, the work is great and quite stimulating. It's Jenkins whom I don't really care for, at least not lately. When I first took the position, he was fine. Recently his attitude changed from when I first began at the company. But, of course, he's been going through a nasty divorce, and that would affect anyone's demeanor."

"If you don't like your boss, why don't you just find another job and leave?"

"I keep hoping things will turn around and smooth out. And, I don't believe that I could find another job around here that pays as well. The other benefits are respectable, I enjoy the work, and

I'm good at it. If I worked somewhere else for less money, I wouldn't be able to provide for the kids as well."

"So it's a trade-off? The kids' well-being comes before your own."

"Isn't that what all parents do?"

"I suppose," smiled, and then stood to leave. "I need to go. Thanks for a wonderful evening. Next time is my treat. We'll take the kids somewhere, your choice."

"Sounds great. I'm sure Mikey and Sam will be thrilled."

"And what about you? How would you feel?"

"Yes. I'd like that very much."

I took Helen's hands, brought them to my lips and kissed them lightly. Giving her a mild embrace, I turned to leave and remarked, "I'll call you tomorrow. Thanks again for a wonderful evening, and helping to keep a bum from starvation. Oh, by the way, I forgot to tell you earlier, the view of the sun setting behind the orchard as I drove in was breathtaking."

"Yeah, I know."

THREE

Springtime in the orchard was the everlasting bond that induced Helen to cling to the farm. The countryside overflowed with a natural beauty provided by the abundant colors and smells that were in constant flux. Most of the audience took nature's wonders in stride, all except Helen.

The clean crisp mornings, and warm afternoons, dispersed scents carried on a small breeze to validate a purpose for being. A simple verse provided the rhythmic cadence of the ever-changing folds of nature floating in the air. With pollen carried from flower to flower, and wind whispering through the trees, the earth was at its finest leaving behind any question the universe happened by chance.

Helen's sanctuary was the orchard, as a young girl. Here was a springboard from a topsy-turvy world to a universe of adventure, and discovery that became her anchor. The down-to-earth pleasures of running through fresh mowed grass, the smell of blossoms, climbing a branch or swinging on a tree limb were constant companions.

She could track an inchworm as it edged around a leaf or explore the composition of a flower blossom without fully capable of comprehending the marvels. So many wonders to captivate a child and ignite her imagination as she lingered, immersed in the unfolding of creation taking place.

From youth through adolescence into adulthood, the orchard mesmerized Helen with its natural wonders. She came to depend on these for the serenity and privacy she craved. The orchard became her place of repose, a hamlet to explore the meaning of life and a respite from the hectic day-to-day activities that could steal so much.

A secluded lair was at the center. A sequestered corner where she became lost to the outside and absorbed nature as it evolved. She pledged that regardless of where life took her, this site would always be sacred. From a gangly, all arms and legs tomboyish child, emerged a beautiful, bright, and popular woman, a transformation from a cygnet to a swan.

The ensuing years brought on additional erudition to separate her from this haven, as she returned on breaks from life at the university. Roommates and friends were welcome to share the farm, the countryside, and to meet the parents, but none valued the beauty or became as spellbound by the orchard as Helen.

When away from the homestead for an extended period, upon returning she zeroed in on the orchard for rejuvenation. Making a beeline to the oasis within its core, gear fell at the front steps. While at home, she would spend hours studying and writing in the place buried deep within the grove that provided inspiration. If away for long periods, she could feel the orchard luring her back, tugging at her heart, and enticing her to return. It was drawing her back to the welcome retreat from a hectic pace that life had tossed in her direction.

Graduating with honors, she extended her education with additional study to a Masters Degree in Business Administration. Afterward, many opportunities for employment opened, but these offered to take her miles away from a place called home and the orchard where she had spent most of her life. Here was where she belonged anchored in central Indiana, with a core of Midwestern roots buried deep.

"I'll find the same opportunities close-by as those offered far from the farm in other parts of the country," Helen declared. "If not, I'll plow a path and furrow a row to create my own prospects."

With an advanced education, she became determined to commit those skills for use in a familiar locale. The corn lined roads and bean filled paths would anchor her to a home and orchard she revered.

Soon after her schooling was complete, Helen's father had a heart attack while driving on the interstate and crashed his automobile. Upon losing control of the car, he rammed an abutment, killing both parents instantly. Upon examination of the wreckage, the vehicle looked like an accordion, leaving Helen to carry on alone as sole heir of the farm, with only her beloved orchard for comfort.

As the years past, suitors arrived on her doorstep carrying flowers, boxes of chocolates, and trinkets. By tempting Helen they hoped to charm her from a life in the country, and carry her off to someplace energetic with a life fast paced, loose, and frantic.

However, as a small-town girl Helen was ingrained in the rural community, and knew the names of every neighbor for miles. She loved the countryside, the fresh crisp air, and new seedlings bursting through the earth in spring. She cherished a breeze filled with the smell of corn pollinating in late summer, fall harvest, and the bitter cold and deep snows of winter. She loved it all, from the Ohio to the Dunes and everything in between.

There were many first dates, fewer second or third. She wouldn't waste time on a person she knew in short order couldn't be a soul mate. Helen wanted someone who could be her best friend, confidant, and with his interests aligned with hers. She was in search of that special someone to come forward and make her head spin.

Whoever this person was she expected to know them for a lifetime, not just a weekend fling. Although, if he never surfaced that was okay. A blasé marriage absent profound love was unthinkable, and she had no intention of tolerating those circumstances.

A frequent dream was to marry and have a couple of kids, live on the farm, enjoy her orchard selling fruit. This would be her life, not glamorous, but a life she chose.

Moreover, if she couldn't find desired employment, her focus would take an about face. She would start her own business and work from home. Young, vibrant, industrious, and energetic, she had the drive to scrape and struggle to build a company from scratch. But providence had other plans.

For some time Helen pondered an update to some of the accessories in her bathroom. The shower curtain hung over the tub to prevent water from sloshing on the floor for as long as she could remember. But it was brittle and in dire straits, long overdue for replacement.

One bright, sultry, sunny, Saturday afternoon in mid-summer, on a whim she drove to the local hardware store to examine the newest products on the market. Strolling into the store, she asked the clerk for directions to the section where the bath accessories were situated. It was then she came face-to-face with Jerry Faulkner.

Jerry was the sales representative who waltzed into Helen's life while on the shopping spree. His bright colored vest and nameplate with the store decal were dead giveaways to identifying him as an employee, and Helen asked for directions.

Jerry stood tall, over six feet, with light sandy brown hair. On first impression, she guessed him about her age. Like many men in the age group, his appearance was alluring in a rough sort of way. Disregarded was any notion of an attraction. She was there simply to look for accessories to change the appearance in her bathroom.

He took special interest in what she was in search of by escorting her to the department, aisle, and then walked her to the shelf where the items were on display.

"Just what kind of look do you want in your bath?" asked the clerk. "Plastic? Or would you like something more delicate and softer, like cloth?"

"I didn't know there was a choice," remarked the woman.

"Oh, the old standby plastic shower curtain that's been around forever will do the job. But newer materials have come on the market that give the appearance of fabric, and provide a much richer look. The cost will be a little more, but the change in appearance will be worth every penny," offered the salesman.

Helen was surprised the man guided her to the section with a display of the items she wanted. This hadn't been her experience with sales people up till now. Normally, they disappeared as soon as her head turned. In addition, this person was familiar with the subject of bath accessories, and hung around to explain the pros and cons of each item.

"The acrylic appears to be cloth because it's so tightly woven, and repels water. Here, feel it," the clerk said as he pulled an item from the box.

"That really does feel like cloth," remarked the woman.

"With this system, two curtains are used to straddle the side of the tub. One controls the flow of water, while the bright pattern on the other panel hangs outside and gives a lavish look to your bath," remarked Jerry.

"Isn't that neat," said Helen.

"If it were mine, I would pay the extra and buy the softer material. The plastic has a tendency to become brittle over time," said the clerk.

"That's exactly what's happened to my old curtain," said the woman.

Helen felt of the material again and remarked, "I believe I like the acrylic, also. It'll look so much better than the old curtain, and certainly brighten up the room."

"If you buy the new curtain, you should probably replace the rod. We carry a nice selection that will flatter the new panel. These come in either wood or brass finish."

"Hmmmm, I see what you mean. There's no doubt a new rod will look better," remarked Helen. "But, should I spend the money? I really don't need it."

To make the sale, Jerry remained with the customer to assist her with the purchases. After rolling her cart with the boxes to checkout, he pushed it to her car to unload. Before Helen got away from the store, she purchased all new garnishes for the bath, and received an offer from the salesman to come to her home and help with installation.

Jerry captured her name, phone number, where the farm was located, and arranged an evening to install the products. Yearning to see her outside of work, she agreed to a movie the following Saturday. The man recognized good quality in merchandise and women, and was selling more than just products from Home Depot. This was one babe he became interested in fast, and had no intention of allowing her to get away.

She walked in to the hardware store, but coming out her head was in the clouds.

Have I met mister right? she wondered.

Planning to reserve judgment until they had been out and knew more about him, she had dated smooth talkers before only to later figure out the guy was shallow and their personalities were a mismatch. Some guys show more interest in their appearance than things of importance, and few considered her stance on life.

Helen thought many times, if I'm to become serious with someone, he has to be considerate and have similar interests. I also expect him to have a strong work ethic, the same expectations from life, and he must love the farm and take an interest in the orchard.

Helen's faith was also important. Her first choice in a mate was to marry someone of the same religion. She felt a similar foundation removed obstacles for contention, and made for a stronger union and gave it meaning. The person she married wouldn't have to be Catholic, but he had to associate with some religion.

"Mom always said, a marriage wouldn't last unless God was invited to the wedding," Helen maintained. "A marriage without Him was a house built on quicksand."

Steadfast a couple's beliefs had to align, they could disagree on the denomination, but the person she married had to attend church regularly.

Helen and Jerry's first date was a disaster from the start. He had a flat tire and was late to pick her up, causing the couple to miss the movie. In an attempt to salvage part of the evening, he offered to take her to a sandwich shop for a burger and small talk. But while in the restaurant, Jerry was successful in dropping food on the floor and spilling a drink in his lap. After these incidents, the couple called it an evening and he took Helen home. His only salvation was to laugh and call himself klutzy.

Embarrassed and ashamed of how the first rendezvous ended, he was surprised when she agreed to go out on a second date.

"I'll make certain nothing happens the next time," he stressed.

The second go around was set for the following weekend and the event ran like clockwork. No flat tires, no dropped food, and no spilled drinks to plague the outing. Jerry was the perfect gentleman, and desperate to impress the woman he hoped would mother his children.

Sharing her orchard with a fiancé was a natural extension of a relationship, a first kiss, and making love in the lush grass. When courageous enough to propose, the orchard became the scene for the preeminent appeal.

"Will you marry me," said Jerry.

"Yes, I will," replied Helen, without hesitation.

So much in love with high expectations, the moment was befitting as the pinnacle of existence, and the orchard a proper setting to commence the hopes and dreams of the future.

After the wedding, the couple used twilight to run through the trees, making love often while stars twinkled overhead. Following intimacy they would lie under the branches and talk about what the future held, how many children they would have, and who they would look like.

When they curled up, alteration of the farmhouse became a topic of conversation to put their own signature on the place. The discussions hinged on changes a young couple envisioned for a future family. Looking forward, the couple could only see their prospects as rosy, happy, and financially stable.

The orchard became a home of cheerful recollection where Helen returned often to ponder, as the duties of life took a toll. While pregnancy and childbirth brought on burdens and hardships, these perplexities evolved as a natural progression of moments to cherish, and satisfy the affirmation of attachment. One-by-one when the newborns arrived, they were introduced to the orchard and enmeshed in the intricacies and wonders held by nature.

FOUR

Jerry was as intrigued by the orchard as Helen, often suggesting, "Let's have a picnic in the orchard."

Sandwiches, chips, a few beers, and a party formed. Following the meal, toddlers slept as the adults tidied up, talked about the future, and with youthful vitality, made love under the stars.

Helen drank an occasional beer, but Jerry downed a six-pack without batting an eye. She wasn't crazy about the quantity he consumed, but accepted it rather than create a ruckus. Although he drank plenty, it seemed harmless and nobody was hurt.

In time, this changed. As the bottles multiplied, Jerry hid them from Helen. In the middle of a drinking bout, he switched from beer to Bourbon, then Vodka or Gin straight up. He was slipping fast down the road to slavery. Hooked, he obliterated all dreams the couple had for the family, unless the cavalry arrived to pull him from the muck.

Helen was slow to pick up on the amount of alcohol consumed until too late. This surfaced and became central when the occasional bout turned into a weeklong drunk Jerry laughed off. He attempted to take it in stride, and chalked-up the intake as letting his hair down.

"I'm just trying to brighten up my meager existence," remarked Jerry.

"What do you mean brighten it up?" Helen became irate. "I thought we were happy. We had a strong marriage and the makings of a good life together. Just where did all that go?"

To hide what he was drinking, the binges moved from home to the tavern. Afterwards, Jerry would arrive in the early morning, falling down drunk and throwing-up.

"You've got to get help. This can't go on," Helen screamed.

"What the hell do you want from me? I work my ass off every day and I'm just trying to have a little fun. What do you expect?" her husband struck back.

Although harsh words ensued, these did little to solve the underlying problem. Slowly, a bitter wedge was dividing the couple.

Drunk became the norm, an everyday occurrence that seeped in and affected job and family. Jerry became incapable of functioning satisfactorily in the workplace.

"Get him sober and keep him that way or we'll let him go," his boss warned Helen.

Failing to meet the responsibilities at home and on a farm he once cheerfully accepted, Helen kept trying to intervene without success.

"You've got to get help," she begged. "You're sick. You can't kick this on your own."

Resolute, Jerry admonished, "I don't have a problem. I'm not sick. You people are jealous because I'm having so much fun."

"I'll go with you and do whatever it takes to get well," said Helen.

Jerry refused to acknowledge a crisis existed or agree to hunt for a solution. A vicious cycle, the unending spiral was repeated day-by-day. Whether working or not, he stopped at the tavern, yet somehow managed to drift home to collapse in the yard. From there he'd crawl through the doorway, if he made it that far.

Fighting off his wife to undress him was a blur. Vomiting, the stench of alcohol, and being propped under the shower before pouring him into bed was an impenetrable fog. Stale alcohol permeating his clothing and the acrid stench that seeped through the pores of his skin were companions she learned to hate.

Each day became a rubber stamp of the one before.

"Goddammit, Jerry, this shit has got to stop," demanded his wife. "You've got two kids to think about. Now stop this stuff and get help."

Cursing, heated words and the shed of tears did nothing to curb his behavior. Aware of the drunken stupor, friends begged Helen to throw him out of the house.

"You don't have to live like this. Nobody deserves to live with a drunk," friends told her. "You don't need the abuse and can do better," they would say.

But Helen was steadfast and firm in her conviction. The vows she recited meant something and not taken lightly, for she was resolute in holding both her marriage and family together.

Helen made an attempt to shield the children from the conduct of their father. Unfortunately, that wasn't enough. As the children became older and his drunkenness became habitual, she would remind them his behavior wasn't normal.

"Daddy's sick. He needs to see a doctor so he can get well," she explained.

"But why doesn't Daddy go to the doctor, Mommy?" the children asked.

Without success, she tried to persuade her husband to join a treatment program to curb his addiction.

"Jerry, I'll go with you to AA," she begged. "You're not alone. We can beat this."

Members from Alcoholics Anonymous met with Jerry and asked him to attend a meeting.

"They're just a bunch of drunks," Jerry cried out. "Those winos are worse than I could ever get." Continually he insisted there was no problem. "I can quit anytime I want," he professed. "I'm just not ready."

But, Helen remained true, and was determined to find the person she married. Somewhere beneath the puke and debauchery was the good man she once knew, and would pray for a miracle to resurrect him.

Each night he was out, she stayed awake, waiting and hoping he would arrive home safe. But she dreaded the aftermath. Unable to sleep, she listened intently for his entrance and anticipated the clamor. When the hour the tavern closed extended beyond the usual, she became unnerved. About the time of expecting his appearance, she became fidgety and braced herself for a repeat performance of the previous night.

A stifled echo resounded from the front lawn. The muffled sound of a car door rang through the night air as it closed, controlled, and forthright.

Helen said, "This can't be Jerry."

And then the doorbell pealed and her senses alerted.

"Something's not right," she remarked.

His usual entrance was loud, boisterous, and intolerant of anyone within shouting distance once the bar closed. Upon approaching the door, a police officer stood on the porch.

"Are you Mrs. Faulkner?" asked the officer.

"Yes, I'm Helen Faulkner."

"Mrs. Jerry Faulkner?" he asked.

"What's the matter? Has something happened?" she replied.

"Mrs. Faulkner, we must inform you that there's been an accident," said the officer.

"Is Jerry in the hospital?" asked Helen.

"I'm afraid it's more serious. Your husband's dead. A car hit him as he staggered into the street."

Helen's fears came home to roost. Until Jerry arrived, she was awake with worry, and prayed for his safety. He may have been a drunk and made life a living hell, but she loved him and lived the promises made on their wedding day.

With a funeral imminent, Helen was dazed and the children too young to understand the implications of a father's death. Helen filled her days with busy work and cried herself to sleep. Throughout the aftermath, friends and neighbors pitched in. They attended to the children, brought food, and ran errands.

The long period of witnessing him drunk and the abuse inflicted on the household had ended. But, Helen was plagued with guilt for being relieved of a burden. Her husband's illness was unruly, but she felt obligated to tend to him in the age of turmoil.

Grief stricken his life ended abruptly, she was overjoyed he was at peace and the demons torturing him vanished. The escalating violence had dissipated, and her children were now safe from the heartache that had long been a yoke strangling them.

Alone after the interment, with the house quiet and devoid of visitors, and with the children asleep, Helen reclined on the sofa. She wanted to catch up on reading from the accumulated stack of periodicals. Words were on pages, but these blurred as moisture formed in her eyes. She began to weep, trickles turned into streams.

Tears formed a torrent that turned raucous. Freed, was the pent-up misery clutched too long. Her body was demanding escape and enrichment for the years and ravages of despair. This violent exchange expunged the crippling affliction and permitted her to move beyond the moment. The release would permit a stable environment for the children to grow in love, admiration, and affection, instead of bitterness and the bottle.

To deal with the day-to-day complexities and run a household alone, Helen needed emotional stability. Before Jerry died this was near impossible. As a single parent the tasks would be tricky, but attainable.

She enjoyed her job. A once sweet man, who turned into an antagonistic and hateful boss and grouch, was problematic. Without adequate means to quit, she had to juggle family, job, and the frills that came with these commitments. Raising two children and meeting the requirements of full-time employment were feats she planned to conquer.

To recharge and prepare for the transition, Helen returned to the orchard. A mug of coffee in hand, she reminisced over the time she met her husband, their first date and how it was a complete disaster. Laughing, she recalled the moment of realizing she was in love. She thought about their courtship and the day of marriage, all happy memories.

Each pregnancy Jerry told her how beautiful she was.

As she laughed at his remark, she told him, "You fool. When I look in the mirror, all I see is a blubbery, bloated, blob, begging to eat everything in sight. I don't feel beautiful."

Preceding the heavy drinking and before the tap was turned full force, the marriage had many good times. These were memories to treasure. Somehow, she would sort through the destructive events that led to the ruin of their marriage, and the untimely demise of Jerry Faulkner.

* * * *

Drawn back to the work world like a moth to a flame, Helen craved a better life for her children. As much as she loved her brood and had the desire to spend every waking moment with them, she also hungered for interaction with adults. Refreshed and recharged after the interlude following her husband's death, with fresh eyes she was prepared to tackle the project she'd designed, sculpted, and tweaked.

During the sabbatical, she had come to terms with the horrors faced by an abuser. Sequestered to a corner of her mind were memories of the slow descent that shifted gears for the race to the finish line, and the dark world of drunken stupor.

Mentally prepared, she gave in to the need to perform. She craved a loving environment for children needing comfort, care, and companionship. Determined to build a solid, nurturing foundation for the future, she would disregard the pitfalls tossed her direction.

Work soon overshadowed Helen's personal struggles. Sympathetic to home life, the company allowed flexible hours, restructured workloads to make jobs function smoother, and create a happier, productive workforce.

For Helen, a routine began to fall into place. Throughout the workweek, she helped the children dress and prepare for the day before catching the school bus. After watching them stroll to the end of the lane, she would dash the thirty-minute drive to the office. As a positive example to the team, she was first on the floor most mornings. And to remain current, unfinished work came home for perusal after the children were tucked-in.

Before her homework began, Helen reviewed school progress and scrutinized the kids' schoolwork. The children completed the daily chores without much prodding. She was grateful her children were loving, thoughtful, and brought out the best in her. The Lord knew she had more than her share of unrest.

Thoroughly examined in the evenings were contracts, agreements, and flow charts. She demanded the department remain current with contract provisions and production schedules. Each project had a different personality to accommodate. To keep projects moving and to accommodate deliveries that ran late required adjustments to the schedule. Volatility in certain countries created disruptions. Procurement was there to ensure goods were available as services returned on-line.

Except for an emergency, weekends were set aside for family, shopping, and attending Mass. Recharging her spirit in the solitude and sanctuary of the orchard was high on her agenda. Unless the weather was uncooperative with snow too deep or a hard rain barred her from the peace and tranquility, she trekked to her favorite place often. She watched the children at play running through grass, the color depending on the season, or swinging upside-down from a tree branch.

In winter, favorites were building a snowman, constructing a snow fort, or to have a snowball fight. Sometimes, simply sledding across the fluffy white was a necessity. Like Helen, her children became involved with anything that challenged a fertile imagination.

Sometime while they played, Helen cleared her mind, attempting to make sense of her many responsibilities. Resurrected was the occasional memory of her husband. These conjured up distasteful thoughts of mopping puke and the mess that followed. The grief and misery brought on the household was hard to forget. Guilt hovered in the air.

Could I have done something different to change him? she often asked herself. Was there anything I should have done that would make a difference in his behavior?

But, on the other hand, she was thankful the drinking, and vomit, and violence were behind her. These were no longer a part of her life and she didn't like to focus on them. Grateful the burden was lifted, he was now relieved of an illness that abducted his soul. Paid with many lives was a cold levy, caused by a selfish sickness that lasted too long and immeasurable to calculate.

Feelings of remorse were a constant, and to place these on the backburner was difficult. But to move on, Helen had to come to terms with the undeniable truth that death provided consolation, and was the only cure for a disease that swindled a portion of her life.

Being young, Helen perceived someone, someday, might show an interest in her.

I met a fellow named Matthew Walker, she thought. He's rather handsome.

The couple had been out a few times, and started to become acquainted. Mister charming caused her heart to flutter and took her breath away. Their get-togethers were fleeting, but right-off she recognized he was special. He seemed like a good man with a good heart, who could make a good male role model for her children. She believed this was something they sorely needed.

Regardless of what materialized, booze wouldn't play a role in a relationship no matter how appealing Prince Charming. At the forefront of observing someone self-destruct and deteriorate into oblivion, was the unbearable reminder the effect alcohol played to consume someone predisposed to the drug. Combine this with a firsthand image that alcohol played to destroy those around the alcoholic, and she became steadfast.

Being drunk will play no part in my future, she thought, or that of the children.

She was determined the nightmare wouldn't affect Michael and Samantha again. All the signs were there with Jerry, but she chose to overlook them.

"There will be no second go-around to re-live a similar experience. Married to a drunk once was enough for eternity," she mumbled. "We've done more penance than necessary for the sins we'll ever commit."

Helen's first priority was faith and family. Employment at a company she thought was a dream job was next on the list, regardless of the boss's current state.

"With minimal contact, I'll tolerate his bad attitude," she remarked off-handedly.

Devoted to Sam and Michael, she never missed a school function or celebrating a birthday or any occasion set-aside on the calendar. Ground Hog's Day, Valentine's Day, Halloween, All

Saints Day, or any other reason she could dream up was fair game.

Allowed freedom to work as the job mandated, with demands balanced against other commitments, she had the best of both worlds. Appreciative of her employer, she was cognizant that many women would kill for that kind of package.

Like a mother tiger with her cubs, she protected her position.

A dozen people would like to fill my shoes, she often thought. But I'll make myself so valuable the company wouldn't consider replacing me with someone of inferior skills or lesser pay.

Beeson International was Helen's employer, a conglomerate with jobs in national defense, energy, construction, and other services brewing around the world. The company worked for the U. S. Government and a number of other countries circling the globe. Ironically, it formed a study group to consider projects that could take place on the moon. At this juncture, the unit was ineffective in finding an approach to make them profitable.

Helen was the head of a department called Procurement. This small section had the responsibility for vendor material and supplies showing up on the worksite just in time. A proviso strictly enforced, meant neither one-day early nor late. Due to the efficiencies of the sector, the company saved billions by eliminating an inventory that fast became outdated, and obsolete. Reduction in labor needed to handle and restock materials was a side benefit.

After Howard sought out Helen for the position and saw her credentials, he hired her on the spot. He explained he needed someone with a fresh perspective from outside the company to fill it.

Helen initially designed and streamlined the system between supplier and jobsite to make the configuration flawless. The process became as simple as palms placed together and fingers threaded.

Bumps arose in due course but the system smoothed out and matured as soon as participants understood their roles. A slight kink would cause Procurement to jump, as these folks were empowered to untangle the mess and keep the flow moving.

Lack of goods at a worksite could shut it down, and escalate costs that would mount into the millions. Stopping a project, and then to bring it back on board created overhead in hours and dollars. Due to familiarity with the system, and designer of the process, Helen could pinpoint a procedural change instantly.

Awarded top dollar were suppliers demonstrating the ability to provide goods and services without excuses. As a rule, the lowest bid never got an order. Helen was a bargain hunter, but the best bargain was the ability to deliver products on time. This was far more important than shaving a few dollars off the front end.

Helen's duties made her aware of every agreement and placed her in the position to call each contractor by name. A priority existed for vendors to work together within the framework of the system. When something cropped up that affected a project, Procurement was tenacious and followed the trail to decipher what happened, where the holdup was, and which department placed the order. Questionable answers could cause a stoppage in the flow of cash until the department was satisfied payment was due. Helen, and the small band of co-workers she corralled, was responsible for goods showing up on jobsites and timed to keep production flowing.

"Do you have any idea what this check for one hundred thousand dollars is for?" asked Eve Blankenship, a woman who reported to Helen. "The vendor is Benson Consulting."

"That's a new one," replied Helen. "No, I don't recall the name. Who signed the request?"

The company issues a multitude of checks. After an initial set-up in the accounting system, payments to a vendor were on terms of the contract. Additional funds disbursed were by check request, with documentation completed with receipt of the purchase order or invoice. However, in every case a manager signed-off on the disbursement. Without authorization on file, the check writing process slowed and materials or services derailed until legitimacy resolved. Solving the problem before remittal of funds was preferable.

In this instance, a check came to Procurement for verification because of an ambiguity. With authorization illegible, somewhere in the process the system became impaired, and the fix fell on Procurement.

FIVE

"The signature's all scribbled. I can't make out the name," Eve commented, "or what department it came from."

Eve was Helen's second in command. She worked side-by-side with her boss from the beginning, and knew the program inside and out.

"How about a contract, or maybe there's a separate order?" asked Helen. "Could somebody have pre-authorized it?"

Eve shook her head warily. "If there's any paperwork for these people it's not in the system," remarked Eve. "Or, maybe I just can't find it? But that would be unusual. I can generally put my hands on any document."

Two years earlier Beeson switched document storage from maintaining paper originals in filing cabinets, to a paperless system. The newer system allows images stored electronically in a Portable Document Format, or PDF file. The electronic storage is offsite and away from the company, readily accessible through computer terminals by authorized users.

Sorting, filing, and searching became effortless. Proven was the cost for the system, justified through reduction in overhead and quicker retrieval of documents.

With a paper filing system, documents are stored by hand and sensitive items were frequently misplaced. In time, this proved detrimental to Beeson and helped justify the system.

The system provided better organization, eliminated rooms of filing cabinets, and recovered floor space for needed offices. These efficiencies promptly realized dividends from the transformation.

"Did you check with the people in scanning? Maybe the contract hasn't been processed," Helen suggested.

The current system tags a document with a bar code at the point of entry to the company. Once marked, a department holds the instrument, and then it's retrieved when scheduled. In essence, tracking a document begins from the moment of arrival until available for viewing. The scanning department takes pride in the goal that images were available for viewing within twenty-four hours the tracking number appends to a document.

"Been there, done that. No record of any kind for this company is in the queue for processing," Eve responded.

"I suppose I'll have to go ask Howard. Maybe he knows something that we don't," Helen replied.

"You'd better take a Valium before you go see the little prick. He hasn't had sex for so long he might jump your bones while you're with him," commented Eve.

"I can take care of myself," Helen assured the coworker.

"He's getting meaner and grumpier by the day," said Eve. "If he gets laid, he might mellow."

Howard Jenkins is Chief Financial Officer, or CFO, for Beeson, and the organizational chart showed Procurement reporting directly to him. He'd been with the company since its infancy, and long before going public. Through Howard's machinations, the company has been instrumental in a wave of successes. But recently stockholders have become disillusioned with profits taking a dive.

Smiling at Eve's comment, Helen chimed-in, "Now be nice. But then again, I don't believe there's any need to worry. He's still so mad at his ex-wife after the divorce, he probably couldn't get it up if he wanted."

When Helen was hired, Howard was pleasant, easy going, even-tempered, and jocular. He told her he wanted the position filled by someone young, energetic, and, "tough enough not to take shit off anybody."

Howard also said she had to learn quickly to handle herself against the company's rough vendors.

"You will have to grow brass balls," Howard remarked, "and make decisions on the fly, for you'll be responsible for keeping products flowing or the inventory project will be shut down. If that happens, and this new concept doesn't work, the company could go belly up and we'll all be out of a job."

Howard, with his new fangled ideas and innovation was the driving force that brought Beeson to be a behemoth. Shrewd, cunning, masterful, calculating, and a risk taker were just a few of the adjectives of how people in the industry described his business acumen. But since his divorce, his attitude toward the company changed and not for the better. He was bitter, resentful, and spewed venom on anybody that got in his path.

Deserting while he was out of town, his wife pilfered an ample quantity of possessions accumulated during the marriage, as the divorce wasn't amicable. It became a bitter split by a couple who had made the usual promises. While their heads evoked endorphins to allow young bodies to feel good, their eyes glazed over with lust. These delightful feelings dissipated, and soon replaced with a contest of who hated whom and how each could make the other pay.

This resulted in Howard exuding a harsh, caustic, and abrasive exterior to those he came into contact. The only exception was the attitude toward his colleagues in the Ivory Tower, as employees referred to the top floor of the Beeson building.

Early on Helen enjoyed working with Howard, and learned from him for he was her mentor. In his present state, though, he had such a terrible disposition and was so impossible to reason with, underlings gave him a wide berth.

When spotted, the person would make a U-turn and go out of the way to avoid an encounter. Due to his moodiness and corrosive personality, Helen's attitude toward him was tainted. Whenever a reason surfaced to interact with her boss, she cringed. Formerly an avid supporter, she became uncomfortable and her skin crawled being in his presence.

The abrupt change in personality made her feel like she didn't want to be near the man, much less work under his tutelage. But, Helen considered herself a professional. She was determined to keep her projects on track, even if it meant an occasional interaction with a tyrant.

Entering the elevator, Helen waited patiently until the car stopped on the top floor. She strolled slowly to Jenkins' office, knocked on the door, and heard his deep gravely voice barking her inside.

Howard had dark, well-trimmed thick hair, when Helen was first hired. It had now turned thin and white. He let his hair grow and it seemed to have a mind of its own. Poking out in all directions, he badly needed a trim.

Now, the stubble covering his face reflected remnants of an undeterminable days of failing to shave, a frown his constant companion. These were newly acquired accoutrements by someone no longer concerned with appearances.

From behind the desk, piled high with papers and books, peeked a surly man. The stacks of materials around his desk appeared haphazard, although he claimed to know the location of every document. An office that once was immaculate now looked like a dump, and Helen felt dirty just entering the room.

"What the hell do you want?" Howard barked.

Not one to dally given the uneventful circumstances of the encounter, with his attitude making her nervous, she answered hastily. "We've come across a one hundred thousand dollars check that was intended for the mail, but luckily we caught it."

"Why the hell are you telling me about it? Last time I looked that's your department," Howard snapped.

"There's no documentation, and we can't figure out where it originated. Do you know something about it, or do you have any idea where it came from?" asked Helen.

"What's it for, anyway?" scoffed Howard.

He sat and stared vacantly at Helen, showing no reaction. He then suddenly snapped at her, "Who's the goddamn check made out to?"

"It's to a company called Benson Consulting. We've never heard of them," said Helen. "It was to have been sent to a post office box in Atlanta, Georgia, although this could be a drop box."

A drop box is a central depository companies use to collect payments.

"I've done a Google search and couldn't find the name listed on the web. I don't understand why it wouldn't show up, unless the company is a startup and too new for a hit. But, if that's the case, why are we doing business with an unproven source?"

"Just leave the damn thing on my desk, and I'll check it out," demanded Howard. "I'm sure there's a goddamn good explanation. Somebody approved it or it wouldn't have printed. That's the way the system works. I'll figure out who did it, and which department it goes to."

Helen turned to leave, and over her shoulder commented, "In the meantime I'll just void the check before it gets lost. We'll reissue it later."

Howard jumped to his feet and growled, "NO! God-dammit, I said I'd look into it," his face turning crimson.

Shocked by the abrupt, and scathing reaction to her suggestion, Helen did an about face dropping the check on his desk. She was surprised by the backlash. His normal response would be to accept her recommendation through a wave of his hand. In due course, he came to trust her judgment and if he objected, would provide some logic, but not now, not this time.

"All right, if that's what you want," Helen yielded. "Tell me if you find out what's going on. We'll know how to handle this situation if it comes up again," Helen said.

He's such an asshole anymore, she thought.

Leaving Howard's office, she realized the hour was late. Helen trudged back to her cubicle to straighten her desk before ending the workday. Her organizational skills had developed early, and she considered it abhorrent to arrive in the morning to face an office in disarray. With a clean desk policy established for her department, passing through, she did a cursory inspection of the area.

The other team members were gone, so she quickly picked up, put up, and darted through the door and down the staircase for home. She took the stairs because this was faster than waiting for a slow elevator ride.

In a normal evening, work would go home with her. But tonight she was looking forward to dinner out with Matt. With a relationship still fresh, she couldn't allow business to intervene. Besides, there was nothing urgent expected to arise that couldn't wait until morning. For something critical, her cell phone was always on.

Scurrying down the stairs empty handed, the door slammed behind her, and before reaching the first landing the stairwell turned black instantly.

"Damn!" she cursed. "The light's gone out."

"Hey is anybody there?" she yelled. "The lights are out."

Silence, no answer, she couldn't see a hand in front of her face, but heard a slight shuffle, and yet couldn't make out where the sound originated.

She shouted again, "Is somebody there? I can't see. It's dark in here."

She listened intently, still no response. Turning, she hugged the stair rail as if a lifeline, and reached for the wall for stability. She began to feel her way towards the door she came through and ascended the steps. Her plan was to return to her desk and report the problem to maintenance. Calling Matt and tell him she would be late was a thought, but decided to wait until she reached her desk where she would have light, and the cell phone reception was better.

It's odd the emergency light didn't come on when the power went out, she thought.

Arriving on the top step, she fumbled for the doorknob. Something latched onto her leg and she jumped, trying to pull free. Surprise, she cried out, "Youch, who's there?" Again, she struggled to pull her leg free without success. Something struck her knee making her wobbly, and caused her to lose balance. She toppled uncontrollably head first down the flight of steps.

As she fell, she reached out, groping in the darkness to catch something that might stop her fall. Useless, the plummet continued until her head smacked the concrete wall below. Barely cognizant, she heard feet shuffle and felt someone press against her. A voice whispered in her ear.

What did you say? She thought. I don't understand.

The mumbled words turned to mush as the world faded to black.

* * * *

Through bleary eyes, Helen looked cautiously about the room when she roused, and attempted to digest where she was. Everything in view was a blur and out of focus. Noises emanating from the background were foreign and unfamiliar.

Where am I? She wondered. What is this place?

After blinking several times to clear her eyes, she thought, I've got to be in bed. But where, and better still, why.

Accepting she wasn't in her own bed, she glanced about and spotted a rectangular box attached to a pole with fuzzy illuminated numbers. A stream of jagged blips moved haphazardly across a small screen. A bag hung overhead releasing a liquid that descended slowly through a clear narrow tube, disappearing under the blanket covering her. She flexed her hands and arms, and moved her legs.

Man that feels good, she thought.

Her head was throbbing, and with a free hand, she reached up and realized some type of bandage was around it.

What am I doing here? She wondered, trying to remember. How did I get here?

Her last memory was from the office. Everything that followed was blank. She couldn't grasp the unfamiliar bed, why her head was hurting and bandaged, or why she was tethered to gadgets parked around her.

Why is everything so blurry? she thought. Why am I here? And what is this place?

The recent past escaped her, and short-term memory was elusive. She tried in desperation, to summon a recollection but unable to do so. The last thing recalled was talking to a co-worker, whenever that could have been. Attempting to decipher the day or time was an impossibility. Questions were easy to dispense, answers unattainable.

Out of the corner of her eye something moved. A figure stood and walked from the shadows to cross the floor. She was disconcerted that someone hid in the recesses of the dimly lit area as the form ambled to her bedside.

"Hello, Helen. Do you remember me?"

Helen stared intently, blinked a number of times to clear her sight and gazed at the intruder with protracted curiosity.

"Of course I know who you are, silly. Why would you ask that?" said Helen. "Why shouldn't I know you, Matt?"

Reaching over, Matt picked up an unrestrained hand and squeezed.

"The doctors weren't sure who you'd recognize or what you'd remember when you came around," responded Matt. "I'm just happy to see you're awake."

Matt appeared scruffy and unshaven. He wore jeans and a knit shirt, both wrinkled and looked as if they were in the dryer long after the spinning cycle stopped. His eyes were puffy, his hair ruffled, and he looked like he'd been dozing.

The touch of his hand on hers was comforting and revived feelings of something pleasant. This assured her that whatever happened, he would make it better.

"What happened to me?" she asked. "Where am I and what am I doing here?" she persisted.

"Well, you had . . ." Matt tried to respond.

"And, how did I get here," Helen continued. "How long have I been here?"

"You've been here . . ." began Matt.

"Where are my children? I wish someone would tell me what's going on." She continued. "Could I have a drink of water? My throat's awfully dry."

Gushing like an open spigot, Matt was unable to answer in the staccato manner questions were fired. Topics spewed forth but Matt was unable to respond.

"Wait a minute. Hold on. I'll have to check with the nurse about the water," Matt said. "As soon as I get back, I'll answer all your questions, but you've got to slow down. One question at a time, okay?"

Matt retreated and turned to fetch the attendant as she appeared from nowhere.

"Well, hello miss sleepyhead. You finally decide to wake up. We were starting to worry about you."

The nurse on the shift was a thin, matronly woman with silver hair and a boyish bob. An identification badge imprinted with her picture and the name, Gerty, hung from the pocket of her scrubs. She had retired from a stint in the military and working on a second pension with this hospital, assigned to ICU for many years.

Strolling smoothly across the floor, she pressed buttons on machines monitoring the patient, and simultaneously ascertained calibrations were accurate.

"May I have some water? My mouth is dry as a bone," Helen begged.

"Let's start with some ice chips," the nurse countered as she continued to punch buttons and responded to the patient while she worked. "If those stay down, you can have some water. Are you getting hungry? We can try some Jell-O. No solid foods yet, I don't want to overload your stomach. You haven't eaten since you arrived."

"No, thanks, I'm not hungry, just dying of thirst. I could use something for a headache," responded Helen. "My head is killing me. How long have I been here, by the way?"

As the nurse pushed buttons and checked lines, she carefully chose her words, and offered, "Let me get you something for pain, and then we'll talk."

While the nurse was out of the room, Helen held her head in pain, disinterested in talking to anyone.

"Do you remember anything about what happened?" the nurse asked upon her return.

"No, everything is a blank," Helen groaned. I'm in a hospital, but can't recall why or how I got here. The last thing I remember is being at work, and now I'm here in this bed. How did that happen?"

The nurse picked up a chart and read the notes. "You apparently fell in a stairwell of your office building and were brought to the hospital. You were unconscious on arrival, and admitted for a concussion."

"Gosh, I don't remember anything. Can anybody tell me what happened?" asked Helen.

"Somehow you tripped," replied Matt. "You must have fallen pretty hard."

"Your condition was touch and go for a while," continued Gerty. "The doctor that diagnosed you wasn't sure you'd wake up. Now that you're conscious and alert, your prognosis looks good."

"Was I out for long?" Helen asked.

"The concussion caused your brain to swell, and when this subsided you woke up," responded the nurse. "During this time your body was healing." Pointing in Matt's direction, she added, "I'll let your friend tell you about the mishap. He probably knows more than I do."

Helen felt her head spinning by the nurse's comments. She looked to her friend, and asked, "Matt, what's going on?"

Matt stepped forward and sat on the side of the bed. He picked up Helen's hand, and began the tale of what he knew about the mishap.

"The night watchman found you on the landing on the stairs while making rounds. He said it looked like you tripped and fell, and must have hit the wall fairly hard. A huge knot was on your forehead when you arrived at the emergency room," Matt explained.

Helen was at a loss and couldn't recall anything except a conversation with Eve, remembering nothing about a face-to-face confrontation with a wall. She looked quizzically at Matt, struggled, and made an attempt to digest the story he was telling, and asked, "Just how long have I been here?"

Matt paused before replying, "You've been unconscious for two days. The doctors have done about every test imaginable, but so far they have been unable to find anything except that you had a concussion."

"Is that all?" asked Helen. "No broken bones or internal injuries?"

"That was enough to concern them. I'd say you were extremely fortunate. As hard as you hit the wall, indications were your life was in jeopardy and could have died. Somehow that was averted," asserted Matt.

"Thank God for that," replied Helen.

"The doctor confided that as long as you slept the chances improved for the swelling to recede. Then you would have a fighting chance for improvement," continued Matt.

"Looks like they were correct," said Helen.

"Although, it's unclear if you'll have any long-term effects from the fall," said Matt. "I'm just glad you're back among the living."

Helen stared at Matt as if in a fog and replied, "Even after telling me what went on I don't remember any of it, and wonder how it happened."

"Like I was told, the guards speculate that somehow you tripped on a step," said Matt. "Your guardian angel must have been watching over you, or the fall would have been more serious. It could have been a real disaster. You're lucky."

"You keep saying that, but I don't feel lucky. I'm sore and I've lost two days of my life that I don't know a thing about," replied Helen. "That bothers me."

Confused and struggling, Helen tried to dredge up the incident. "Where are Michael and Samantha?" she asked. "Where have they been all this time, and who's been watching them."

"They're with me. I've been sleeping over at your house. I hope that's okay," replied Matt. "They're with the sitter, now. If you agree, I'll stay with them until you get home and on your feet."

"I'm glad you were there for them. They were probably scared to death, the poor things," reflected Helen. "It hasn't been that long ago they lost their father. Thanks for being there."

"You're welcome. Now that you're awake, the kids will be excited to know you're okay," remarked Matt. "They will be happy to see you. They're in bed by now, since it's so late. But, I'll bring them to visit tomorrow."

"Oh, I can't wait to see them," chimed in Helen. "I miss them so much,"

"It's getting late, and the sitter needs to get home. She has school tomorrow, you know, so I'd better go. I'll bring the kids by after work," promised Matt. "Get some rest."

Helen stretched and moved around in the bed to get comfortable and remarked, "I am tired. Kiss the kids for me, will you?"

"You bet," Matt answered, while leaning over pecking her on the forehead. "Welcome back, stranger. Now, go to sleep. I'll see you tomorrow. Oh, I forgot to tell you, you look gorgeous, and I love you."

"Yeah, I can just imagine what I look like. Thanks anyway. I love you, too."

* * * *

Matt walked from the room and flipped the switch to the overhead light as Helen settled for the night. Although quite fond of Mike and Sam, knowing that their mother was no longer unconscious and on the mend relieved his mind. The big question nagging him was how he would provide for two small children for the long haul if they were not his own. If Helen's absence extended much longer, he realized Child Protective Services and a judge would become involved with the children's fate.

He was overjoyed she was awake and would be coming home soon. By then, maybe life would return to normal. He had no experience at being a parent and no legal authority to care for the children, but loved them just as if they were his own. Through this disaster, he came to realize how much he cared for their mother. But still he wasn't a parent, just a temporary surrogate.

* * * *

As Matt ambled from ICU, Helen was awake trying to recall what took place. She attempted to conjure up an image and fit the puzzle together.

To make sense of what Matt and the nurse had told her about the tumble and the hospital was impossible. To imagine being in a coma for the past several days was unthinkable. Wrestling with her memory, the pieces just didn't fit.

If someone else had concocted a story like this, she would have called them nuts and said it was a tall tale. But in this instance, signs of what they told her were apparent. Along with her head bandage, she ached, and was acutely weary and sluggish. These were all signs the explanation was correct. Until something else was apparent, she had to accept it.

But how did it happen? she thought. I've gone up and down those steps a hundred times and never fallen. There's just nothing to trip on. What happened to cause me to fall?

The event pestered her as she turned it over in her mind. The injection given by the nurse was taking effect, her eyelids began to droop, and she slowly drifted off.

SIX

A battery of tests suggested Helen had no repercussions from the accident. She walked frequently through the hospital corridors, and met with a physical therapist to improve mobility. Upgrading her prognosis, there was no medical reason lingering for her to occupy a hospital bed. Discharged under Matt's watchful eye, she could recuperate in familiar surroundings.

Headaches persisted and plagued her erratically, although abated through medication. Doctors treating her expected the discomfort to subside in time, although, the symptoms were inadequate for continual detention at the hospital.

Matt agreed to stay at her home during transition. His intention was to hang about long enough for her to recoup strength and fend for the children.

Arriving home, Helen stuck to Mike and Sam like glue, which resulted from the gnawing insecurity developed while separated. Rekindled was the bond set aside while disconnected.

In Helen's estimation, the hospital interlude persisted far too long.

Taking advantage of Matt's good-natured support over the days that followed, with children in tow she strolled often to the orchard. She reveled in her brood, and absorbed the natural beauty emanating from this hidden corner of the globe. Sitting quietly, she attempted to nudge from hiding the forerunner to the fall that placed her in this predicament. Unfortunately, the exercise was useless.

"The doctors said with time you'll remember what's happened. Maybe someday it'll come back suddenly," Matt offered. "But, if you'd care to talk, I'll listen."

Matt accompanied the group on occasion, and tried to help Helen jog the episode free from the hidden recesses.

"Maybe talking about the unpleasant event will resurrect details from your subconscious," Matt remarked.

"I'm not sure it will do any good," Helen responded skeptically.

"Whatever happened is buried deep. A conversation might cause the pieces to fall into place," acknowledge Matt.

Carefully chosen were questions to unlock her thoughts.

"You know, Matt, I've been going over everything in my mind. I've tried to remember, and search for answers, but I keep coming up blank. The only thing I find is an empty black hole," said Helen. "It's useless, and unless something happens to cause me to remember, I have to accept that part of my life is lost."

"Maybe you're trying too hard," Matt responded.

"Could be, nothing seems to click," Helen remarked. "It's like working a puzzle with some of the pieces missing. I can remember up to a point, and then it skips. I can't get a handle on what happened."

"Well, relax and try not to think about it," offered Matt. "Someday maybe it'll come back."

"Like you said, maybe I'm trying too hard. God knows I want to resuscitate the incident, for no other reason than my on satisfaction. I need to figure out what happened for me to miss those days," continued Helen. "Yet, for the life of me, I can't."

Sympathetic, Matt responded, "Don't beat yourself up. After all, it was just a stupid accident. It could have happened to anyone. Someday you'll know exactly what you've missed. If that happens you might wish you hadn't. Sometime ignorance is better than reality."

"God, I hope not. When I can't remember something it bothers the dickens out of me," said Helen.

"The important thing now is to concentrate on the kids, and regain your strength," Matt continued. "Have you considered talking to Eve? Maybe she might know what happened."

"She doesn't have a clue," said Helen. "The last thing she remembers is that I went into Howard's office, and was in there so long she eventually went home. She doesn't have any idea what happened because we didn't talk afterwards."

"Would anybody else know?" Matt asked.

"Apparently everyone was gone before I came back. They all learned of the mishap the following morning. Eve said the entire floor was abuzz. That's all they wanted to talk about," responded Helen. "But, I find it odd that I can't remember going to the top floor. It had to be for something important or I wouldn't have gone otherwise."

"How about asking Howard if he remembers?" asked Matt.

"One thing I do remember and that's his damn moodiness," remarked Helen. "So, no thanks, I'd rather walk down Main Street naked, before I'd ask him anything, unless there's simply no other way. I'm hoping my memory will return before that happens."

"Well that's a start. At least everything hasn't been forgotten, like Howard's temperament," Matt chided. "I'd like to see that, by the way."

"What are you talking about?" asked Helen.

"You, walking naked down Main Street," Matt snickered.

Poking Matt gently with an elbow, Helen continued, "You know what I mean. Nobody could forget how crabby he is. He's been a real pain in the ass. When he and his wife separated, the divorce nearly destroyed him, and it almost ruined the department by the tantrums he threw. We couldn't do anything right."

"Okay, next question." Matt said, "Who found you in the stairwell?"

"You said the night guards found me stretched out on the landing during rounds," Helen replied. "But I don't recall anything until I awoke in the hospital. It's weird, just as if someone hit the delete button on that part of my memory. It's a complete zero."

"You don't have any recollection of what you went to see Howard about?" Matt remarked. "If you dislike him so much, there had to be a big reason for you to talk to him face-to-face."

"I don't know the answer," Helen raised her voice in disgust. She was irritated by all the questions, but settling down, said, "The next time I talk to Eve I'll ask her. Maybe that's a starting point."

"If I were you, I'd try not to think to hard about the whole thing," said Matt. "After all, it was just an accident."

Matt asked no further questions, and a lull hung in the conversation like a bird in the air. Matt thought whatever transpired during the interval was trivial. He was happy Helen was home and on the mend. Nothing else really mattered.

The couple snuggled on the bench, arms entwined, enjoying the simple pleasure as a family while they watched the children frolic among the trees. Breathing in the sweet, aromatic, country air, they both smiled at the performances of the children.

Matt reached over, picked up her injured hand, brought it to his lips, and lightly kissed it.

"I can see why you like it here in the orchard. It's so easy to get caught up in the surroundings," Matt remarked.

Helen paused, wiped away a tear that had welled in her eye, and said, "Matt, I want to thank you for all you've done for me and the kids while I was in the hospital, and, for staying with us now I'm on the mend. It was thoughtful and sweet. I don't really know what would have happened if you weren't here."

"You're my best friend, and the three of you are my most favorite people in the whole world," remarked Matt. "I'm just glad I could help."

"Thanks. It was unexpected but appreciated. This was something you didn't have to do. You really put yourself out."

Pulling Helen closer, Matt responded, "Hey, it was the least I could do. Thanks aren't necessary. I'm just glad I was available when I got the call."

"Matt, I've been thinking," Helen said.

"Oh, oh. Am I in trouble?" Matt asked.

"Hardly," Helen reassured. "You know I love you and I've told you I care about you."

"I love you too," Matt said.

"Would you consider moving in with us for a while?" Helen asked. "At least until I get back on my feet. I could use the extra hands, and the kids love having you around."

"Are you sure that's what you want?" Matt asked. "I wouldn't want you to do something you would regret."

"This will only be until I begin to feel better," remarked Helen.

"We haven't been seeing each other long, so I'm not ready for a committed relationship."

"Don't misunderstand what I'm asking. I'm not saying this is permanent or we should live as a couple," responded Helen. "I know you're not ready for that and neither am I. It's too soon."

"Okay," replied Matt.

"I'm not getting my strength back as quickly as I thought, and I need someone here to help out. It's going to take longer than the couple of weeks we agreed on," Helen continued. "I'm getting stronger by the day, but these incessant headaches really take a toll. I've never had this kind of an ache before. And, when one hits I can't function."

Matt paused, reflected on her comments, and then responded, "Helen, I've told you many times how I feel about you and the kids. And believe me I want to get married, someday. But time will prove if my feelings are real. For me to make a statement like this is a huge step. I've never felt this way before, so I'm walking on new turf."

"I'm not asking for marriage," Helen replied. "I just need some help till I get back on my feet."

"I understand. With your last husband being a lush, I'm sure you're not ready for another marriage either," responded Matt.

"From how you described him the marriage was on a constant roller coaster. You still have issues that you need to come to terms with before we consider getting married."

"You're right. There are a lot of things that I need to work out," responded Helen.

"But I will say this, since we've met my whole life has turned up-side-down. I've never felt this way when I'm around another woman, and I'm not sure how to interpret it," continued Matt. "Until I iron out all of the kinks, I want to tread lightly. It wouldn't be fair to any of us."

"I'm glad you're thinking with your head instead of another part of your anatomy," responded Helen.

"That has a bearing on this also. But, for the few months since we've met, I want to think we've become a family," remarked Matt. "I feel some responsibility for you and the kids, and would like to make a home for us. I'm here now for a few days to help out. But moving in without being married is a big step. I'm not ready for that."

"Well think about it and let me know when you make a decision," said Helen.

"Some guys would jump at a chance like this," remarked Matt. "Couples today live together with the idea it'll ward-off a divorce. But, if a couple really loves each other, they'll make the commitment and work through problems as they crop up. There are no guarantees in life."

"I feel the same way," Helen smiled. "And this promise must not be taken lightly."

"My buddies laugh when I tell them that, say I'm crazy," said Matt. "They tell me I'm old fashioned and out-of-step. But, give me some time and let me think about it."

"Matt, I appreciate your honesty. You have no responsibility for me or the kids," said Helen. "I just need some help for a while. If you're not comfortable with that, I'll have to figure something else out. I have no other family."

Matt was quiet for several minutes, pondering.

"If I do this, I'll continue to sleep in the spare bedroom," asserted Matt.

"That's fine, we'll take it slow. Whatever this turns out to be is not set in stone," remarked Helen. "You can leave any time."

"Okay, for now I'll agree to stay until you feel sure of yourself and the headaches are gone, or as long as you need me," acquiesced Matt. "But I'm not giving up my apartment. I'm the hired help, just unpaid. So let's see how this works."

* * * *

Over the weeks that followed, ever so slowly Helen began to regain strength, and picked up the pace around the house. A routine fell into place. Daily she walked, a half-mile increased to a mile, and then two miles. She pushed herself, and the expanse stretched farther on each jaunt. But the headaches persisted and inconveniently cropped up, and she couldn't function when this happened. Pain pills helped, but to make them disappear, retreating to a darkened room to sleep was the best alternative.

Although the pain was persistent, the doctors proposed she return to work. This was to keep her mind occupied in hopes the aching would dissipate sooner. They were optimistic that work would be therapeutic.

Procurement was flying by the seat of its pants without Helen's supervision. Howard was of no benefit, and the department was floundering.

As she gained strength, installed in Helen's home were a computer and a T1 line. Now tied-in to the company network, she could remain in touch and up-to-date with the goings-on as items were either couriered or e-mailed, and the fax utilized to the fullest.

Later, while on the phone with Eve to discuss a business deal, Helen thought to ask about the day of the fall.

"Eve, do you remember what happened the day I fell? Was anything special going on?" Helen asked. "Do you recall just what we were talking about before I went to see Howard?"

"I'm glad you brought that up. I was thinking about that over the weekend and meant to say something. There was an irregular check that came through," Eve responded. "and everybody in the department was trying to figure out where it came from, because some of the paperwork was illegible and others missing. I remember you were determined to track it down. As much as it killed you, you decided to go ask Howard if he knew anything about the check. The reason I thought about the incident is because we've had several others to come through while you've been gone, and some were for much larger amounts."

"Has anyone determined who's sending these through the system?" asked Helen. "Or, has anybody even asked the question?"

"Lordy, I don't have any idea. That's not in my job description," responded Eve. "When I get one like that, I send it to the fat guy. He takes care of it. That's why he's paid the big bucks. I like my job too much to ask questions. That ain't in my pay scale and way over my head."

Helen asked, "Do you know if the checks are actually being cashed?"

"No, I don't, honey. I don't get involved in that part of the business. I just handle the paperwork and make sure the deliveries get made when they're supposed to," replied Eve. "There's always somebody above me who makes those types of decisions around here. And, while you've been gone, it's Howard. What he does or doesn't do, I don't know anything about and don't ask any questions. I ain't rocking the boat."

"What was the name of the company on the check?" Helen asked. "I've forgotten."

"Hold on, I'll look it up," responded Eve. "The check was to a company called Benson Consulting. As I said, some of the other checks that followed were for larger amounts. And others have come through with different names besides Benson. Do you want me to look them up?"

Helen jotted the name on a pad of paper, and replied, "Not now, maybe later. But I still don't remember doing business with a company by that name."

"We don't, and that's exactly what you said before trotting off to see Howard," Eve replied. Don't you remember any of that?"

"No I don't," related Helen. "Right now everything's a blank."

Eve replied, "After I came to work the next morning and found out you fell down the stairs, the subject has never been brought up."

"Really, I wonder why?" said Helen.

"Howard is supposed to know more about what's going on so I don't ask," replied Eve. "And with his rotten attitude, I'm not going to say anything. Does that help you any?"

"Maybe," said Helen. "And thanks, Eve. It's probably best you didn't ask too many questions. I'm going to look through the checks clearing the bank."

"I don't have the authority to do that," Eve added.

"I know you don't, but I do," responded Helen. "If money is being sent without proper documentation, somebody needs to have their feet put in the fire. Someone's going to answer for this. I need to figure out why this is happening, and I'm also curious who's behind it. This could all be legitimate, but I'm going to find out one way or another."

Typing in a user name and password, Helen logged onto the company's accounting system. Entered in the search box was the name Benson Consulting. Within seconds, a list appeared of checks issued to the company. Paid-out in less than six months was over one million dollars. A one million dollar consulting contract for a company as large as Beeson wasn't unusual. But company policy required a paper trail.

Typed on the first line was the amount of one hundred thousand dollars she had asked Howard to clarify. A number of other checks marked cleared were also on the list.

Procedures established compelled fund disbursements to identify the division head authorizing a transaction. In addition, although circumvented at the moment, the policy required supporting documentation for payments. Simple paperwork, these controls were in place to protect the company and prevent pilferage. And the mundane activity to make certain the paperwork existed fell within Procurement's jurisdiction.

Helen tried to determine who could be involved in a funds diversion. "What if there never was a written agreement?" Helen asked. "If that's the case and money's being paid without a contract, this sounds like fraud and we have a huge hole in the accounting system that needs fixed."

The excitement of learning about the checks soon made her realize how exhausted she had become and felt drained. Matt would be home before long, so she needed to rest for a while before starting dinner. Powering off the computer, she laid her head on the sofa. Benson Consulting would be put on hold and wait until tomorrow, or whenever the time came to sniff around again.

I just need to rest my eyes for a few moments, she thought.

* * * *

Startled from a deep sleep, Helen screamed and jolted upright in bed. Disturbed, she was shaken and clammy by the images evoked. Her aquamarine nightgown was drenched as beads of sweat stood on her skin. Gasping for air she sprang forward, her blonde hair ruffled from rolling in bed as she tossed and turned. Confused, she attempted to regain her bearings upon dredging up unpleasant memories.

With screams from down the hall, Matt jumped from bed, ran into Helen's room to see what was going on, and rushed to her side to comfort her.

"Shush, calm down, be quiet. Everything's all right now. It's just a bad dream. I'm here. Everything's okay," Matt said, trying to relieve the anxiety she experienced as he held her in his arms.

He rocked her back and forth as if holding a baby. His dark hair was messed and uncombed. The T-shirt and pajama bottoms he wore were askew from abruptly being startled from slumber. Dashing to Helen's aid, he hadn't taken time to straighten his clothing.

In a shaky voice Helen said, "Someone pushed me down the stairs."

"It was only a dream. Shush, calm down."

"No, Matt, you don't understand what I'm telling you. I remember exactly what happened," Helen related. "Falling down those stairs was not an accident. Someone tripped me, and made me lose my balance. That fall was intentional."

"Helen, it was just a dream," reassured Matt. "No one would do that and walk off and leave you there. Would they? What would be their motive for making you fall?"

"I don't know why they did it, but I'm absolutely certain that's what happened. I remember the details as plain as I can see you now," replied Helen. "After I came out of Howard's office, I was in a hurry to get home. I rushed down the stairs to leave, because I was running late. We were supposed to go out to dinner that evening, remember?"

"Yeah, I remember," replied Matt.

"As soon as I started down the steps everything turned black. I couldn't see a thing," said Helen. "I called out for help and no one answered, so then I tried to feel my way back to my office. It was when I got to the top landing and reached for the door that someone grabbed my leg to trip me. This was why I fell and hit so hard. Somebody actually gave me a shove."

"Are you sure?" asked Matt. "Maybe your mind is playing tricks on you."

"And another thing," Helen continued. Before I blacked out, a man leaned over and whispered into my ear."

"What makes you so certain it was a man?" asked Matt. "What did this person say, do you remember?"

"Yes I'm absolutely confident it was a man," replied Helen. "But, I haven't been able to make out what he said, but I'm going to find out. That fall was no accident it was deliberate. Somebody tried to kill me."

"That sounds rather ominous," remarked Matt. "Just how are you going to figure it out? If somebody pushed you, you could still be in danger."

Helen responded. "As long as the person thinks I'm still out of it, for the time being I'm safe. I'm not going to tell anybody what happened. And don't you tell anyone either. We've got to keep this to ourselves."

"Who in the hell am I going to tell?" cried out Matt.

Helen was still shaking profoundly as Matt held her, gently rocking on the side of the bed while she regained composure. To be comfortable they reclined on the bed.

Helen was too upset to sleep, but casually placed her head on Matt's chest. Her eyes wide open, she was weighing what happened, trying to piece together details. Racing through the event, her mind was tossing what happened around like bowling pins. She retraced every bump as she tumbled down the steps. Then she tried to discern what the person whispered.

I ought to remember, Helen thought. I've got to remember. It's on the tip of my tongue. What is it?

SEVEN

"That goddamn bitch is still breathing," Howard barked while scolding his accomplices. "You sure screwed that up. Whatever happened to, 'I'll handle the job,' as you made such a big deal of strangling the bitch with your bare hands."

"I didn't know it would turn out the way it did," responded Camp.

"All you did was to give her a smack on the head, you dumb ass. What you did was to create another problem," berated Howard, "and, gave her a vacation at company expense. What in the hell were you thinking?"

"I can't help it she smashed into the wall and it didn't kill her," Camp claimed. "Her head cracked when she hit so hard, there's no reason she isn't dead."

Wearing a neatly pressed Navy suit, Eric Camp was Vice President over domestic operations. At six-six, he was muscular, his physique preserved by morning workouts, a daily run of five miles, and all on company time.

"But, Jesus Christ, she's still alive. After she hit, why didn't you choke her like you said you would?" demanded Howard. "Goddamn, why did I ever listen to you? Where's your mind?"

Howard stormed about castigating his accomplice for the foiled mission he volunteered to complete. With Camp's calamity, Howard went wild. His temper flared and the agitation bubbling, certain to erupt. His nostrils flared, and his countenance gnarled as he pranced. Contributing to this persona was a rumpled shirt and slacks that sagged due to a recent weight loss. Howard felt caged like an animal yearning to escape, because of Camp's failure, although, apprehensive of the next move.

"You have one damn job and can't even do that right," yelled Jenkins, "Just one goddamn job."

Ranting, Howard pointed his finger in Camp's face, and then looked at the entire group and declared, "I hope all of you bastards realize that if this son-of-a-bitch did what he said he would do, we wouldn't be in this mess."

"Don't point your finger at me. I thought it would be a lot easier," responded Eric. "This was the first time I've tried to kill someone. How many people have you killed?"

"We're not talking about me. If you didn't have the stomach for it, you should have said so," Howard blasted. "We could have engaged a real man who wasn't squeamish, like I wanted to do in the first place."

"I figured as hard as she whacked her head on the wall the fall would have killed her," remarked Eric.

"What you did was make matters worse," Howard bellowed. "Now, whatever happens must look like the real deal after this fiasco."

Howard blamed Camp squarely for the current predicament, as he wagged his finger at the group and warned. "I remind you bastards again, we wouldn't be in this pickle if you sons-a-bitches had listened to me and let me get a pro."

"It's too late for that," conceded Camp. "So settle down."

"We shouldn't be facing this problem. She should be dead, d-e-a-d, squashed like a bug," Howard shouted. "But you're too damn cheap. You wouldn't let go of some of that precious cash to save your asses."

"Dammit Howard, if you'll recall we didn't have time to wait. We had to act before she got out of the building," said Camp. "It couldn't have been put off."

"That's what you said to convince the others. It was bullshit then and bullshit now. Time was on our side. We could have taken her anytime, and made certain she was gone. We weren't pressed to kill her, not then, not the way you guys wanted to handle it."

"It's too late," said Camp.

"What happens when she remembers, and believe me she will," Howard cautioned the group. "She has a memory like an elephant."

"What do you mean?" remarked Camp.

"Don't you know? That's why the program she runs works so damn well. She's goddamn good at her job," remarked Jenkins. "It's not because of anything I did. Hell, if we'd hired anyone with lesser skills, this just-in-time thing would have died long ago, as I designed it to do. The damn thing was too complex not to fail. But somehow, she made it work."

"That's to our benefit," Camp smiled as he responded. "She made a lot more money for us to take."

"You're forgetting that the plan backfired. The ship was supposed to sink, and all eyes would be on her for screwing up. Except now, with our goddamn luck, the bitch will dredge up Camp shoving her down the stairs and blab it to someone," remarked Howard. "She's somebody we don't want around, and we've got to make it look like a real accident or somebody will get suspicious. Does anybody have any ideas?" Looking at Eric he said, "I could kick your ass."

"Yeah, I'd like to see you try, you little prick," Camp responded.

Eric stood and towered over Jenkins. He was younger, taller, and more strapping, eclipsed him, and could easily subdue him in a scuffle. But Howard was the key to his fortune, and Camp wasn't eager to become testy.

"Now, everybody calm down. Bickering won't solve the problem or get the job done," Compton injected.

Gordon Compton was President of Beeson International. He and Howard had been cronies for as long as they had been with the company.

"Let's focus. We need to figure out our next move," Compton added.

Laugh lines extending from the corner of his eyes evidenced a peacemaker with an amicable demeanor. To disarm and place an opponent at ease, he often used a warm handshake. The current circumstance, though, prevented his normal charming disposition.

As an executive, he played the part with tailored suits and custom ties, and his exterior aligned as a person leading a major corporation. In reality he was a mere figurehead. The person in charge and controlling the purse strings stormed about the floor.

Howard continued to pace and bellow at his fellow associates. He was perturbed, fearing the situation was spiraling out of control.

"We've got to come up with a solution damn quick. Our asses are on the line," Howard demanded. "So, let's find a way to fix this."

"I think this thing has gotten completely out of hand. I won't be part of a murder," said Compton. "Howard, we just need to cash out and disappear,"

"Get a backbone, Gordon," Howard scolded his friend. "Your hands are just as dirty as ours. Did you think this would be a walk in the park, or some goddamn slot machine you could cash out anytime you wanted?"

"I'm certainly not in favor of killing anyone," replied Compton.

"You didn't hesitate when you decided to push her down the steps. It's too late to turn back. We've got to see this through so we can get the hell out, without a trail leading to us," Howard scoffed. "And, another thing, we can't all disappear at once. That would really throw up a red flag. Like it or not, we've got to get rid of the meddlesome bitch or she'll keep digging. And, we can't allow that to happen."

"I don't care what I agreed to earlier, I'm not in favor of killing anyone. That's just unacceptable. There's got to be a better way," said Gordon.

"Unacceptable my ass. What other choice do we have? Unless you've got a better idea, we'll all go to jail if she doesn't disappear. Look, when that woman was hired, the plan was she'd take the blame for the missing money. Now that we're at that juncture, we've got to make it happen," barked Howard.

"I don't want her blood on my hands," said Compton.

"Gordon, I see no other way. I've worked with her enough to know she going to figure out what happened and it won't take her long. That woman is a pain in our collective asses, and much smarter than I gave her credit."

"Then what do you think should be done?" said Leonard Busby. "Hire a hit man? Is that what you're saying, Howard?"

Busby was VP of Overseas Operations. Habitually, he dressed in cheap clothes bought off the rack, and had little interest in a flashy exterior.

"How much have you put back so far?" asked George.

"Last count was over eight hundred million," responded Howard. "We're currently sending a million a month. But even that will come to a screeching halt if we don't find a way soon to stop that woman, permanently."

"I thought her name was tied to all these accounts? Let's keep to the original plan, fire her and have her arrested. Then, we can turn her over to the cops. That'll solve the problem," squealed Busby. Every tooth in his head was shining through the smirk he sported. "We're cashing out anyway before someone else finds out what's going on."

"That's not smart, Busby. If the woman's alive, she'll yap, yap, yap and convince someone she didn't know anything about what's going on, and we can't take that chance. Until we set a trap for the nosey bitch we can't leave, not yet," replied Howard. "She's still on medical leave because of Camp's screw-up. So, we need to wait till she's back at work to finish the job. This may take a while, but will give us time to plan what we need to do. Until she's history, we can't pin anything on her. But, when she returns, we'll be ready."

"At least we can keep sending cash out of the country. Can we speed it up somehow? I want a bigger cushion," remarked Compton.

"No," snapped Howard. "Don't you think eight hundred million split five ways is enough for retirement? Where is Clark, by the way? Why isn't he here?"

"He's in Aruba at the company retreat. He'll be back next week," responded George.

Howard nodded and continued, "A couple of the directors have been questioning cash flow. There's just so much I can cover up in those reports. And, the auditors will be here soon. I've got to move some things around before they arrive."

"Better cover up any loose ends," remarked Busby.

"The pension fund will be scrutinized. I have to fix a few things there," remarked Howard. "So, for now, we've got to back off or someone besides that woman may ask questions. A million a month, until we can crank it up again, should be enough. Let's not get greedy just when we can see our way out."

Eric asked, "What do we do if she remembers what happened on the stairs?"

"There won't be a next time, we're getting rid of the bitch," responded Jenkins. "I just decided. I'll take care of her before she comes back to work. And this time for sure. There will be no third chance."

"How are we going to do it, Howard," asked Camp.

"Don't worry, I'll set it up," said Jenkins.

"Well, I guess some people are just accident-prone," replied Busby.

"And when it happens, all of you better show up at the funeral and shed tears," remarked Howard. "Tears of joy. Just be damn glad she's out of our lives. Otherwise she's going to cause us a lot of grief."

Busby remarked, "Good, I don't want to take the chance of someone finding out how much we've taken, and I don't want it traced back to us. Before somebody starts to sniff around, I plan to be long gone and live comfortable on my share."

* * * *

Her mind raced and she wrestled with the covers as sleep eluded her. Helen rolled from bed, traipsed to the computer and typed a string of commands. Lines filled the screen with dates and numbers.

"I was afraid I would find something like this," she mumbled. "What the hell's going on? I don't know most of these companies, and that's my job."

After sorting, the list began in alphabetical order, Adams Consulting, Baker Consulting, Beaver Consulting, Benson Consulting, with a long register trailing. Page after page the screen filled, and appeared reluctant to end. Bewildered, Helen sat back incredulous, she looked at the monitor and shook her head.

Is this the tip of the iceberg? she wondered. Or are there other names besides these?

Some names she recognized. Beeson had legitimate contracts with vendors and worked with them regularly. Helen knew the people in charge, and could pick up a phone and talk to them anytime.

The identity of others on the list was baffling. The report of undocumented cash paid out exceeded twenty million dollars.

Who's behind all this? She questioned. And who's sending this money to companies I know nothing about? This isn't chump change by any stretch of the imagination.

With a few keystrokes, Helen saved the list for future reference. Next, she searched a file that contained copies of cancelled checks, and cross-referenced the images to the unidentified names listed.

Helen perused and scrutinized the replicas for anything unusual. She found it odd all checks cleared through a bank in Belize, a country situated on the Caribbean Sea in Central America.

Why would all these companies be using the same bank, and outside the US? she wondered. That's weird. First checks go to Atlanta, but then cashed in Belize, why?

Perplexed, she deliberated, attempting to unravel the puzzle.

This can't be a coincidence, she reflected. There has to be a common denominator.

Helen typed in the web browser's request box the name of the financial institution, *Providian Bank and Trust*. In a matter of seconds a website appeared beckoning her to open an offshore corporation, and an offshore bank account, but only on condition the account holder wasn't a resident.

Scrounging further through the web pages offered information on the relaxed banking laws, and the bank's relationship with financial institutions of other countries. These provisions permitted fund transfers around the globe. Channeling cash through this bank soon became clear. After speculating a relation between the names, she now knew why.

Whoever's behind this operation is using multiple companies to siphon money away from Beeson, Helen reasoned. It's a shell game, and made to appear the transactions are legitimate. I wonder, how many dummy companies are they using? And who at Beeson could orchestrate something so intricate, and have the know-how to pull it off?

Mentally, Helen ran down a short list of those who would know the system and could manipulate the records. The CEO and President she had seen on occasion, but doubted their involvement. Disconnected from financial matters, familiarity with internal accounting controls would be foreign to them.

These guys are just pretty faces, she thought. They're only visible when the company needs an image. No, whoever's doing this has to be hands-on, know the system inside and out, and be able to by-pass the checks and balances.

Helen continued with her analysis of the possible players.

Then there's the company controller and a few accountants. The controller, maybe, but I doubt it. He's a number cruncher. None of these would have knowledge of the entire system, she realized. These guys couldn't pull off a scheme this complicated, and not for these kinds of transactions. Whoever's behind this must be higher up the food chain, and be able to divert attention to know how the pieces all fit together.

As CFO and her boss, Howard Jenkins was the only executive she knew well enough to fall in that category.

He could put this type of a plot together, she thought. He designed the accounting system and knew exactly where all the soft spots were.

Pausing, she contemplated. Surely, Howard wouldn't be involved in something this elaborate. Although, he did handle the check I asked him about that I found had later cleared the bank. Why would he do something like this? He's been with the company forever and helped build it from the ground up. This goes against everything he taught me.

Helen realized the only way she'd find out for sure was to rummage through his office and try to find anything that would eliminate him from suspicion.

That's going to be next to impossible, Helen thought. How can I do that, and when? He practically lives at the place.

Mulling over the concept, Helen began to formulate a plan.

What if I went to the office for a visit, she thought. While I'm there, I could look through his office to see if he was somehow involved.

Technically, on medical leave, a clear-cut rationale to visit didn't exist. Therefore, she had to conjure up a motive.

Now that I'm feeling stronger, I should go in for a short while. I need to check on my department, she rationalized. Making an appearance wouldn't look suspicious under these circumstances. Besides, it's time to get out of the house. An outing would do me good.

If she found something to show Howard wasn't involved, Helen couldn't think of another person it could be.

Nobody has access like he does, she thought. But, if it's not him, well, I'll have to cross that bridge when I come to it.

She was doing a convincing job of talking herself through Howard's office door. At this juncture, Helen would use any pretext as justification to find the truth.

She remembered the Board of Directors held a meeting once a month. At these meetings, Howard was required to report on financial matters, specifically problems in troubled areas. This portion of the meeting drew a lot of interest and always ran long.

If timed properly, she could slip in, look around, find something to redeem Howard, and be gone before he realized she'd been in the building.

Admitting she had no idea what to look for, she held out hope he wasn't into some devious operation. If he was, she wanted to know to what extent. If not, she would clear his name and solicit his help.

Howard had hired her and had been a good mentor. Before his attitude changed with the divorce, he treated her as an equal. Therefore, she wasn't eager to make an unsupported accusation. If innocent, she was obligated to point the finger in another direction. And, whoever tried to kill her, she wanted behind bars.

Traditionally, Director meetings were on Wednesday and an all-day affair. If the schedule held true, the next meeting would be the following week. To assure the visit would go without a hitch, she had to begin immediately.

With Howard preoccupied, she would have ample time to explore his office. Hopefully, whatever was found wouldn't be damning. Pilfering through Howard's office wasn't a pleasant thought, but neither was the company going bankrupt, nor the idea that someone had tried to kill her.

When I can determine he's not associated with an embezzlement, I'll take everything I have and give it to him. Then, he can deal with it. I'm in over my head already, and uncovered more than I want to know.

Helen wouldn't accuse anyone of a crime without proof of guilt, and hoped to find evidence to vindicate Howard.

Matt won't like what I'm about to do, but I'll tell him afterwards, she thought. I'll have to explain why I did it. Until then, I'm on my own.

Powering off the computer, Helen sauntered back to bed stopping in Matt's bedroom. Stretching and yawning, she curled up next to her companion and laid her head on his chest. Feeling like she was about to betray a friend, the warmth of his body was needed to appease the small voice in her head shouting danger, danger ahead.

Wide-eyed, her mind was pushing full throttle as she reflected on her plan, considered options, and created scenarios that might play out, considering every known contingency. With her head on his chest, she could hear the gentle rhythmic heartbeat of her soul mate. Feeling secure, she was lulled into slumber.

* * * *

Gray was the sky, and a mist hung in the air like smoke at a campfire. Chills spread through Helen's body that matched her mood. The coat she wore was drawn close to her chin to ward off dampness and gloom. Feeling uneasy about returning, even temporarily, to an office under false pretenses, the weather didn't improve her disposition.

This wasn't a pleasure trip and a nasty climate wasn't encouraging. To make the trip under a drummed up pretext was disheartening, the possibility of turning up something damning troubling, but, based on an amateur's analysis, all indicators were pointing in one direction. Helen had to resolve in her own mind if Howard was engaged in an illegal act before searching for another culprit.

Even though his mannerisms changed with the divorce, she was hesitant to believe he would stoop so low as to steal from a company he helped build. Without conclusive proof, she wouldn't readily accept his involvement in something underhanded.

But, if it's not him, who could it be? She thought. There is no one I can think of that has the knowledge or ability to manipulate the records on such an elaborate scheme.

Whoever's behind this brainchild knows the system throughout. They have complete comprehension of the checks and balances to avoid setting off alarms. And whoever they are must be well versed in company operations, and Jenkins fits the bill.

Alerted that something was amuck was only by chance.

Helen reflected, just one check sliding across my desk raised the flag. If it wasn't for that, I'd still be in the dark.

Even when confronted with the evidence Helen wanted to believe the check was legitimate.

Boy, am I gullible, she scolded. I should have known instantly something wasn't right. Beeson doesn't make payment without documentation, period, at least not through my department.

Helen attempted to find goodness in everyone. For a few, this was difficult and she had to look deep. With others, impossible, they were bad to the core. But, whoever was behind this larceny was evil. Exposing this conspiracy was a must.

If the company went belly-up, good people and their families would be devastated, she thought. Disappearance of large amounts of cash has to inflict a heavy toll, and eventually Beeson couldn't pay its bills.

Michael and Samantha were with a sitter for the day. Being apart for a short while was awkward because she hadn't fully recovered from the anxiety of separation experienced during the stint in the hospital, and grown accustomed to keeping them within hailing distance. Each time she left them in the care of another, a feeling of abandonment returned, even knowing the disconnection would be short-lived.

As she turned into the lot, she eyeballed a parking spot through the windshield. The wipers worked overtime wagging back and forth as precipitation pounded. Crops sorely needed rain, but she wondered if the poor weather on the day she chose to snoop around was a bad omen. Slipping into an empty visitor's slot with the idea of being here a short while, by dodging raindrops she ran to the front entrance.

"God, why couldn't this be under better circumstances?" she mumbled.

I feel awkward returning to the office, especially under these convoluted circumstances, she thought. Will anyone be able to tell why I'm here, she wondered. Will there be a sign hanging over my forehead and everybody will know? God, I hope not. Howard's tied up all day, but what if somebody else catches me. Well, I've come this far, I can't let that stop me now.

The doctors gave Helen the okay for a short visit, provided she would rest when tired. Her condition remained fragile and stress could cause a setback. The headaches persisted, but seemed less frequent and intense.

Passing through the main entrance, Helen collapsed the umbrella and glanced about to find the lobby was comfortably unchanged. The massive hall with forty-foot ceilings and decked out in marble and polished steel was immaculate. Giant trees and greenery filled the open space and splashed about for color. The hall had the aplomb expected of a large company to impress the finickiest of visitors.

Helen smiled and nodded at Scotty stationed at the information desk. He'd been the guard she greeted every morning since employed. Returning her wide smile, he expressed, "It's good to see you up and around."

As she passed the checkpoint, a picture identification badge attached to a long flexible tether hung from her neck, and showed the department assigned. An embedded security chip allowed an employee access to authorized areas.

A badge given each employee when hired provided each with identification to pinpoint the department ascribed, and level of access. Helen's badge allowed her into all areas due to the requirements of her job.

Upon learning of the sudden visit, hastily thrown together to catch-up was a departmental gathering to welcome Helen back. Workers in Procurement anticipated her arrival by preparing a small celebration. A co-worker baked a large Danish to share with morning coffee.

"How thoughtful, I didn't expect this," Helen acknowledged.

"We just wanted to let you know we're glad you're up and around and doing so well," remarked Eve. "If we had more notice, we would have done more."

"Thank you," remarked Helen.

"Do you have anything special on your agenda while you're here?" continued Eve.

"Well, I probably won't be here long," she announced. "I tire easily and have to rest. But while I'm here, I want to review the workload and get up to speed on our job progress. I've got to feel comfortable we're meeting expectations."

"Believe me, we've been working our tails off to keep up. We don't want nobody coming in here to replace you," responded Eve. "I think Howard will be happy to see you're back. He's been in such a tizzy."

"Hasn't he been helping the department?" asked Helen.

Eve scrunched up her face and shook her head. "No," she replied. "And, I think his disposition is getting worse. We should probably take up a collection and hire a hooker. He probably hasn't had sex since his wife left. Might make his attitude straighten out, along with something else," she laughed. "Anything would be an improvement, he's so grumpy."

Helen smiled and remarked, "If there's a board meeting today, I don't think I'll see him. I'm tired by lunchtime and need to lie down."

"I'm sure he'll be sorry he didn't get to see you," replied Eve.

If what I suspect is true, Helen thought, he'd wish I hadn't come into the building, especially if I find something.

Reviewing orders, schedules, and flow charts, Helen became current with the progress, and then turned her attention to new endeavors started during her absence. Working from home and through ongoing conversations with team members, she was aware of the activities. But, to refresh her memory and appear interested in the goings-on of the department, she reviewed them again. She didn't plan to tip her hand for today's stopover.

She'd been in Howard's sanctum often and recalled the layout. She knew where to look, but not exactly what to look for but ideas rolled around.

A few last-minute jitters were beginning to creep in as the time arrived to do what she came for. This visit had to be fruitful and produce evidence, otherwise, if somehow connected, Howard may get away with a crime.

Another stab at me breaking and entering was nil and out of the question.

To an outsider he wasn't organized. Howard was infamous for keeping paper copies, regardless of office policy. He always claimed policies were for others. Rules were for the hired help.

The guys in charge were exempt. Although, paper scattered about was the primary reason his office was in shambles.

Howard kept a black leather-bound notebook he either carried with him or placed beside his computer. It contained all his contact information for people and websites, the book a key to user names and passwords. He was paranoid and these key items changed often. Without a traffic cop such as the book, he would be lost.

Once, Howard bragged to Helen identities were changed on a whim, with the journal the only record for keeping track. She watched him reference the book, and hoped it was beside his computer today because he wouldn't need it in the meeting.

As the morning niceties drew to a close and the hullabaloo over Helen's return subsided, she slipped from the department and made her way through the building to the Ivory Tower.

She was tense, but wasn't a stranger to the top floor. However, this trip was but for one purpose, to find evidence if it existed. She hoped to somehow find Howard exonerated of wrongdoing, and a suspected diversion of funds from company coffers. She also wanted to learn if employee pensions were intact, and a connection to the bank account in Belize if one existed in Howard's domain.

This was a tall order to fill in the short span available. She held out hope that her boss was not complicit in a crime. But, all her senses told another story.

EIGHT

Helen moved effortlessly through the building swiping her badge in the provided slots. Gradually, she meandered until reaching the executive offices on the top floor where top management congregated.

Howard despised the idea of a personal assistant. He didn't want anyone questioning every move or scrutinizing his actions. Although infrequent, if he needed a typist he requisitioned the assistant from the clerical pool. Absence of a helper contributed to his sloven propensity, therefore, Helen didn't need to skirt someone guarding his door.

Helen had to move swiftly to identify key features, and then disappear or be caught in the act. Although, locating anything would be impossible without prior knowledge of the layout.

When the elevator doors separated, the silence beyond was deafening. The place was empty and it gave Helen a creepy feeling. All the big wigs were with the directors, and assistants either were with their bosses, or had abandoned their posts.

Without a hum from the overhead light fixture, there would be no sound. The floor was dead, and this gave Helen some idea of what a morgue might be like, as she shuttered.

Is my imagination getting the best of me? she wondered.

Strolling nonchalantly, Howard's station was to the left of the elevator, isolated in an alcove at the end of a hallway. Helen slipped through his doorway, surprised it was unlatched and standing ajar.

He must have believed everyone was going to the meeting, she thought. On occasion he locks the door while he's away.

Helen went to work immediately. Uncertain of what to look for, she reasoned if he was involved in something devious, evidence had to reside around the desk or the computer. From earlier experiences, she didn't believe he would put something away just because of a meeting. As expected, everything was a mess and it was apparent he didn't expect someone uninvited to visit his office. He met with directors sporadically, but only when scheduled and then in a conference room.

The search began by thumbing through papers lying about haphazardly. Although doubtful of the topic, she was certain that when found a connection would be self-evident.

Stock reports were of no interest. Phone slips with reminders to return calls, useless. Post-it-notes were stuck about with hand-written tidbits glanced over and dismissed. A few looked interesting and might be of use, but this wasn't the time or place. None of this stuff was pertinent, and she turned her attention to the computer.

Suddenly a low rumble emanated from the far end of the hallway and she froze. The voices grew louder and it became apparent these were flowing in her direction. Abruptly bodies burst through the unchecked entry.

* * * *

"What the hell is so damned urgent we had to get together and talk?" snapped Howard as the group arrived in the sanctuary of his office. "Couldn't this wait until later? We don't have a lot of time."

He seemed to be as gruff and hateful with his colleagues, as he normally was with others he came in contact.

"The directors will be wondering where we are," Howard continued. "It's a good thing we went in opposite directions, or someone might get the wrong idea."

At the monthly meeting, the executives remained through the day until the get-together concluded. With meals catered and phone calls held, unless a dire emergency, video links were set up for direct communication with project heads. The board wanted a progress report firsthand.

The company's exposure remained too great for directors to remain in a haze. The scrutiny wasn't designed to micro-manage, but provide oversight to the team leading the company in a new century. The course was particularly useful in the ambiguous era and unsettled locales where the company operated.

The board expected monetary rewards to be abundant with the high risk of the projects, and the significant investment of people, time, and infusion of cash. But the numbers conveyed a different picture. Profits were marginal, with losses recognized on several ventures.

Four people had filtered through the entryway with Jenkins.

"I believe some of the directors might be on to what we're doing," said Clark Ford.

Ford was the Chief Executive Officer. In theory, it was his responsibility to develop new opportunities for company investment. His book of contacts was endless.

In reality, he was waiting to retire with the money from the subterfuge Howard formulated. Living beyond his means, and hounded by three ex-wives bleeding him, he looked to make a killing on this deal and vanish into oblivion. His health was deteriorating and he appeared twenty years older than his fifty-three years. His simple wish was to live out the remainder of his time pampered and in peace.

"Bill was asking questions about some of the jobs we're pulling cash from, and I wasn't sure how to answer him," Clark said. "His questions were direct and he seemed apprehensive."

"How in the hell could he be suspicious of anything?" replied Jenkins.

"He was extremely interested in cost overruns," continued Ford.

"Those bastards don't know shit. You're paranoid," snarled Howard, with a show of agitation by the question. "Settle down, you're too damn jumpy. What the hell did you tell him anyway?"

"I told him there was a lot of risk, more than we had anticipated, and the operating cost far exceeded expectations."

"Good. Just what you should have said," remarked Howard.

"Then I told him he needed to talk to you about specifics because you're putting all the numbers together. What else could I tell him?" remarked Clark.

"That's exactly what you should have said. But, no one is getting uptight. Apparently, he saw me after he spoke to you. He understands where we stand now. If it'll make you feel better, I'll talk to him again," replied Howard.

"I wish you would. It's much better when it comes from you," responded Ford.

Like hell I will, Howard thought. That damn Ford has no balls.

For today's meeting, Howard was dapper with a new suit and tie, shoes shined, and a fresh shave. A guise befitting of a CFO, and an expectation of the position, instead that of a slob.

"Your office is a damn pit. Why don't you clean up this hole?" remarked Gordon Compton. "Hell, I don't see how you find anything. Get one of those secretaries to come in and throw out all this shit."

"Go screw yourself. Take care of your own damn office and leave mine alone," snapped Howard. "I know exactly where everything is."

"Are you sure a trail won't lead back to us? If someone finds out what we're doing, we're going to prison." Eric quickly jumped into the conversation to change direction, and keep it from turning into a shouting match.

"Don't get so worked up. Don't you have a backbone either? You may be going to jail, but I'm not. I've made sure that our tracks are well covered," remarked Howard. "There is nothing to connect us. That woman is set to take the fall."

"Are you sure?" asked Eric.

"It's her name on those bank accounts, and the transfers all look like they're through her department," boasted Jenkins, as a laugh replaced his usual frown. "She's screwed. Her fingerprints are all over this thing. There's no way Helen can wiggle out."

When Howard established the offshore accounts he used Helen's identification, and personal details hijacked from company employment records. An electric bill lifted from her desk showing her home address verified U. S. residency.

"Nevertheless, I don't plan on going to jail," remarked Camp. "I want my share of the money so I can get the hell out of here before anybody figures out what's happened. I'd like for that to be yesterday, then I'll feel better. I'm feeling uneasy about this whole thing."

"You should have killed her instead of just bashing her head into the wall, and we'd already be out the door," admonished Howard.

"I told that bitch she should have kept her nose out of our affairs," remarked Camp.

"When did you say that?" asked Compton.

"On the stairs, when she fell," said Camp. "Before she passed out, I told her it was her own damn fault, she brought it on herself."

"It doesn't matter now, she'll be dead soon," Jenkins interjected.

"What if she starts to remember things and talks to someone before that happens?" asked Busby. "What do we do then?"

"I've made some calls. She's going to have an accident, and all this is going to happen before she comes back to work," responded Howard. "But it's not going to be cheap, and the cost comes out of the money in the bank. But we need to get back to the meeting before somebody misses us. The morning break is about over."

"I want to see how much we have in the bank," said Clark.

"We'll do it later," Howard dismissed the remark with a wave of his hand.

"No. I want to see it now," Ford demanded.

Sternly, Howard insisted, "Dammit, I said we'd do it later."

"I'm not leaving here until I see how much is there," said Clark. "You haven't done something with the money, have you, Howard?"

Howard was standing to leave, but turned briskly and sat at the computer. Clicking an icon, he selected a website and the page for Provident Bank appeared. From the notebook, he entered a name and password, and an access portal opened. The screen soon filled with the account balance.

Irritated, Howard remarked, "Now are you happy?" He arose and began to leave the room.

"That's just part of it," submitted Gordon.

"You know the rest of it's in a numbered account," replied Howard over his shoulder.

The CEO was adamant. "Show me. I want to see it," demanded Clark, standing his ground.

"What's got into to you. I'll show you after the directors are gone," Howard gruffly responded.

"I don't want to wait till later," said Ford. "I've made plans and want to know how much is mine."

Howard returned to his desk and called up another address. The website for the Swiss bank appeared, and again Howard referred to the black book to retrieve the logon for the account. A balance of eight hundred thirty-seven million dollars appeared.

"Are you satisfied now," said Howard as a big grin replaced the frown, and he wrapped an arm around Clark to appease him.

"That's a lot of cash to be split five ways," remarked Ford.

"Yeah, you can live like a king anywhere in the world," said Howard. "But, we've got to get back before we're missed."

"When are we going to divvy it up?" asked Eric.

"We'll figure that out later," responded Howard.

The five men strolled from the room with wide smiles. Symbolically, the group was patting themselves on the back for pulling off yet another successfully scheme. Each anticipated this undertaking would soon be coming to a close, and held visions of living the good life.

* * * *

Helen was stone faced. Speechless and appalled by the confessions of the five-men, and panic-stricken by what she'd overheard. She wanted to reject the entire demonstration as someone playing a bad joke. But, a voice whispered from deep inside, "Believe your eyes, what you saw was true."

Witnessing the planning of crimes by a band of white-collar thugs changed the perspective of everything she came to pursue. The question now wasn't who was involved, but what to do with the affirmations. The person she wanted to trust was the leader of the bunch and dispelled the possibility of talking to him. Now where could she turn?

Instead of protecting the company, these people are involved in a conspiracy to fill their own pockets and rip the company to shreds, she thought. If they get away with it, Beeson will be blindsided and won't survive.

A parallel to how these confirmations would ripple through the organization began to soak-in like a sponge submerged in water. Helen didn't consider her fate, and concern for her own welfare hadn't hit home. She was concerned about the health of the company and the state of the employees.

What's caused these guys to get so far off track? Helen wondered. They have positions most people only dream about. They've worked hard to get where they are, and the jobs weren't handed to them I know, but something happened. Where'd they go wrong?

Beeson International expanded by taking on projects other companies shied away from for lack of expertise or undercapitalization. Yet, due to this small group Beeson thrived, met the challenge, and driven with an entrepreneurial spirit of accomplishment.

This was a company with a take-charge attitude, conquered obstacles through innovation, and found ways for projects to work that shouldn't. Ventures became profitable beyond expectations where other companies failed. These were the leaders responsible for pulling Beeson into the future and making things happen.

But after thinking about it all, I still don't understand, Helen reflected. Why build a company to turn around and destroy it? Haven't they thought about how this will affect so many people? The damage inflicted will be catastrophic and bankrupt the company. These men will now be responsible for the financial destruction of lives that can never recover.

Helen realized that somewhere along the way these guys began to look out for their own skins. They were prepared to go to any length to protect the scam they created, and this included murder.

Abruptly, Helen became quiet and shuddered. Like the flip of a switch, reality sunk-in.

"Eric Camp is the one that tried to kill me," she said clearly.

Those guys are nothing but a bunch of thieves, she thought, common criminals who put their own greed above everything. And for what, money, and what it'll buy, or to achieve their own self-serving ambitions? For them, this is just another challenge. But these men had a duty to the company and its employees, not just fill their own pockets. Apparently, they forgot all about responsibility and chose to disregard what's happening. What a legacy to leave behind.

Now certain a conspiracy was taking place under her nose, Helen was dubious of the outcome. She knew something had to be done, but was not sure where to turn or how to reverse course. But first on the list, she had to secure her family. The bloodthirsty group had plans to kill again.

Next time their mission may be accomplished, she reflected. My children are in grave danger unless I take steps to prevent whatever Howard has in mind. He has no qualms about another so-called accident, and I could wind up a statistic.

Helen vowed to somehow stop the impending train wreck after securing her family. With the many lives affected that hung in the balance, to sit back and doing nothing wasn't an option. She recognized the urgency to thwart the actions of the criminals, and prepare for contingencies. Laying the groundwork was essential. The question was where to begin.

* * * *

With the approach of unexpected voices, Helen slipped through the only available opening. Often, she had been to Howard's office but never in this space.

The lavatory was spacious. It contained the usual accoutrements of a sink, and toilet. But in addition, a urinal, bidet, sunken tub, shower, sauna and a chaise lounge. The real quirk, the fixtures were ostentatiously gold.

No one will believe me if I told them a private spa adjoined this pigsty, Helen ruminated.

The room was clearly to impress someone who came to his office, or perhaps provide alternate entertainment. Helen cringed when she considered intimacy with Howard.

The floor was marble. The decorator used bright colors and muted lighting to augment the ambiance, and mirrors to increase the expanse. The entire theme Helen considered too elaborate and uncanny for an office venue. She was surprised such lavishness extended to the room or that Howard's taste ran in this direction.

Once inside, Helen encountered a storeroom and scooted through the door. This was on the off chance the voices might have use for the facility, and she sought to mask her presence.

Entering the smaller space, a thin shaft of light flickered through a crack in the corner. Inquisitive, she shoved firmly and the wall moved freely, opening to an obscure chamber. Here she watched and listened to the interaction between the parties through a glass panel. Light stemming from the opening filled the room.

As the banter persisted, Helen watched spellbound and observed the players as if she were a member of the party, seemingly close enough to touch them. A sense rippled through her that one of them could tell she was watching.

A large mirror hung behind Howard's desk, and she soon grasped the concept. The mirror was dead center behind it, exposing every square inch of his repugnant abyss. Helen stood in the unimpeded opening and watched the exchange unfold.

In the cramped quarters was a bookshelf backed against the wall. The floor carpeted, a computer sat on a small desk and adjoined the bookcase. Someone was serious about security, with a Sentry Executive safe standing in the back corner, although poorly managed with the door breached. And apparent from the lack of precautions, no fear existed of someone finding the room.

The hinged door moved effortlessly when Helen tugged on the corner and pulled, the lower section partitioned with shelves, the upper small drawers. Computer discs were in sheaths lined up in rows and stood vertical on the top shelf, labeled, and dated.

Bundles of hundred dollar bills packed the bottom shelf. Helen counted the packages and concluded one million dollars stared at her.

Pulling on each small knob, diamonds, rubes, sapphires, and emeralds danced as light struck their polished surface. She picked up an emerald and turned it in the light. The radiance of the deep green color flickered brilliantly.

Returning the jewel to the drawer, she remarked, "Whew, I don't know much about gems, but I'm guessing a small fortune is in this safe. My, my, Howard, you've been holding out on your wife."

She turned back toward the window. Aimed at Howard's inner sanctum was a camcorder. The camera was recording when Helen entered the compartment, and abruptly switched off as the men departed.

A motion sensor must activate the machine by movement in his office, Helen thought. This was his warped way of keeping track of someone coming into his office, and maintaining a record of the event. He planned to use this as insurance to keep the bunch in line. I'm guessing those guys don't know the room existed, or have any idea the pictures were taken.

Those men wouldn't have been so free to speak out if they'd known he bugged the place, Helen concluded. And knowing Howard, he brought the group to his office for the sole purpose of recording the meeting.

This is a perfect set-up for Howard, Helen reasoned. To maintain the equipment he could simply lock the bathroom door. There's no telling what sort of shenanigans he's captured on those discs. I wonder if he had some way to take pictures of anything happening on the lounge in the bathroom. Now that would be interesting.

Helen pressed the playback button. Instantly, a picture showed up with a short segment of the recording. She watched as the proceedings repeated.

My picture's farther back on the disc, Helen reflected. I wonder how Howard came up with this idea.

Punching eject, the new video slid into a protective jacket retrieved from the supply shelf. The CD eased into the handbag hanging around Helen's neck, and a blank disc took its place. After snatching a handful of CDs from the safe and transferring them to her bag, she flipped the camera's switch to standby.

When I review these at home, she thought, I might be able to see just how deep this conspiracy goes in the company, and find out who else is involved.

Through the storage closet and across the lavatory, Helen darted to Howard's desk. She flipped the pages in the small notebook and jotted down websites and access data for contact with the banks. Now her mission was to leave unimpeded.

Cracking the door, she peeked to ascertain who was milling about in the hall. The floor was deserted. Casually she strolled to the elevator for the ride to the lobby.

The stairs were off limits with the fall so fresh on her mind. She didn't have the courage to tackle the steps, but opted for the quickest alternate route, an unhurried elevator.

Helen pressed the button, quickly a second punch, and then a third, the entire time praying the doors to open. Impatiently she waited and willed the doors to part like the Red Sea. With a sensation she had to pee, she crossed her legs and squeezed to relieve the pressure.

Cautious, she looked over her shoulder to spot anyone watching as she fretfully awaited the car. Scurrying inside when the box arrived, she pressed the button and poked again and again hoping the doors would close quicker and the car descend faster. No such luck. After a lifetime, it began to move.

Apprehensive the elevator cab would stop any moment, Helen felt fortunate when it descended smoothly and stopped at the bottom of the long shaft to open in the atrium. As the doors parted, she waved and smiled at Scotty and walked briskly crossing the endless span. Passing through the front doors, when they separated she ran toward the safety of her car.

Abruptly she stopped, bent over, and threw up retching violently. Witnessing participants of a crime in the making, she'd observed an intricate scheme perpetrated by traitors to swindle the company. She was caught off-guard, and unprepared for the chaos that repulsed her.

Squatting beside the curb, she attempted to regain her composure. She also had to pause and take stock of what she'd learned. Due to the shock of the event, her actions to this point were awkward, haphazard, and not well thought out. There was no plan of attack, a counterattack, or preparations to do anything, period. She was living in the moment.

What these animals were capable of is obvious, she thought. I heard them boast as if they had no regard for anyone.

Until this second, she had been reactive.

This has to change, she thought. What I need is to develop a strategy and anticipate what will come. Clearly, to remain alive and protect my family, I've got to become the aggressor.

Wanting to scream, Helen felt rage as a result of the event she witnessed, and thought, those bastards hired me for only one purpose. It wasn't due to my education, how well I did the job, and certainly not my intellect. Efficiency in running the program had nothing to do with it either, or not even how I looked. All they wanted was a scapegoat to cover their asses and make me the bad guy. That makes me so damn mad. Those assholes aren't going to get away with it, not if I have any say in the matter.

Her body heaved, and she threw up again, and again.

God, I'm sick. But I've got to pull myself together and get home so I can tell Matt about this. Together we'll figure out what to do. I can't even think straight right now. Two heads are better than one, anyway. I've just got to sit here a couple of minutes till I feel stronger.

Weak and unable to move, Helen was motionless sitting on the curb. Her head hung low trying to regain some feelings in her tingling limbs. Eventually, she conjured up strength to move and dug through her purse to find a tissue to wipe her mouth. Her hand brushed against a plastic sleeve that held a silvery circle of the evidence collected.

This disc confirms what they've been doing, she thought, and this was the same bunch who handpicked me to take the fall for their crimes. Matt will want to see this CD. I swear, as long as I have breath in my body, those guys will not get away with this fiasco.

As she regained her strength and the nausea subsided, Helen stood, weak and trembling, and wobbled the few remaining steps to her car, clutching the handbag firmly as if treasure.

NINE

When Matt arrived home, Helen was waiting. In anticipation, she chewed over how to present the reason for the makeshift outing, and the discoveries found. After withholding the idea she was making the excursion, she sensed he might be perturbed, and braced for the irritability he could display.

Once the visit was divulged, Matt became noticeably upset.

"Why in hell didn't you tell me you were going? I would have made arrangement to go with you," Matt bellowed. "But, you didn't want me to know. You withheld telling me because you knew I wouldn't agree with the idea."

"Matt, this was something I had to do alone," replied Helen.

"What were you thinking? If you had a relapse while you were there, what would you have done?" he clamored. "Did that ever occur to you?"

"I thought about it, but everything turned out alright," she responded.

"Helen, I've watched you. You're not strong enough to be running around all over creation, not yet anyway," he remarked sympathetically. "Were the doctors in on this?"

"Yes, I told them I was going and they thought it would be a good idea," she remarked calmly.

"I just wish you had told me about your plans before hand." Matt scolded. "But, you knew I wouldn't approve, and would have tried to convince you not to go."

"I didn't want to worry you," Helen admitted. "Besides, everything turned out okay."

"That's what you keep saying, but you don't look like everything's okay. You're white as a sheet," Matt snapped. "You're just damn lucky. This little episode could have taken a wrong turn and setback your recovery. Then you would have been stuck at home a lot longer before returning to work."

"Well, it didn't happen and I'm home safe now," Helen confirmed. "Matt, this was something that was eating at me, and I had to do. Besides, it was a good thing I went. I found out stuff's going on that you won't believe. Things I didn't have a clue were happening. It puts a whole new light on that spill I took on the stairs."

"You don't still think it was something other than an accident?" remarked Matt.

"Me falling down the stairs was just part of a larger conspiracy," Helen offered. "Let's get the kids put to bed, and I'll show you what I found. You won't believe it."

"Wait a minute," Matt replied. "Just hold on. Why don't you just give me a bird's eye view before we get too involved here? What really went on today?"

"Oh, nothing really, I just ran across a bunch of executives talking about stealing from the company. They've designated me as their patsy to take the blame for what they're doing, that's all," she said and erupted in tears.

Matt looked at her and was speechless. Wrapping his arms around her, he remarked, "You are kidding, aren't you."

Through watery eyes, she blubbered, "Do I look like I'm kidding? Those bastards have plans to make it look like I've taken money from the company. There are five people involved that I know about. I'm not sure whether this goes deeper and if others are wrapped up in the mess, or who they might be."

"This has got to be a joke," replied Matt.

"Hell no, it's not a joke," Helen screamed at him.

"Just how did you find out about all this? Did someone come up and tell you what they were doing while you were at the office today?" asked Matt. "This sounds rather bazaar."

"Matt, I went to the office to figure out why checks were being sent to vendors I didn't know about," Helen responded. "These checks are being deposited at a bank in Belize, and made out to names of companies I've never heard of before."

"Do all checks come across you desk?" he asked.

"No, but checks as large as these would have had some type of written agreement, and that's why our department got involved," Helen replied. "I later found out that the missing money amounts to millions."

"Wow," Matt remarked. "That is serious."

"Do you remember the dream I told you about?" Helen asked.

"The one where you thought someone shoved you down the steps," replied Matt.

"Yeah, that's the one. Well, after that I talked to Eve. She helped me remember why I went to see Howard in the first place," Helen remarked. "Then I did a search in the accounting program and a whole list of names was brought up, showing checks sent to businesses that I knew nothing about. Also, the documentation to support them is non-existent. Nothing, absolutely zilch, no contracts, no invoices, not even a hand-written note was in file."

"Did anyone try to run these down to find out where they came from?" Matt asked.

"Before the fall, I came across a large check I couldn't identify. It was one of those companies I didn't recognize that Beeson had never done business with before," remarked Helen. "I took it to Howard to ask him if he knew anything about the company or the check. He got extremely defensive, had me to leave it on his desk, and told me he would look into where it came from. The day I met with him was the day I fell. Don't you see? Because I began to ask questions, they tried to kill me the same afternoon as I left for home."

"It does sound like a coincidence," responded Matt.

"Everything makes sense. When I became inquisitive they panicked. I became a threat to their little secret," continued Helen. "I was too much of a liability and needed to be silenced to keep their scam under wraps."

"Well, that much makes sense," reasoned Matt.

"I found out later that the check I left on Howard desk was on the printout of items clearing the bank. When I found that, I suspected something funny was going on. There's no telling how long this has been happening. My guess is long before I was hired, or at least the plan was thought up that far back, and they have been siphoning off cash ever since."

"What did Howard say when you asked him about this?" said Matt.

"I haven't talked to him since the day I fell. But, while I was in his office today, I overheard a conversation between the whole bunch," continued Helen. "They were talking about setting me up to take the blame for money they took. One of them, Eric, something or other, is a VP I've seen around the place a couple of times. He let it out that he was the one who shoved me. After I hit the wall, he leaned over and called me a nosy bitch, and said I should keep my nose out of their business. This whole thing was a setup from the start."

"How can you prove any of this?" asked Matt. "It's just your word against theirs."

"Proof, you want proof? You bet your ass I've got all the proof you need," replied Helen.

Matt's eyes opened wide and his ears perked up.

"I have the entire conversation recorded," admitted Helen. "I'll show you after we get the kids in bed."

"What do you mean, show me?" remarked Matt. "What are you talking about?"

"That's what I've been trying to tell you all along. I took a DVD from a camcorder that recorded the entire conversation," Helen erupted. "When those guys got together it was recorded, sight and sound."

"How did you pull that off?" asked Matt.

"Howard has a secret room behind his desk with a camera that records everything that goes on," Helen revealed.

"You've got to be shitting me," Matt exclaimed. "Let's hurry, I want to see this."

"I thought you would."

The couple threw a meal together for the kids, and the entire time chatted about what was on the video. Tonight's bedtime story was shorter than usual, with the kids hurriedly tucked in for the night. Afterwards, Helen popped the disc taken earlier into the DVD player, and the couple settled on the couch.

Matt became mesmerized as he watched the interaction and exchanges between the men, the bickering between the players, and admissions of complicity in the conspiracy to steal from the company. Helen identified Eric Camp, the person who shoved her on the stairs, and witnessed once again an open discussion of the plan for her annihilation.

After the show, Matt groaned. "God almighty, that's enough to send chills down your spine. What do you think should be done about this?"

"I don't know yet. Maybe I ought to go straight to the cops. What do you think I should do?"

"I'm not sure. But whatever you do, the disc needs to be put somewhere safe," suggested Matt. "That bunch would kill in a heartbeat if they realized you have this. Would you like me to hide it for you?"

"It's been taken care of. I made several copies before you came home," replied Helen. "The original is locked away."

"Good thinking. How do you feel about what that bunch has done?" Matt asked. "You're not really considering a return to work under these circumstances, are you?"

"They said they were going to kill me before I go back," Helen responded. "And, as soon as Howard finds out the disc is gone, he'll be ready to strangle me himself. He's smart enough to figure out someone's been inside his office, and he'll suspect I'm the one who took the CD. After that, I'm not exactly sure what's going to happen."

"Why do you say that," Matt asked.

"By now he may already know the disc is gone. I'm quite sure the other guys don't have a clue about the recording. One thing is for certain, Howard won't tell them. My guess is he'll think hard before retrieving the discs himself. He'll hire someone to do his dirty work to keep his hands clean. He's tried to kill once and boasted he would do it again."

"That's a frightening thought," said Matt. "Regardless, the kids need to be taken away from here until this blows over or they could be in jeopardy."

"Where can I leave them? I don't have any place for them to go," Helen responded. "I have no family, and if I left them with someone, those bastards would find out where they were and go after them. No, for now the kids stay with me. That disc is my ace in the hole. As long as I have it and he doesn't, Howard's going to be careful and won't be eager to do much of anything until he gets it back."

"I'm not sure I agree," responded Matt. "The kids might be safer somewhere else."

"He'll think long and hard about whatever he does, and you can bet he won't do anything stupid. One thing Howard's not, and that's stupid," remarked Helen. "Whatever he has up his sleeve will be well thought out. The others will never know about those discs unless they're made public. He just won't tell them."

The couple continued the discussion into the wee hours of the morning. They talked about options available to handle the untenable situation, and concocted a scenario of what might happen when Howard learns of the disappearance. Howard would suspect Helen immediately. All hell would then break loose, and his screams heard for miles, maybe all the way to the small orchard in central Indiana.

* * * *

Howard's butt dragged as he dawdled to his office after a grueling day ensnared with directors. Wiped out, the board members hammered him with pointed questions. They drilled him on the poor performance and losses sustained on every front, and he was tired of answering questions from a bunch of idiots.

He held firm to the assertions that cost overruns were due to locked-in contracts bid far too low. Operational costs were too high, he insisted, because of unforeseen overhead in the regions. He claimed the ventures were located in eccentric countries where bribes, kickbacks to ethnic leaders, and payoffs to government officials, were a way of life. As fodder to chew on, he threw-in any spurious defense he could provide.

Howard would never reveal the ventures were highly profitable, and losses sustained resulted from skimming. Siphoned off under the guise of cash payouts were earnings by any means of murky accountability. His crew was doing this with regularity with efforts stepped up in recent years, as the group of deviants wanted to abandon the company, and soon.

Howard surmised the directors singled him out and held him responsible for poor performance and a declining stock price. The directors were pummeling him, seeking justification to avert up-in-arms stockholders, the SEC, and any other regulatory body from knocking on the door to nose around. Howard was prepared to go the distance to forestall an ill-fated event until the crisis stabilized, or he was gone. Wrung out at present, he could care less. He felt like the condemned walking to the gallows for a lynching.

Grilled endlessly concerning company operations as CFO, scrutinized were reports from every undertaking around the globe. The directors expected answers on his fingertips with challenges tossed his direction. Entering his office, out of habit he picked up the small remote from his desk, pointed it toward the mirror, and pressed stop.

I'm so damn tired of these inquisitions by those bastards, he thought.

He sat at his desk gazing out the window overlooking the tranquil gardens below. The view took in White River State Park, a mall near the city center. Here people gathered and events took place in a vibrant and bustling Midwestern metropolis. People from all walks of life normally milled about in the commons. But the crowd appeared unusually scanty this evening.

Overhead streetlights had begun to flicker as twilight was approaching. Soon darkness would envelope the city as lovers stroll arm-in-arm along the water's edge, absorbing the soothing romance in the air.

A short distance beyond, towering buildings overshadowed the city. For miles, massive signs erected atop tall structures were visible to announce its occupant. Proud skyscrapers owned by companies as names changed overnight following a merger.

Oblivious, Howard was blind to the beauty of the skyline. He was numb from the day's antics and had become callus to the backdrop. His mind was still in the room with the bloodthirsty eyes focused on his demise, seeking opportunities to devour him. As the events replayed, the inaction of the other members of his faction who remained muted during the bloodbath perturbed him. They were voiceless, leaving him to flounder on his own with no support for the explanations he provided.

Why do I need those sonsabitches? Howard reflected. After they did this to me, I'm going to hang every damn one of those bastards out to dry. I'm the one who made this company what it is today. I'm the one who came up with the ideas on how to rake huge profits by moving into other countries. And I'm the one who had the idea to channel cash to offshore accounts. Then they wanted to jump on the bandwagon after I showed them how to do it.

"Screw them," Howard whispered. I built this company with no help from anybody, he considered. This is my company and always has been. Why, it's evident by how everyone looks to me for answers. I'm entitled to every dollar I take from this damn place. Without me, this company would be nothing.

Hell, I've done everything, and those bastards have just been tagging along for the ride. Frankly, I never needed any of them. Now this has happened, they're not getting a penny. They've outlived their usefulness, and when this is over and I'm out of here, they're all going to be dead in the water. I'm going to hang every last one of their asses.

Turning to his computer, he logged on to the Swiss bank, entered his password, and a screen appeared showing the cash balance.

Eight hundred million and change, I love looking at that number knowing it's mine.

He smiled and pondered what he would do with it. All mine, he thought.

I'll be able to live quite comfortably. But, I'd like to get it over a billion before I leave, although I'm not waiting around. I'm leaving real soon.

He shut down the machine realizing the hour. Pointing the remote toward the mirror, he pressed record.

After today's inquisition, I need a hot shower. I'm going home. Tomorrow will be another day. As soon as I see those assholes, I'm going to chew their asses for not speaking up. They hung me out to dry, those assholes, and they'll pay for it.

Howard turned out the light, took the elevator to the lobby, and walked the few steps to his Mercedes. Absorbed with the injustices inflicted on him, he was formulating a plan to disappear and cutout the group.

"Those bastards, those goddamn bastards," he remarked.

* * * *

"How can I stop that bunch from taking off with the money?" Helen muttered. What can I do?, she wondered.

The riddle spun through her mind for hours as she sought a solution to an inexplicable question. Tossing, turning, and unable to sleep, she got out of bed and flipped the computer switch. Opening a web browser, she typed in the Internet address to the Bank of Switzerland. Meticulous, she entered items to open a new numbered account.

Her name was already on file. Starting a second account was matter-of-fact. She had settled on the first step to a solution to expose the deceit of the men. Adamant, she didn't plan for the criminals to get away with the cash.

Reporting theft at Beeson to the police remained an option. Initially, she rejected the notion because it wouldn't get quick attention, and going through channels would take forever. She could visualize useless studies conducted before any accomplishment, and with her family placed under a microscope. This was something she couldn't allow. The embezzlement had nothing to do with her children, and she wouldn't allow them to be the subject of suspicion or pulled into the milieu.

Time was in short supply, and the legal mumbo-jumbo would consume an exorbitant amount. First-hand observation supported her contention the accomplices were preparing to bolt. With an inquiry opened, cash and crooks would both disappear. And if the prosecutor dropped the ball, the villains would disappear like Casper.

Convinced local authorities were incompetent and unable to avert a mass exodus, deciding on an aggressive approach, to move the money out of the reach of the thugs was a beginning. At least the funds would be secure even if the scoundrels vanished.

Helen opened the web page for the bank account in Belize. Signing on using the name and password from Howard's notebook, an impressive string of digits appeared.

"I wonder how often they've been making transfers to Switzerland?" she muttered.

The answer came upon looking through the account history. Transfers were made weekly with regularity. Clicking an icon, she selected Wire Transfer, and inserted the account balance. Questions, plucked from Howard's notebook that appeared on screen, were completed. Immediate transfer selected.

A grayish box appeared in center screen and provided a sliding bar to signify progress of the transmission. Soon, TRANSFER COMPLETE, appeared. With a few mouse clicks, Helen logged out.

The Swiss bank account showed the funds she transferred as a new deposit. Initially, Helen thought the total had to be a mistake. She had never imagined so many numbers and digits as those filling the screen.

"This is incredible," she said. Her mouth flew open, as she gawked in amazement. They've apparently been stealing for years to build up this balance, she thought.

With a few mouse clicks, the entire amount moved to the newly created account opened on the previous visit to the website. Afterwards, she ascertained the funds were safely in the new account. Now confident the cash was beyond Howard's reach, she closed the browser.

At least the money is no longer available, Helen thought. Now, let's take the next step.

Helen typed a note, placed it in a cardboard pouch along with a copy of the DVD, and addressed the package for delivery. Feeling drained, she wandered back to bed.

As she reclined and attempted to sleep, her body ached from weariness. Still too worked up from the course of action chosen, slumber eluded her. Helen rolled from bed, but this time she was up for the day, earlier than usual. The sun hadn't begun to rise and the sky outside remained dark, as she became aware of a morning chill. Draping a bathrobe around her shoulders, it was tied at the waist. The robe was old and had been hanging in the closet forever. A coffee pot was bubbling in short order.

The aroma of the brew filled the air with its specialty blend. She loved to start the day with the smell of fresh coffee. The whiff flowing through the air was comforting, something she could rely on like a pair of old broken-in shoes. Matt and the children were still in bed and she decided to let them sleep.

There's no reason for the entire household to be awake, she thought, at least not at this hour. After delivery of the package there will be so much upheaval around here, they're going to need all the sleep they can get.

Helen needed this time alone to reflect on the solution she had settled, and consider how the undertaking might play out. Once the package was out of her hands, life as she knew it would change forever.

There wouldn't be a change of heart, or an about face to alter the path she had set in motion. Releasing the information from the CD would affect many lives. Shredded in an instant would be a once vibrant institution that provided jobs for thousands, and trust long endowed on company executives. Helen had to come to terms with the enormity of her decision, and have confidence the action she chose was the correct path to take.

Light began to appear through the windows as Matt sauntered into the kitchen carrying Samantha with Michael in tow. After a "Good Morning," Helen kissed them and began to pull cereal from the cabinet shelf, retrieve milk from the refrigerator, and prepare breakfast for the bunch.

Mumbling, "Morning," the children wrung sleep from their eyes with their fists.

"Good morning," Matt replied as he yawned, and leaned over to give Helen a peck on the cheek. "Not able to sleep?"

"No. I've struggled throughout the night with what to do, and I had to think this situation all the way out. Decisions I make will affect a lot of folks. I just pray the company and the employees are strong enough to survive," remarked Helen. "I'll have to look for another job if I can find one. Not many places are looking to hire a whistleblower, at least none that I know of. And management will have a complete turnover. But, in the long-run Beeson will be stronger after the dust settles. Other than that everything is peachy."

"Are you sure you're doing the right thing?" asked Matt.

"No," she replied. "But I've got to do something, and this is the best solution I can come up with. Whatever happens must be soon. That's the monster I've been wrestling and has kept me awake. The affects of what I'm about to do will reach far beyond anything I can imagine."

"Why do you say that?" asked Matt.

"Because I'm certain the ripples will be much greater than I can envision. Yet, if I sit back and do nothing, that whole bunch is going to scatter like ants at a picnic and be long gone. Then it would take forever to ferret out the bunch and bring them to justice, if they would ever be caught."

"Do you want to be known as a whistleblower the rest of your life?" asked Matt. "This label will be awfully harsh."

"I know, but at least I'll be able to sleep nights, and my conscience will be clear. In time, maybe people will forget what I did except for the good parts," Helen remarked. "It's better to be a whistleblower than a coward."

"Branded and fired," responded Matt. "Whistleblower might as well be tattooed across your forehead. That term will stick like glue."

"But Matt, are you saying I shouldn't do anything? If I sit back, good people will be hurt, and the bad guys will get away. I've got to try to stop them. That's the reason I can't put it off," responded Helen.

"I understand," said Matt. "But at least for a while, people are not going to think too highly of you."

"Yeah, undergoing scrutiny will be tough, but I hope in time things will change. If I don't do something, it'll always be on my conscience, and I'd be constantly questioning if I did the right thing by not coming forward," Helen responded.

"Whatever you've got planned, are you sure it'll work?" asked Matt.

"No. I'm not certain it's the best choice or that it is the right thing to do. But if I do nothing, I'll regret it," Helen replied. "This is something that has to be done regardless of how it plays out."

"If you feel that strongly, I'll support whatever you decide and tag along for the ride," Matt responded.

Raising Helen's chin, Matt looked into her eyes and professed, "I love you, and believe me when I tell you this, you're no coward. You're the bravest person I've ever met. Beautiful, too, by the way, even this early in the morning," he said kissing her on the forehead.

"At the moment, I don't feel very brave."

TEN

Howard had another night of truncated sleep. He arose, surrendered to insomnia, stepped in the shower, and decided to return to his fiefdom at the office.

Twenty-four hours earlier, he was dressed for success. Since then he caved to the homeless mask of disheveled hair, rumpled clothing, and the reemergence of gray stubble. But after a shower, at least he wouldn't stink.

Although resembling a derelict, he cherished hot steamy water pouring over his short plump frame for a morning pick-me-up. The ritual heightened his senses and prepared him for battle.

Every day was combat, somebody was out to get him. He had to be ever vigilant, watch his back, and scratch for every morsel.

As the water flowed, his eyes closed and his mind drifted to surroundings where he soon intended to live in luxury. Standing by the sea he could hear the roar of the ocean, visualize the whitecaps created by a storm at sea, and the salt air burning his nostrils. Here he would command respect, and be pampered with any depravity to satisfy a hedonic appetite. This was the place where he would be king.

I'll never be stuck behind a desk again, or hurry to meet some damn deadline, he resolved. And, no more goddamn board meetings, I hate them. My only regret, I won't be able to tell those damn bastards to go to hell. By nightfall, I'll be gone.

Howard had made an instant change of plan. Today was the day. Returning to the office to gather a few things was all that stood between him and freedom.

This godforsaken job has handcuffed me far too long. Before anybody figures out what's hit them, I'll be out of here. The lousy bastards don't have any balls and I'll leave them holding the bag. Screw that woman. I'll let someone else sort out who took the money. Let's see them dance for answers while they're swinging in the wind. They'll be sorry they left me hanging. Hell, I'll show all of them who they're dealing with, and the cash will go with me. I'll show them, those bastards.

Arriving at the office, Howard parked in his usual space, waved to the guard, and took the slow elevator to the high rent district. Here was where he hashed out major decisions, including embezzlement.

He pressed pause on the remote as he strolled in the room. There was no need to record his every move rustling about the office. Packing light, he would take only a few things along with the hard drive from his computer.

Can't leave that, he reflected. It's full of too much good stuff that would create a scandal if abandoned. But for all the other junk, I'll leave for some other bitch to clean up.

Through the bathroom and into the hidden compartment, Howard began his usual routine to make certain the camera was live. Previously, a power surge or the lights flickering would shut it down. To prevent this, a power pack with a surge protector was connected.

He had no plans to use the camera in the future, but couldn't leave it for others to speculate. A creature of habit, he had become accustomed to performing the routine, and old habits were hard to break. Besides, a fresh disc needed manual insertion.

Until I'm gone, this camera stays put, he thought. There's no telling what tidbits I might pick up.

Howard pressed preview to inspect the recording from the previous day. Snow appeared on the small screen. Again he hit preview, and once again, snow. Queued to the beginning, he pushed play yet again, still no picture from the disc. He looked closely at the equipment and found it set on standby.

"This camera wasn't working," he muttered. "How the hell did that happen?"

Punching eject, the disc slid into the CD drive of a nearby computer. Howard clicked the button on the machine and found there were no files, only snow filled the screen.

"What the hell is going on here?" He murmured.

Turning to the camera he carefully observed the setting.

The last time I was in the room was yesterday when I changed the disc, he reflected. The switch was then set on automatic, he recalled. It wasn't on standby. Somebody's been in here. What asshole could have found this room?

Fuming, Howard darted to the safe. A mental count was made of the cash, and detected it was intact. Pulling on each drawer, the stones appeared untouched. Picking up a disc, he realized the date was older.

"Why wouldn't somebody take the cash and stones?" he mumbled. "Those would have been easy pickings and untraceable. What the hell were they after?"

Howard paused, remembered the camera and the lapse in dates of the discs, and became weak kneed. He felt like collapsing and unexpectedly became sick to his stomach, wanting to puke.

"Goddamnmit," he yelled. "Those discs in the right hands are worth more than the rest of this shit. They'll put me in jail. Goddamnmit," he bellowed. "I've got to get those damn things back. Which one of those bastards could have taken them?"

He recalled the gathering from the previous day.

Shit! One of those assholes found out about this room, he thought. The bastard has yesterday's recording. That blows my plans for certain.

Howard knew he had to retrieve the discs before leaving town or face jail time.

Let's see, we talked about the money and doing away with Helen, he thought. Shit! Shit! Shit! What the hell else did I say? They'll find plenty once they look at those CDs closely. SON-OF-A-BITCH! One of those assholes will unravel everything. This goddamn party might just be over if I don't get those things back.

"Who swiped my goddamn discs?" he shouted.

Abruptly, he recalled accessing the banks and ran to his desk. Calling up the web page, the Belize bank account was zero.

"Goddamnmit, where is my money?" he hollered.

Looking through the history, he found a transfer made in the early morning hours.

"I didn't do this. What the goddamn hell is going on here?" he shouted.

Dumbfounded, Howard logged onto the Bank of Switzerland and found the account empty.

"God-damn-son-of-a-bitch," he shouted. "What in the hell is going on here? Who took my money? Which asshole is dumb enough to do something like this?"

Searching the activity, he spotted an entry to empty the account. Blood drain from his face, his legs went limp as he plopped in his office chair. His arms and legs tingled, his chest ached, and his heart was pounding.

"Who would have taken all my money?" he shouted. "When I find out I'm going to choke them with my bare hands."

Springing from the chair, he paced the room. Sensitive to a renewed strength and rush of adrenaline, he knew it was imperative to remain calm and think, think clearly. Picking up the phone, he dialed the Bank of Switzerland. With a six-hour time disparity, in that country it was early afternoon.

"Guten Tag. Herzlich willkommen in die Bank der Schweiz. Wie kann ich von Nutzen sein?" (Good afternoon. Welcome to the Bank of Switzerland. How may I be of service?), responded the operator.

Although a small country, Switzerland had four official languages, with German used in Zurich, the banking center of the country.

"English," Howard barked.

"How may I help?" the operator said in perfect American English.

"Customer Service," snapped Howard.

After a short wait, a woman answered.

"Good afternoon and welcome. My name is Gretchen. How may I be of assistance?"

Howard explained that he looked online and there was an obvious error with a transfer from his account.

"I'm sorry you're having trouble. Upon looking at the information, we don't show you are an authorized user. I can't provide you with any information. I'm sorry."

Howard was speechless. For an instant, he'd forgotten the account was set up using Helen's name and documents.

Sweating bullets, he quickly responded, "I used another name on the account," and gave the attendant the security data.

"I'm sorry. That's not the current information on file."

Howard pounded his fist in the air, as his blood pressure elevated and he pulled at his hair.

"NO, GODDAMNMIT, THAT CAN'T BE," he screamed loud enough to be heard across the ocean. "I'm the only one with access," he remarked lowering his voice.

"I'm sorry," Gretchen replied and disconnected.

Someone found the account number and password. Whoever did this couldn't have just guessed, he thought. That information was in my locked desk. The last time I looked at the account, the only people around were the guys in the meeting, he thought.

"They were with me in the board meeting the whole time and didn't have an opportunity to copy it," he said. "So who the hell could have done this?"

Shit, I've got to get out of here before somebody finds out about this, he thought. I've got enough cash to last for a while, and the jewels will bring a pretty penny when sold. I have my passport and can leave right away. I'll take the company jet and fly to South America. I'll go to one of those countries with no extradition, he thought. Venezuela would be good.

Howard considered the possibilities as he paced and circled the room, stepping over and around objects. His strides were steady as he tried to grasp the severity of the circumstances. He reversed directions, and counterbalanced the situation placing him in this position. Reminded to remain calm, his decision was crucial.

"No goddamnmit, I'm not going anywhere. That money is mine, I've earned it," he said. "I've worked too damn hard to get it, and I'm going to find out which sonofabitch took it. I'm getting it back, and whoever the prick is, he's not getting away with my money."

Howard called the mailroom and ordered whoever made the deliveries sent to his office. The clerk was a petite woman, twenty years of age, five feet tall. She had short brown hair, and her complexion held remnants of severe acne from early teens when the skin condition was an all out battle. On her arrival, Howard was still pacing and he demanded she sit. Without a hello, he stared down on her and at once began his inquest.

"Cassie, this is extremely important. When you delivered on this floor yesterday, did you see anybody milling around here?" Howard growled. "Think hard."

Shaken by Howard's abrupt demeanor, she hesitated knowing if she didn't answer correctly, she could be jobless in a heartbeat. She knew to stay calm and think. With the company only six months, she had the opportunity to wander through every department. She loved talking to people, and hoped this would improve her chances of a move out of the mailroom.

The woman had her finger on the pulse of interoffice gossip due to the free movement her job allowed. Picking up on bits and pieces as she roamed, she carefully weighed the answer.

"No, Mr. Jenkins. There wasn't anybody around when I delivered here. You were all in that big meeting, remember? How did it go, by the way?" She was interested in fresh chitchat to spread, and tried to lighten the tension in the room.

Howard ignored the question and barked, "Did you see anything unusual going on anywhere yesterday?"

She paused and gathered her thoughts.

"No, sir, I don't remember anything like that. Ms. Faulkner came in for a while. She got tired and went home early."

"Get the hell out of here," Howard screamed at her.

He turned to his computer and called up the swipe log showing employees that accessed sensitive areas, the Ivory Tower the most vulnerable.

"Helen. Goddamn Helen," he shrieked. "I should have known it would be that bitch."

He picked up a book and threw it against the wall. It hit hard, and made a dent, as he screamed.

"Here she is," he confirmed, scrolling through the names. "She swiped her goddamn badge on this floor during the morning. That woman would have been here when we met during the break. She was in my back room watching the whole time. That damn bitch. That goddamn bitch, I'll strangle her with my bare hands. I've got to find her and get those discs back, and find out what she did with my money before she does anything else foolish."

* * * *

After the children were on the bus and Matt took off for work, Helen gathered her package and drove to the center of the city. Locating a parking space on Pennsylvania Street, she sauntered the block and a half to the entrance of the *Indianapolis Star* newspaper building, and meandered to the front counter.

"Hi. May I help you?" said the perky blonde behind the desk.

"Would you please see that Pete Drucker gets this envelope?" asked Helen.

"I'll be happy to give it to him. Is there a message?" the receptionist asked as she took the package.

"Everything's inside. But please be sure this goes to him personally, without delay. It's extremely urgent," Helen remarked.

Everything anybody brings in here is urgent, the blonde considered as she replied, "I'll deliver it to him at once," and took the package with a broad smile.

Helen did an about face and strolled briskly from the building. The receptionist watched as the woman hiked smartly through the door. The pouch dropped to a ledge behind the counter in the next instant, so the young woman could answer a ringing telephone.

* * * *

Howard punched wildly at the digits provided to make contact. He didn't care who the person was, he wanted Helen dead and his property returned. He would pay the unconscionable fee with assurance of returning his things.

The number was from a trusted source, and assured the contractor would do the deed without question. The compensation was unreasonable, but the person wouldn't go squeamish over the assignment.

Howard initially had reservations about making the call concerning the endeavor. Once arranged, changing his mind wouldn't be an option.

He'd been responsible for hiring Helen, and taken her under his wing. Indoctrinated on how to perform the job, he had allowed her enough rope to hang herself. A tinge of regret hung in the air knowing that with one phone call a life he nurtured would end.

This contract would be permanent and allow for no backing out. That wasn't the case with Eric Camp. Howard always doubted his abilities. He played along with the group to appease the gnawing urgency from the others to take her out, but had no faith in Camp's aptitude to complete the job, and he was right.

After considering his present circumstance for an instant, he was convinced his freedom was far more essential than her life. One phone call would keep the fat man out of jail and restore his property, and at the same time a formidable foe eliminated.

Someone not expected to provide resistance had become a pain in his ass. In reality, he had come to admire her ability to adapt and land on her feet.

Helen Faulkner, that damn bitch, he thought. Maybe in another life we could team up.

Without a connection to the outcome, Howard had no reservations on the eradication. He wasn't interested in what took place, as long as the problem was rectified and he got what he wanted. The phone call would remove the problem, keep him out of jail, and his hands clean. The arrangement would be worth the ridiculous price. Her life for his dream was a regrettable alternative. Getting his possessions back was the only concern for Howard Jenkins to remain free and rich.

The voice told him to be at the far end of the parking garage of Clarion Hospital, second level. Early morning allowed free reign through the tiered edifice with no gatekeeper on duty.

The instructions were curt and precise. Fill the briefcase with the fee, and enclose pictures and relevant information.

Howard was to provide a list of items to retrieve, and was emphatic the new account numbers, passwords, and security authorizations were salvaged. He was precise in his instruction, "If you try to take off with any of the goods, I'll hunt you down and you'll never live to enjoy them."

Howard added a caveat, "If she resists, use the children as leverage to extract information."

Howard's intuition told him her motherly instinct wouldn't allow harm to come to the children. What happened afterwards was unimportant after retrieval of the articles. The man could then eliminate everybody who could talk.

Wheeling through the maze to the second level, Howard parked in the shadows, alone, and away from a handful of scattered vehicles. He asked how he would find the caller, and was told, "I'll find you."

Inside the briefcase, Howard included the list requested. In addition, he proposed a bonus if the items were brought back within forty-eight hours. This would provide an ample opportunity for a quick getaway before someone linked him to the killing. Normally, the gunman would decline the offer, but the money was easy and too good to pass up.

"For that kind of dough, the stuff on the list must be important," he tersely remarked to Jenkins.

"Don't ask questions," scolded Howard. "Just do the deed."

"And you'd better have the cash ready. I don't intend to baby-sit for long," offered the assassin.

* * * *

Always carrying a smile, Mandy Carter handed the cardboard envelope to Pete Drucker. "Some woman just dropped this at the front desk, Mr. Drucker, and said it was urgent. You know, just like everybody else does." She rolled her eyes without giving the package credibility after dealing with the obnoxious behavior of a few. For some, everything carried in the door was crucial.

"Thanks, Mandy," said Pete. "Who was she?

ELEVEN

On her nineteenth birthday, Marie Dominique married Joseph Drucker, two years her senior. A son followed within a year named James, James Peter Drucker.

Astute and mature, more so than most children his age, the boy absorbed knowledge like a sponge. He thrived on learning, and with a ferocious appetite for reading, the child's natural curiosity was encouraged. An inherent fondness for words was cultivated, as he became fascinated with vocabulary.

Astounded with the use of diverse terms, he learned early a discriminating word could be a powerful tool, although limp if used improperly. Often he played rhyming word games with his parents to develop an understanding for the usage of certain terms. The meaning of a phrase or paragraph, he soon realized, could hinge on the exploit of a single anomalous expression.

Entering college he gravitated to Journalism, worked for the school newspaper and later became its editor. After bouncing from one newspaper to another after graduation, he got wind of a rag seeking a reporter in Indiana.

Indianapolis was a town he'd only read about and was a long walk from family and a home with familiar surroundings. A move to the Midwest was a big sacrifice for a fledging correspondent who had never been outside the state of his birth. He would be alone, encounter strange people, and stranger surroundings. Without family, he would struggle and scrimp, but after mulling over the options, in the end he was willing to give it a whirl and applied for the opening.

Pete Drucker inherited traits from both parents. His father's handsome Polish features, and his mother's high cheekbones and olive complexion, the tinge of a pallid suntan. He inherited good qualities from each parent, and women considered him quite appealing and easy on the eye. At six-two, he was slim at one-ninety, and unmarried.

Work was his passion, yet he held out hope to stumble upon a woman that could one day provide passion for his heart. Until that juncture, he was married to a career with little time for anything else.

* * * *

Smiling cheerfully, the petite blonde replied, "Don't know, I've never seen her before."

Mandy was effervescent and well suited for the post she held. Although young, she emitted an eagerness to perform tasks in good spirits and ingratiate coworkers. Regardless of what took place at the front desk, her attitude was positive and demonstrated a maturity to handle situations delicately. She was a people pleaser.

Pete glanced at the name scrolled across the package as he turned it over and around, examining the pouch to search for a return address. There was none.

"Beautiful handwriting, wonder who sent it," he remarked and looked at the neat scrawl on the jacket. "I wish my scribbling was that pretty."

He hesitated, seemed reluctant to open the envelope remembering the news stories of certain high-level people receiving inexplicable packages laced with anthrax.

I'm not that important, he thought. Who'd want to hurt me?

Curiosity won out as he pulled the strip and the contents were exposed. Surprised, he found a DVD and a short note.

Play this video and watch it carefully. The contents are self-explanatory, the participants easy to identify. Afterwards, if you want more information, contact me at hf83271@yahoo.com.

An air of mystery surrounded the envelope causing Drucker to become intrigued when the package first appeared. Now that he read the message and had disc in hand, his interest spiked as he placed it in the reader. Getting comfortable, he sat back in the chair with his feet on the desk.

I need some popcorn and a soda, he thought. I wish I knew the name of the movie. I wonder who made it.

The picture began slowly, stopped abruptly, and jerked a number of times as people shifted from view. In the bottom corner was the date, time, and sequence number of each frame.

This was from a couple of days ago, he realized.

He became bored watching the jerky sequence and thought it was some kind of joke.

I think I'm wasting my time, this thing is trash. Weighing its importance, he thought, I actually have other stories to work on that are more important.

Although bored by the jerky action, his reporter instincts provided enough interest to find out what was on the disc. He watched for a couple of minutes as a sequence began so he could get a gist for the content. The picture stopped jerking and a woman came into view as she sheepishly peered around the doorframe.

Glancing through stuff strewn about the room, the woman zeroed in on the oversized desk in center screen. Searching for something, she looked through messages and papers piled on the desk. And then she began to rifle the desk drawer but stopped. A low roar began in the distance. As the voices moved closer and became palpable, the woman vanished.

Five well-clothed men burst in. They were agitated and upset as reflected by the rude lingo flung about. Talking at the same time, tones gradually lowered and the conversation became civil.

"Damn, is this for real?" Pete said.

He was a captive as he listened to remarks hurled about.

The men were wearing expensive suits, ties, and shoes, all custom. These were obviously high rollers with lots of cash at their disposal.

"Couldn't this wait till later?" snapped the short pudgy man who seemed to be in control of the get-together. "We don't have much time. What the hell is so damned urgent we need to talk about?"

The man seemed to be in bad spirits, ill mannered and vile with his colleagues.

Pete turned up the volume. He didn't want to miss a syllable, and feverishly took notes with his ears on alert listening intently. He watched the men as they rambled about the room, stepping over things as the conversation heated. He could tell that the discussion was eroding and could come to blows. Jumping from his chair, he anticipated a punch. Another man wedged into the fray to distract two of the men and sidetrack the squabble to prevent the disagreement from turning into a fistfight.

Seeing the situation cool, Pete sat back in the chair.

"Man, I thought I'd have to become a referee for a second," he commented.

The conversation was moving so fast, Pete could only jot down key words for later recall of the event, and relieved he could replay the disc to remind him of the confrontation. This was a luxury he didn't have most of the time, and relied on a small recorder he carried in his pocket.

Suddenly the person called Howard, sat at the computer and called up a web page. After entering certain information, numbers appeared.

"Now are you happy?" asked the pudgy man.

Unsatisfied, the man demanded to see a second account. The fat guy called up a different web address and another bank website appeared.

Pete wanted to see the details on screen but a man blocked his view. Damn, I wish he'd move over, he thought.

After the exchange, the five men strolled from the room smiling, and offering praise for a job well done and a successful scheme about to be wrapped up.

* * * *

Amazed with the matter-of-fact discussion the men had of their involvement in crimes, Pete construed from the chatter the characters were involved in a scheme to steal from the company that employed them. The conversation included a failure to kill a woman, and the intent to make it look like an accident with a follow-up plan in the works.

Man, these topics come up in everybody daily conversations, he thought facetiously. Where'd this thing come from?

As the picture turned to snow, he was mesmerized and fixated on the screen. For several minutes, he remained seated, looking at the blank screen.

"This can't be real. Somebody's playing a joke on me," he said upon reflection.

He stood and looked around the newsroom to see if anyone was watching to get a rise out of him. Over the top of the cubicle he announced, "If someone's trying to play a joke, well you did it, it worked. I fell for it."

He glanced around the newsroom and laughed to see if anyone was watching for a reaction. People stopped and looked at him oddly as if he had two heads and continued with what they were involved.

Accepting the video as authentic, he turned his attention to the computer and played the movie again from the beginning, the disc set to where the five men entered the room. As he observed and listened, he came to the conclusion he had seen some of these men before. Printing pictures, he took them to Joel Sumner, his editor.

"Hey, Joe, I have some photos here, do you recognize any of these people?"

Joel looked at the grainy prints carefully and remarked, "This guy is Clark Ford, and this one is Gordon Compton. They're executives at Beeson International. This short heavy guy is Howard Jenkins. He's the CFO. I believe the others might work there but I don't know their names or position. Why do you ask? What's going on?"

"Maybe the biggest story this newspaper has ever seen," replied Pete. "I'll let you know as soon as I figure it out."

Drucker returned to his desk and wrote the names of the men on each photograph. He pounded out a response to the email address listed on the note.

WANT TO MEET AS SOON AS POSSIBLE, TELL ME WHERE AND WHEN.

He dated and signed his name, and wondered how long it would take to get a response.

The disc played several times, and with each revolution the reporter became more aware of the interactions of the men. Immersed into the conversation, he listened intently and considered the inflection of each word or phrase. He needed to discern its exact meaning, or conclude another underlying connotation was evident.

A student once again, he remained alert, attentive, and challenged to comprehend an underlying gist if one existed. Coming to a conclusion the conversations were genuine was critical, or if they should be denounced for some reason. Taking the dialogue at face value, with each viewing he became more astonished. He shook his head in amazement, and found it difficult to believe what was happening.

As he wrapped up viewing the disc for the final time, he jumped when a voice heralded, YOU'VE GOT MAIL.

* * * *

After delivering the package to the receptionist, Helen returned home. She entered the narrow drive then walked the front steps. Overly cautious, she'd placed clear tape across the ledge of the doorway and felt for it before opening the door. On the tip of her finger she could feel a break, the tape was torn. Someone was inside and she wouldn't take a chance on confronting an intruder.

Turning on a dime, she scampered to her car and sped off. She was fearful, yet infuriated that someone had violated her sanctuary, as she dialed Matt's cell number.

* * * *

A man watched as a car fitting the description he was seeking moved up the lane toward the house. The residence was in the open, and he had concealed his vehicle in a grove of trees a half-mile away and walked the distance. Gaining entry he tossed the place, dumped bookshelves, and scattered stuff everywhere searching for the shiny discs.

Unable to uncover them, he waited. He was hoping the woman would return soon so he could get what he wanted and finish her off, then be on his way with the job done in record time and collect his bonus.

He was in place to snatch her when she came through the door, but instead watched as she hesitated. Something had spooked her and she hurried back to the car. Unsure of the reason, he realized the timing was off and slipped away. Upon her return, she would find someone ransacked her house, put her on alert, and complicate another attempt.

* * * *

"Have you been back to the house since you left for work this morning?" she blurted out as Matt answered his cell.

"No, I had no reason to return home," responded Matt. "Why do you ask?"

"After I delivered the package, the tape I marked the door with before leaving was torn. Somebody broke in."

"My God, are you sure?" said Matt.

"Yes, I'm sure," replied Helen.

"What'd you do?" Matt asked.

"I'll talk to you about it later," Helen responded. "I'm not going back in there unless somebody's with me."

Matt responded, "I don't blame you, but where will you go?"

"I don't know," Helen remarked. "I've got some things yet to do so I'll be in touch."

Helen proceeded to the public library to use a computer and check her e-mail, anxious to know if a she received a response about the package dropped at the *Star*. Calling up her account, she was happy to find a message waiting. With the response in caps, she knew his interest was clear, and she punched out a reply.

* * * *

A side street was the closest spot Helen could find to park near Matt's lofty office building. She planned to tell him about her upcoming meeting with the reporter and she could be late for dinner. Entering the front lobby, a bustle of people were milling about as she spotted Matt standing by the newsstand holding the *Wall Street Journal* in one hand and a large coffee in the other. Her hand flew in the air to catch his attention, and just as quick carefully lowered it. Stopped in her tracks, she attempted to become inconspicuous. Standing beside Matt was one of the men in the video taken from Howard's camera.

Was Matt part of the conspiracy the whole time and been concealing it? If that's the case, whom can I trust? Is everybody taking me for a fool?

Before Matt realized she was in the building, Helen made an about face and hurried out the way she came. She was bewildered and uncertain of what to do.

* * * *

On a park bench at the Indianapolis Zoo near the gateway to the Dolphin pavilion, Pete Drucker sat twiddling his thumbs, waiting as instructed. Helen had the area under surveillance long before he arrived. Making his appearance, she watched him meander through the walkways and in due course settle on a park bench.

Just waiting, he watched and looked around studying every female patron to distinguish if this was who he came to meet. He scrutinized the expression on every face and wondered, could this be the person he was to interview? He realized he needed to cool it or someone might get the impression he was a pervert.

Wouldn't that be great headlines? he thought.

He changed his tactics and observed them from the corner of his eye. Hoping he wasn't too obvious, he watched carefully in his quest to connect with the person he was there to meet. This story was too important. So he waited, and watched.

* * * *

A bomb had dropped on Helen with the visit to Matt's office, and she was befuddled and tentative by what she saw, and unsure what to do about the circumstances. They had become close, seemed to share the same interests, and discussed marriage. But she was the holdout, hesitant to acquiesce because of a roller coaster first marriage.

Before considering nuptials, she was searching for some assurance the marriage would be lasting. She kept watching for hidden traits, such as alcoholism, buried and waiting to surface. She wanted assurances the two were compatible, and planned to use her head in addition to her heart to confirm the verdict.

I trusted him with the kids, and he's now living in our home and acts as if he cares for us. But was there ever a bond? How can we be intimate if I can't trust him? How could I trust him again after this? There has been no indication he knew anyone at Beeson. He's home every night, but now I feel betrayed and the only reason he was here was to spy and carry tales back to those bastards. Was I the fool all along, and what I saw today the real Matt? If he's part of the conspiracy, this relationship never got off first base.

Before the unplanned stop at Matt's office, Helen had set a meeting with the reporter. Stumbling on the guy from Beeson with Matt was a shock. After seeing the two men together, she darted from the building to meet with the journalist, and didn't need a confrontation at the moment. There was a lot of thinking she had to do and would deal with the status of Matthew Walker later. At present, she could think of only one real solution to this episode.

Throw him out and never have anything to do with him again, that's what I need to do. But, could there be a logical explanation? She wondered. Oh, hell, I'm not sure what to do.

* * * *

Helen arrived early to scope out the zoo. Given specific instructions, the newspaper guy must follow them to the letter or she wouldn't show, and he would never get to see her. Just a hint of an accomplice or someone trailing along would cause her to jump ship and find another outlet for the story.

Maybe I should've gone straight to the cops, like I thought of doing in the first place, she contemplated. God almighty, I'm nervous, she thought, feeling jittery.

If a balloon popped, she would have jumped through the ceiling. At this juncture Helen was skittish and tentative on whom to trust. Until she could tell the difference, she planned to be wary of everyone. And to be safe, she would select her path with care for the short run.

Watching the man stroll through the entrance, she paralleled the walkways that carried the reporter to the Dolphin arena as directed. Satisfied the people milling about were just visitors interested in the exhibits, after observing for a reasonable period she meandered over and sat on the opposite end of the bench from the newsman.

* * * *

"Helen? I wondered if the person in the video might be you. Now I know."

"Hello, Mr. Drucker."

"Call me Pete." He stood and shook her hand. "I was beginning to think you wouldn't show. I was about to leave."

"I wanted to be certain you were alone like I asked," replied the woman. "At the moment I don't feel comfortable with strangers."

"I can appreciate that," said Drucker.

"Did you have a chance to look at the CD?" Helen asked.

"A number of times," Pete fired back.

Surprised by such quick response, she asked, "What did you think about what you saw?"

"If what I think I saw is happening at Beeson, this is one heck of a story," he responded.

"Can you tell what's going on by watching the video?" asked Helen.

"I believe so."

"Tell me about it," said Helen. "What exactly is it you think is happening."

"Here's my take in a nutshell," Pete responded. "These five guys are involved in stealing from Beeson. I couldn't tell, but there are indications it's a lot of money, just how much I'm not sure.

"Take my word for it, the amount is substantial," replied Helen.

"I'm also not sure of much about the group, or a lot of the details, however, they all appear to be an angry bunch and can barely tolerate each other. One thing is certain, the scheme must have been going on for a while to accumulate the dollars they've skimmed, based on how they were acting," Pete said.

"I believe it's been going on as long as I've worked at the company," replied Helen.

"I couldn't get a clear shot at the monitor, and there was a lot of glare on the screen. People were blocking my view so I couldn't make out how much was in the accounts," said Pete.

"I've never seen a number that big, or a string of digits that long before," interjected Helen.

"Well, somewhere in this whole mess," Pete continued, "you somehow stumbled onto what was happening. When you began to ask questions and get to the root of the problem, one of those men tried to shut you up by trying to kill you. They wanted it to look like an accident and keep the crimes under wraps as long as possible. How am I doing so far?"

"You're awfully close," replied the woman.

"What else can you tell me?" Drucker asked.

"Are you going to print the story?" Helen responded.

"It will be the headlines of the next edition, provided we get enough background on the events," replied Drucker. "In addition to the disc and the information you've provided, we'd like to know as much as possible about each of these guys and somehow confirm the details. We've got to have our guns loaded before the story breaks. The legal department is all over the matter, and other people are doing background investigations as we speak."

Pete Drucker never sat so patient or focused as he was at this moment. This was the biggest scoop of his life, and he was silent as he sat taking notes with the story handed to him. He made a point of interrupting only to clarify a point so Helen's concentration wouldn't be broken. Although obligated to grasp an accurate portrayal, a lot of the facts she conveyed he was already aware. But her discourse would fill in the blanks and improve his perception and sequence of the events, and provide a broad spectrum of how things worked at Beeson.

Beginning with a brief overview, she jumped to the part of becoming suspicious by diversion of money from company's coffers. She explained the siphoning off and flow through the door using dummy vendors.

"You can tell from the video, it was when I began to ask questions they decided to kill me," Helen continued. "You already know one of the men shoved me down the stairs and put me in the hospital. I've been off work since the fall."

She told of the loss of memory, and nightmares as she realized it wasn't an accident. As her memory returned, she became suspicious as small tidbits dredged up. It was then she began her search for clues to support her uncertainties.

"About the same time I concluded someone high up had to be behind the plot. I thought of Howard and hoped he wasn't involved, so I could hand everything over to him," continued Helen.

"Was Howard's the short, chubby guy in the video?" asked Pete. "He looked like the ring leader."

"Yes, that's him," replied Helen. "Based on his actions at the meeting, I figured out he was the instigator. When I was searching his room, I lucked out and found the camera as I watched the group plot their next move, which was to shut me up permanently. After that, I sent a copy of the disc to you."

"Why me?" inquired Pete.

"You were a name I recognized from other articles. In those stories you came across as fair and honest in your work," replied Helen. "I respect that in a reporter."

"Thanks for the compliment, but why didn't you just go to the police?"

"I don't know any cops I could trust. But, I feel they wouldn't act soon enough. Whatever is going on will not drag out. Those guys are going to bolt, and I believe the police would have been left in the dust and those men long gone before something was done," Helen responded.

"Don't you think someone would look into this?" asked Pete.

"If an inquiry began, they would smell a rat and take off. I'm sure they have friends in the right places, if you know what I mean. With the cops involved, the case would have died a slow death before making an arrest. By the time they finished screwing things up, those men would be out of the country somewhere untouchable."

"It doesn't sound like you have much confidence in the authorities," said Pete. "But there's no assurance a story in my newspaper will cause someone to act any sooner."

"That's true, but if the story's in print, the employees and the public will be alerted. Together they should be able to raise the dickens and create a backlash that might prevent these people from getting away," Helen responded. "They may even be brought to justice."

"Where are you going from here?" Pete asked.

"I'm not sure. I found out earlier my house has been broken into, and my friend might be involved in this mess. He's been living at my home helping out while I'm recuperating," she responded. "I decided to stop in to tell him I was on my way here, and saw him with one of those men on the CD. He didn't see me so I skedaddled. I'm going to pick up my kids when I leave here, then disappear. It'll be best if you don't know where I'll be."

"If you're in danger, we can see you're somewhere safe," offered Drucker.

"Mr. Drucker, you write stories for a living, and I'm grateful for that. But, I don't know you well enough to put my life in your hands. Until I do, and see some results from your articles, I'll fend for myself. I promise I'll stay in touch."

"Do you need any money?"

"I cleaned out my bank account earlier. For now, I'm fine. I'll be in touch."

"How can I get in touch with you?" asked Pete.

"Don't worry. I'll call you," responded Helen.

The woman was on her feet and gone, dissolved in a sea of humanity strolling through the park before Pete realized she was no longer on the bench.

TWELVE

CASH DISAPPEARS AT BEESON INTERNATIONAL

The morning edition of the newspaper painted a bleak narrative of embezzlement at Beeson's corporate headquarters. Strategically placed photographs of the wrongdoers entangled in the thievery were conspicuous, and arrayed with each article. Side articles provided a chronology of achievements by the accused during the tenure and growth of the company.

The exposé brandished the front page and bounced national news to the back. Blowing the cover from a crime at a leading public corporation was a major story for most newspapers. For a smaller publication like the *Star,* it was enormous. To divulge corruption on a large scale will have a profound affect on the lives of workers, investors, and companies doing business with Beeson.

Whether a large corporation or a Mom-and-Pop shop, working relationships at Beeson would become dicey and distressed. With Beeson's stock owned by copious shareholders, few investors would be immune from the fallout. The transgressions of a handful of people would trickle down and encroach on many lives.

With jobs at stake, and the impingement of pension funds, the story was vital for public consumption. But beneath all the babble, a question forestalled. Could the company survive?

The clanging bell to begin trading on Wall Street created new shivers for investors. Uncertainty prompts a healthy market to react quick, and adversely. Value in Beeson securities plunged, the stock declining in anticipation of the worst possible news. With the freefall, shareholders panicked from the grim news reports as trading in the stock halted.

The FBI dispersed agents to round up the named members. Caught boarding a private jet departing for Brazil was the Chief Executive Officer, Clark Ford. Collared on the border crossing into Canada was Gordon Compton, the company President. Using a passport with a fictitious name, he had a one-way ticket to Switzerland.

Seized at his home, Eric Camp was in the gym when the news broke and caught off-guard, failing to act.

Leonard Busby, was out of the country living the good life, and informed through the Internet. Without delay, his itinerary changed and he disappeared. Interpol was turning over every rock to find the weasel.

Howard Jenkins was on the run. The agent in charge expressed confidence he would be picked up soon, although, critics weren't sure because the man was so devious.

Special Agent Joe Doyle was the FBI Fraud Task Force team leader and visited the *Star* to meet the reporter behind the story.

"I wondered how long it would take you guys to show up," Pete remarked when summoned to the front lobby.

"When something this big happens, the Bureau responds rather quickly," replied the lead agent.

"What can I do for you fellows?" said Pete.

"Is there someplace we can talk?"

"Sure, let's go to the conference room. It'll be more comfortable and we can all fit in there," Pete said. Turning to the receptionist, Drucker asked, "Mandy, would you show these gentlemen to the conference room? I'll be right along. I need to let the editor know we have visitors."

A coterie of FBI agents followed Mandy to the second floor. She made certain the room was accommodating, and before leaving offered everyone beverages, which they declined.

Not one to dally, Drucker and the newspaper's editor strolled in followed by Fred Washman, the in-house counsel. With introductions passed around like a copy of *Playboy*, Pete began the convocation.

"What can we do for you gentlemen?"

"We're here about the information for the source of the articles on Beeson. We would like to see your notes on the articles," responded the agent.

"I realize that's what you want, but you well know I can't give them up without permission."

"By the way, who is your source?"

"I can't tell you that either, you know the drill. But I believe the person will cooperate if given protection. They're in hiding because someone tried to kill them, and they still feel threatened. Their home was broken into recently, and apparently someone was looking for the same stuff you guys want."

"We could get a court order."

"We're aware of that, but an order from the court would require a lot of extra time and effort, and be unnecessary," responded the paper's editor. "That would delay your investigation. I don't believe that's what you really want, and neither do we."

"Would you call this person so we can talk to them?"

"I would if I could, but I don't have a way to get in touch with them," remarked Pete. "The last time we were together, I was told they would call me. That hasn't happened, but I expect to hear from them soon."

"If they call, tell them the FBI wants to talk. We'll give them all the protection they need."

"The arrangement will be in writing, I presume?" remarked Washman, the in-house counsel.

"Yes it will," confirmed the agent. "You have my word."

* * * *

Later that day, Helen called the newspaper to congratulate Pete for engineering the layout. With his name attached to the main article, she wanted to express appreciation for keeping his promise.

"I take it you caught the morning edition," Pete remarked.

"I did, and thank you for printing the story so soon. Maybe someone will take action and the company and jobs can be salvaged." Helen said.

"The FBI has been here wanting to talk to you," remarked Pete. "I told them I couldn't give them anything without your approval."

"Give them anything they ask for," Helen countered.

"With your permission I can do that, but the head agent wants to meet you personally," Pete replied.

"That could be a problem. I'm off the radar and not eager to be in public. When I do go out I've got to be careful and watch everybody," Helen remarked.

"Do be careful. I don't want to hear you're a statistic," warned Pete.

"I thought there were two different people following me earlier, but lost them in a crowd. Since then I haven't seen any frequent faces, and try to keep my distance from everyone."

"The FBI has agreed to give you protection. They've willing to keep you safe and give you a written statement," responded Pete.

"A piece of paper doesn't mean much if you're dead," Helen responded.

"Why don't you come into the office and I'll set up a meeting? Better yet, let me come and get you."

"I don't know," remarked Helen. "Let me think about it."

"Then you can tell your story and hand over the disc," added Pete. "I'll be here till late. Just give me a call."

"I'll have to figure out how this will work," commented Helen.

"We can send a car to pick you up. That would be best, tell me where you are," offered Drucker.

Hesitant to reveal her whereabouts over the phone, Helen remarked, "I'll be in touch. Let me work out the details and I'll get back to you."

Helen was in a phone booth on Meridian Street, two blocks from the newspaper. After the call, and on impulse, she began to wander toward the *Star* to meet with Drucker, but suddenly felt something stiff and round shoved firmly in her spine.

"Don't turn around. Keep walking or you'll be a paraplegic in a heartbeat," charged the male voice.

Taken by surprise, the affront stunned Helen. Momentarily, she was apprehensive and didn't know how to react. She had never before had, what she believed to be, a gun shoved in her back. And from the tone of the man's voice, little doubt remained about him starting to shoot if he felt threatened.

For just a few seconds she had become distracted and vulnerable. Blind-sided, she was exposed after dropping her guard for the few moments while talking to the reporter. Inwardly she was kicking herself for complacency and allowing the assailant to gain the upper hand.

"Keep walking to the end of the block," he demanded. "At the corner turn right."

"Where are you taking me?" asked Helen.

"I'm not going to hurt you. I just want those discs you've got hidden," replied the voice.

"So you're the one who broke in my house," said Helen.

"A real Einstein, aren't you? It didn't take you long to figure that one out," remarked the man. "Keep walking and turn into the parking lot."

Ahead on the street, a police officer had pulled to the curb and stepped from her scooter to write a ticket for a parking meter violation.

"Keep quiet and keep walking, or I'll shoot both of you," the man said as he pressed the gun deeper into her backbone.

"If you shoot me, you won't get your discs back," Helen remarked.

"Shut up and keep walking," said the man. "I'll tell you what you're doing."

Helen knew she had to do something, but her choices were limited.

If I get into a car, I'll be dead before sunset, she thought. If I don't cooperate, I'll be dead anyway, only sooner.

She recalled the self-defense class at the YWCA. Helen glanced at the gunman and saw he was distracted, his eye on the cop. She found her opening. Before the man could react and in a smooth fluid motion, she planted her foot, twisted away from the handgun, raised her leg, and stomped on the crown of the assailant's foot.

With him compromised, she jerked from his grip, kicked, and caught him dead center in the groin. This threw her off-balance as she fell to the ground. The man bent over in agony and Helen screamed.

"GUN! GUN! HE'S GOT A GUN. HE'S GOT A GUN."

The attacker's foot was throbbing, and the man was on the verge of vomiting from the intensity of the blow gravitating from his testicles. His gun had fallen to the sidewalk while he held his groin, and he rolled from the ache spreading through his mid-section.

With Helen's yell, the officer threw the book of tickets in the scooter, drew her gun, and ran to subdue the attacker. After calling for backup she handcuffed the man. But, by the time the officer remembered the victim, Helen was long gone. She folded into a crowd of onlookers that had gathered during the confusion.

* * * *

"What's happened to you?" Pete asked smiling at Helen. She had an abrasion and smudges on her face, and her clothing disheveled. "Come back to the washroom and get cleaned up. Do you need to go to the hospital?"

"No, I'll be fine. The guy who broke into my house just tried to attack me, but I was able to break away," Helen said matter-of-fact.

"Where did this happen?" asked Pete.

"On Meridian, a couple of blocks from here, just after I hung up the phone," Helen replied.

"You're the one the cops are looking for," Pete remarked. "I just heard something come across the scanner about a woman missing from a crime scene."

"You got me. I guess I'm the one," admitted Helen.

"Are you sure you're okay?" Pete asked.

"Yes, I'll be fine," Helen replied.

"Are you up to taking questions from the FBI?" Drucker asked.

"Yeah, let's get this show over with," said Helen. "How quick can those guys get here?"

While Helen went to the washroom, Pete called Agent Doyle and reported the person he wanted to see was at the *Star* office. The reporter suggested that if he planned to speak to them, he should come immediately, or the person might change her mind.

"I'll be there in five minutes," the agent remarked.

The FBI field office was within walking distance of the newspaper.

Helen and the reporter waited in the Board Room anticipating arrival of the agent. The conference table was immense and crowded the room. It was a black Granite oval with a reflective luster. Forty black, high-backed, sheepskin captain chairs that could swallow someone, lined the impressive slab.

Visual aids, a television, and a DVD player were at the end of the table, and the disc loaded and queued to the desired spot. The men from the FBI arrived, breathless, and seemed to have run the entire distance.

Helen was resting with her head on the table after she became dizzy and nauseous. The light-headedness began to dissipate when she closed her eyes and remained quiet with her head lying on the cool top. The lady remained seated as the men entered the room, but Pete Drucker stood to greet Agent Doyle and his minions. Turning to the woman, Pete introduced the FBI to Helen Faulkner.

"You look like you've been in a scuffle. How bad does the other guy look?" the lead agent chuckled in an attempt to provide some levity.

Helen laughed along with the agent, and remarked, "It's really not as bad as it might seem. I had an altercation a short while ago and fell on the sidewalk, but I'll be fine."

"Oh, I'm sorry, I was only kidding. That eye of yours may turn out to be quite a shiner," responded the agent. "I hadn't heard what happened."

"No, that's alright," Helen smiled. "Everything turned out fine. I got away from him, and the police did the hard part and captured him. That's what's important," assured Helen.

"Can we do anything for you?" responded Doyle, showing concern for Helen's welfare. He realized contrition might help to gain a rapport after sticking a big foot in his mouth.

"No, I'm fine," replied Helen.

"Well, I'm glad of that," responded the agent. "May I call you Helen?"

"Yes, if I can call you Joe," replied Helen.

The agent approved, and continued, "Now that we're on a first name basis, we should begin. I understand you're the person who brought information to Mr. Drucker about some missing money at Beeson," said the agent.

"Yes, I did," Helen replied.

"Will you tell me what happened?" asked Joe.

"Weren't the newspaper articles enough? They covered quite a bit," replied Helen.

"You're right. The articles did include a lot. But we'd like to hear your perspective," responded the agent.

"Okay," said Helen.

"May we record the conversation?" asked the agent.

Helen nodded agreement, and after the recording equipment was ready, she proceeded to recount the story.

Summarizing the job she performed, she explained how long she'd worked with the company. Soon she skipped to the part where the whole thing began to unfold as she became suspicious of payments made to certain vendors. Companies she didn't recognize and couldn't find contracts to justify payment.

"Supposedly, I was in charge of the department," Helen explained. "My primary job was to coordinate efforts with vendors we did business. My department was responsible to make certain deliveries were on time to a project. It was really a matter of synchronization, and because of this, our unit became closely associated with these contractors. If another department sent a request for payment through with no contract, we were responsible for running it down to figure out what was going on."

"Why didn't you do that when the one check showed up?" asked the agent.

"I did, or at least tried to," remarked Helen. "I took the check to Howard Jenkins, my boss, and asked him if he knew anything about it. He told me he would handle the matter. It was after that I fell head first down the stairs and woke up in the hospital."

"I'm sorry to hear that," said the agent.

"Thank you," said Helen. "While I was recuperating, I realized that what happened was no accident."

"How did you come to that conclusion?" asked the agent.

"Actually, it came to me in a dream," said Helen.

The agent stopped, raised his eyebrows took a hard look at Helen, then to Drucker, and remarked, "Dreams can be very powerful."

"My friend Matt didn't believe me either," remarked Helen, "but I knew something wasn't right, so I kept digging. I started my own investigation and discovered millions flowing out the door to unapproved vendors. Why I didn't see this sooner, I don't know, so maybe I'm partly responsible for this debacle continuing as long as it did. But I knew one thing for certain, whoever was behind this mess had to have top clearance and full knowledge of the system to circumvent our department. The check caught was merely by accident. Later, I discovered a whole list of vendors consistently paid over a long period. A plan like this wouldn't work unless somebody higher up in the company was involved. The only person I knew with enough knowledge on that level was Howard Jenkins."

"Did you confront him?" asked the agent.

"At first I didn't want to think he would do something like this. But I also knew that whoever it was, had to have in-depth knowledge. I made the decision to try to exclude my boss before I said anything about what I'd discovered."

"So, you were trying to isolate whoever was involved to identify the correct person?" asked the agent.

"That's right. During the process I learned that not only was Howard caught up in the scheme, but he was the quarterback and had a squad of four others that I could count in the mess with him."

"How did you find all this out?" said the agent.

"With the number of unanswered questions, things just didn't seem to add up. So, while on sick leave I set up a visit using the pretext of checking-in on the department," said Helen.

"I remembered a monthly board meeting would be taking place, and timed my visit to coordinate with the meeting. That was the only idea I could come up with to look through Howard's stuff to see what I could find. I secretly hoped something positive would come out and he would be exonerated. If I eliminated my suspicions about him, I intended to turn everything I had over and let him deal with it."

"So what did you do?" said the agent.

"Like I planned, I went to his office to nose around. In the process, five men burst through the door," Helen remarked. "I narrowly escaped being caught by hiding in the bathroom. Once inside, I stumbled on a smaller room overlooking Howard's desk. Anything going on in his office could be seen from behind a one-way mirror."

"Really," responded the agent, looking around at the others in the room.

"This room had sophisticated camera equipment, and money and jewels were in a corner safe." Helen said. "The safe contained DVDs labeled and dated. When the guys left for the board meeting, I took the disc from the camera, grabbed a handful from the safe and ran. They bragged about intending to kill me because the first guy botched the job, but I had no intention of hanging around long enough for them to have the chance."

Pete pressed the button on the remote, and the television came to life. The show began as the men entered Howard's office. The agents took notes, and scrutinized the movie as it played. During the video the agents watched as men confessed to participation in crimes they were accused, and a plan to eliminate Helen.

When the picture concluded, Agent Doyle sat silently for a long while. "I'm going to confiscate this DVD as evidence. We'll give you a receipt for it," he said.

"That's not necessary. What you have is a copy. The original is in a safe place," replied Helen.

"I have to do it anyway," said the agent. "We've rounded up three of the five men. One is on the run out of the country, and we can't locate Howard Jenkins. We've had every form of transportation being watched, planes, trains, and highway, but no Howard."

"I didn't know a lot about his personal life, but a while back I overheard him say something about a cabin in the woods of southern Indiana, in Brown County, I believe. Knowing him, it would be hard to find," offered Helen. "The deed may be recorded in his ex-wife's name. You might look there."

* * * *

Hauling the bunch to jail, articles concerning the embezzlement appeared in the newspapers, with each member charged with a litany of crimes. To stabilize the company, Beeson's directors convened to fill the vacancies with people purporting ethical backgrounds. Silencing a growing public furor demanded new blood.

A newly hired independent auditing firm began its examination of company records to report the magnitude and scope of corruption. The directors were demanding answers the former auditors couldn't provide, as the desire arose for answers to why the scam stretched out so long. In addition, and becoming known of the depth and duration of the crimes, the directors were determined to ascertain if the previous accountants were complicit in the embezzlement. If so, prosecution would result side-by-side with the other criminals.

The SEC halted trading in all of Beeson's securities to afford a cooling off period. The ailing stock price had to stabilize to avoid ancillary panic by investors and employees.

To restore confidence, company stock selling halted. When a stock in a certain industry shows unusual signs of distress, trading may spill over to similar stocks and adversely affect a sector. Forestalling panic was a significant concern as the stock price stabilized and before trading began again.

To survive and ward off bankruptcy, the company must retain skilled workers. Disruption of operations was a two-way street, therefore, workers and company had to pull together to attain victory or all would suffer defeat. The company was at a crossroad and it became the responsibility of every person associated with Beeson to coordinate efforts and circumvent a disaster. Rather than abandon the business, all employees had to pull together to save the ailing company.

A seasoned captain was no longer at the helm to steer the ship to calm waters. Morale was scraping the bottom of a leaky vessel because of the few who believed they were above the law. The group responsible had placed personal desires above the hopes and dreams of workers dedicating their lives to the institution. But to evade a catastrophe, retaining workers and to avoid a mass exodus was the goal.

Confidence evaporated over the destiny of the company. The public sensed Beeson might sink with uncertainty concerning pensions, and sharks were circling and smelled blood in the water.

Because of the number of government contracts, examiners scrutinized every cost allocation. Each line item was under a microscope. Unsubstantiated expenses charged to a project were isolated, and the company faced significant penalties for faulty accounting.

The FBI Fraud Team worked feverishly to unravel the deception. Untangling a complex grid of deceit enmeshed within the company, and designed to divert attention from the chicanery was a protracted endeavor. The use of phantom vendors inflated costs and evaded detection. By routing illegitimate costs to projects, scrutiny and security through established measures went unnoticed. Funds destined for pensions were a portion of monies diverted, as employee retirement was of no concern to thieves.

The tally kept rising and projected to amount to one billion dollars. An amount so large most folks couldn't comprehend the significance of how many integers followed the number one. Regardless, the cash was gone.

Although reluctant, the government of Belize was cooperative. Unfortunately, bank accounts in the country were empty.

The Bank of Switzerland was less forthcoming and noncommittal on deposits. It was protective of clientele identities and transactions. This was not just bank policy, but the rule of law of all Switzerland. Concealment of financial transactions was a prized commodity.

A bank's customer held funds in this sovereign nation with the assurance their affairs would remain private. Unlocking secrets of the JFK assassination would be easier than to acquire unauthorized information from a Swiss bank.

"I believe we need to talk to Ms. Faulkner to find out what happened to the money," remarked Joe Doyle to his colleagues. "We know the money's in Zurich. What we don't know is where. An electronic transfer of a large amount of funds out of the country hasn't happened."

Stationed at Helen's home were several FBI agents in the event an assassin had the idea of completing an open contract.

Two of the thieves were on the loose, Howard Jenkins one of them.

For now, Helen and her children remained safe and out of danger, and Matt couldn't make contact with the Faulkners until authentication of his status. This was a protective measure due to the observation Helen overheard when the men threatened her life.

THIRTEEN

The lead agent was on a mission. He needed answers to a confusing matter while Beeson was flipping topsy-turvy and sideways. To obtain an accurate measure of the crimes, he arranged a daytrip through the countryside to the Faulkner farm. The drive proved to be a delightful diversion from his normal day, as he basked in the scenery from the narrow byways.

Helen was all smiles to see Doyle once again. After a jovial reunion, the agent expressed concern for her well-being before jumping to the heart of the matter for his trip. He came for answers to questions he couldn't find elsewhere, and gave him a purpose to leave the city.

"What can you tell us about the money?" Doyle asked. "Where did it go? We can't locate it, but I have an idea you know exactly what happened to it."

The agent intended to see Helen face-to-face as he asked the questions and observe her reaction. He needed to cover specific details that couldn't be traced another way, primarily the whereabouts of the cash.

In the short time he came to know her, a concern for her well-being arose, and also how the family was coping with the uncommon circumstances. Told of the difficulties the family had undergone, he was sympathetic to their plight.

"We've done an extensive search for the notebook you told us Howard kept for his passwords and notes, but can't find it anywhere," said the agent.

Helen was excited to see anyone. Normally the home streamed in and out with people, but that all dried up and she began to feel like a prisoner. Except for a few phone calls, severed was all contact with the outside world while in protective custody.

"When I went to Howard's office and realized those guys were up to no good, the only thing I took was the discs," Helen replied. "Before I left, I jotted down what I needed to access the banks and left the book beside his computer. I suspect Jenkins took it with him. Something like that he wouldn't leave around."

"We'll probably never see it then," responded the agent. "But, what happened to the money?"

"After finding Howard's back room and hearing their conversation, I knew if I didn't do something, those guys would be gone, along with the money."

"So, what did you do?" asked the agent.

"During the night I moved the cash to a separate account so that I was the only person with a way in," replied Helen. "I originally considered simply changing the password, but I had to be certain Howard, or one of his cronies, didn't have a back door to access the account. A new account prevented them from getting away with the cash."

"That was smart," responded the agent.

"The men bragged about my name being on all the bank records, so I figured starting a new account would be simple. I opened the account and switched the balance."

"I'll bet Jenkins was upset when he found out."

"Upset! Oh, I'm sure he was livid, absolutely beside himself."

"Would you care to tell us where the money is so it can be returned to the company? I'm confident everyone will be thankful, and morale will surely get a boost," said the agent. "Once it's recovered everybody'll feel better. The company is on the verge of being insolvent, and the present circumstances hinder its ability to borrow. If the funds are returned, everybody'll breathe easier."

"Let me show you how much those creeps took," remarked Helen.

Walking to the computer, Helen called up a website, and digits filled the screen. Upon seeing the long string, the agent did a double take and whistled.

"Man alive. It's not every day you see an amount that big. I never realized that much cash really existed" the agent remarked.

"Oh, it's there, and I'll be happy to move it where it belongs. But, before I do, I need to know if I'm going to be charged with anything because of what's happened?" asked the woman.

"I haven't heard any talk about that," replied Doyle.

"To keep anyone from getting that idea, I want immunity from everything and everybody. Federal, state, local, or any other persecution somebody might think up before making the exchange. And, I want it in writing," Helen stipulated.

"Your name is scattered on all the documents, so it appears you're implicated. Those guys knew exactly what they were doing, and did a good job setting you up to take the fall. The video goes a long way to exonerate you. My suspicion is that everyone will be so glad to get the money back no one will consider prosecution. Although, I can't speak for the others, I presume all parties affected know you weren't really involved," remarked the FBI man.

"You believe that, but there's no assurance the others do. I want an iron clad document that exonerates me from all wrongdoing, real or imagined," Helen demanded. "If some hot shot prosecutor gets a bee in his bonnet somewhere down the road, I don't want him making political hay at my expense. And, I also don't want some ambitious politician trying to embolden his name and accuse me of anything around election time. This must end now, before I give the money back."

"That's smart. Somehow I'll see that happens," the agent promised.

"What about Matt? Have you figured out if he was tied up in this mess?" asked Helen.

"We questioned the man Matt was standing beside. He doesn't seem to know how to shut up. Actually, none of the accused knows how to quit talking. They're all pointing the finger at Jenkins for getting them caught up in the deal. They say this entire plot was Howard's idea from the get go. And as the money began to flow, it became easier and gave them a free hand to rationalize what they were doing. But, according to what the fellow told us, he was in Matt's building on another matter. Further legwork supports that fact. It was simply a coincidence you saw him when you did."

"There is no such thing as a coincidence. My Guardian Angel was telling me something. I'm just not sure what it was. But I'll wait and see how this works out, and time will tell," remarked Helen.

"I wouldn't be too concerned about Matt," said the agent.

"Could the bunch have been aware of my relationship with Matt and making plans to harm him? If that's the case, I fear just how far they would have gone to get what they wanted."

"My guess is the bunch would have done anything to make sure their plan worked. They were willing to kill, weren't they?" responded the agent.

"That's scary," replied Helen. "But I've known Matt for a while now, and I'm having a tough time believing he was somehow connected to those men. Is Howard still free? If he's out running around, he might have someone come after me yet."

"No, he hasn't surfaced, but we'll find him. He's got to come out from under that rock sometime. He won't stay underground forever," Doyle remarked.

Helen stood as the agent started to leave. As she did, she became faint and sat down.

Taken by surprise, the agent asked, "Are you okay? Can I get you something?"

Joe was concerned. In the short while they had been acquainted, he had come to appreciate her, and suspected she was someone who thought of others before her own needs. He believed she was authentic and an honorable person. These traits were hard to come by.

"No, I think it's just the excitement. We'll be better off when things settle down and return to normal," responded Helen.

"How are your children? Are they holding up through all this?" asked the agent.

"They're taking it in stride. I try to keep as much of the bad stuff from them, but I think they know more about what's going on than I realize. Most of the time nothing seems to faze them, and they appear unconcerned. I'm sure they'll be fine."

She didn't tell the agent before he left, but her head was spinning and her stomach queasy. Once gone, she rested her head on the arm of the couch, closed her eyes to shut out the world to make it stop spinning, and dozed off.

* * * *

The sun had begun to wane as Helen awoke, her first instinct was to locate the children. With trepidation she called out for assurance they were safe, and it was a relief to hear mumbled voices from the staircase. Confident they were playing upstairs, she arose, wobbled, and started toward the kitchen. She wasn't sure how long she had been sleeping, or the hour, but surmised the children would be hungry soon. The dizziness was gone although she remained unsteady.

"I'm glad to see you're among the living," a familiar voice echoed from across the room.

Quickly, Helen spun in the direction of the male voice that emerged from the shadows. She became disheartened by the eyes locked on her, and a gun pointed at her heart.

"Howard! Where did you come from? How'd you get in here?" Helen was stunned to see the uninvited guest. "How'd you know where I lived?"

Howard smiled and started to answer, but Helen interrupted, "And, just how long have you been sitting here?"

"You're forgetting there's a lot I know about you. After taking care of that fool sitting out front, I walked in," replied Howard. "How in the hell did you think I got in here? I'm not some damn ghost who can appear whenever I take a notion. By the way, you ought to keep your doors locked, and get an alarm. There are too many kooks running around out here in the country for you to be alone."

You're one to be talking, Helen thought.

"I'm surprised, that's all. I never expected to see you again," she remarked. "I suspected you'd be half-way to South America by now."

"I'll just bet you did," Howard replied. "Not without my money I won't. Now where is it? I'm not leaving here until I get my discs, and the money. Now, hand them over."

"Howard, you know darn well the money doesn't belong to you, and I'm not giving it back."

"Yes, you will, or you'll wish you had," threatened Howard.

"Howard, you can threaten all you want but you don't scare me," the woman responded.

"If I get hold of your little brats you'll change your tune," said Jenkins.

"You wouldn't do anything to hurt kids, would you?" remarked Helen.

"Until I get what's mine, you bet your ass. In fact, I'll do them one at a time, and you'll be watching," said Howard.

"Howard, I used to think you were a decent person. Now I know you're just sick," said Helen.

"Say what you like, but until I get my things those kids are open season. And after I'm done, you'll wish you'd told me a lot sooner. Now where's my goddamn money?" yelled Jenkins.

Unfamiliar with firearms, Helen wouldn't recognize one model from another. But the handgun pointed in her direction was black and ugly, and Howard was chaotically swinging it in her direction. Gazing down the center hole of a gun barrel causes a person to rethink priorities. Life is so fragile.

"Howard, have you ever shot a gun before? The way your hand is shaking, it doesn't look like you know what you're doing," remarked Helen.

"Don't you worry. My aim is steady enough to hit you. Now where's my damn money," he shouted.

Helen's mind was racing to arrive at a strategy to thwart his demand. She must keep her children safe, but so far couldn't think of a way to do both. Once he gained access to the bank account he would be gone forever, and would spare no one.

The family was expendable when he no longer needed her, and would kill them once he had access to the cash. If he got away, the money wouldn't go to where it belonged, workers would lose their jobs, and the company would be unable to pay its bills. Somehow, she had to stall him.

"Why are you doing this? Don't you have a conscience? You were my mentor and taught me everything I know about the business," Helen tried to reason with him. "Am I suddenly supposed to believe all the stuff you told me was a bunch of crap? Look at all the people you're going to hurt."

"Look, bitch, I don't give a rat's ass about those stupid idiots at that place," rattled Howard. "The only reason you were there in the first place was to take the blame for the missing cash. Now, you've fulfilled your role and it's time to go. This whole thing was set up long before you came along. You're just a little pawn in a much bigger picture."

"So, that's it. You're going to take off and leave everyone high and dry, and me holding the bag," replied Helen. "What kind of a person are you really?"

"You stupid bitch. Everything was in place to make this whole plan believable. I'm the one who made that company what it is today and I've never been given credit. I'm going to finally take what's coming to me. NOW, WHERE'S MY DAMN MONEY?" Howard had a scowl on his face, had become querulous and shouted viciously. He turned crimson, and the veins in his neck were bulging.

"Howard, sit down. You're going to have a heart attack. Let's talk about this. Give yourself up. You can't get away."

"You must be dumber than I thought. What do you think this is, a democracy?" remarked Howard. "I'm the one holding the gun. Now do as I say and fork over the cash. Then I'll leave you and your brats alone."

"You can't get away. You know you'll never get out of town," Helen responded. "And you'll never be able to use the money."

"Why is that?" the man asked.

"The account has a hold on it. Howard, just give yourself up," pleaded Helen.

"You're lying. Like hell I'll give up," replied Howard.

"How can I be certain you won't hurt us? What's going to keep you from killing us after I tell you how to get at the money?" Helen remarked. "That's what you planned all along. Somebody else was supposed to do your dirty work before and keep your hands clean."

"You'll just have to trust me. Now, for the last goddamn time, where's my damn money?" demanded Howard.

Helen's mind drifted to her dead husband. In time of trouble she thought of him often, remembering the good times they had together before alcohol took over.

Jerry, dear God, help me. I don't know what to do, she thought.

With a spark of determination, Helen blurted out, "Howard, I can't believe a word you say. No, you're a coward and I'm not giving you the money," she boldly remarked, drawing her line in the sand.

Howard became irate. "You stupid bitch, where are those damn kids. Get them down here."

"No, they won't come, and if you kill me you'll never find the money. I'm the only person who knows the password."

Helen was watching for her assailant to make a blunder. If she could turn the tables and get the upper hand, she would have an advantage over these miserable circumstances.

Howard walked to the staircase and shouted, "Hey, kids. Come downstairs. Uncle Howard's got a surprise for you."

"DON'T YOU DARE," Helen screamed. "RUN AND HIDE."

Howard was red faced and rushed toward Helen. "You bitch. I'll fix you. I'll beat it out of you. Before I'm finished you'll wish you'd told me a lot sooner," his voice elevated as he pointed the gun in Helen's direction. He dashed toward her and reached out.

Helen stood her ground and as he tried to grab her she ducked, and his chubby hands missed the mark. As his arm grazed her, she instinctively pushed. Losing his balance, he fell over a chair and the gun flew from his hand, hit the floor and discharged. The explosion was deafening, the blast made her ears ring. Thrown off kilter when shoved, the man forgot the safety was off. Stunned, the loud eruption caused their ears to ring for several seconds.

Helen saw her opening. The advantage was hers and she hastily ran and stomped his chest, placing a solid blow to the breastplate. His lungs expelled rapidly as he choked and coughed, and sucked air. He rolled on the floor gasping as Helen moved the gun from his reach.

"I guess you won't need this anymore," she said.

"Looks like you didn't need my help after all," a familiar voice cajoled as he walked down the stairway holding two small people.

Surprised, Helen remarked, "Well, it took you long enough. Why didn't you just wait until after he shot me?" she said sarcastically to Matt. "What are you doing here, by the way? I thought you had to keep your distance and weren't supposed to be around the house. But now that you're here, help me get this character tied up so I can call the police. They'll be glad to see this creep."

Howard was reeling on the floor, struggling for air. Matt fetched a roll of duct tape to bind Howard's hands, and wound the tape around his ankles. He was making noises so they knew he could speak, although, to keep them from listening to him yell, taped his mouth.

After calling the FBI, the couple waited for agents to arrive and move the fourth member of the cabal to a jail cell.

"You didn't answer my question, what are you doing here?" asked Helen. "How did you know to come over at such an opportune time? The cops just might throw you in jail along with this character."

"Helen, I had to talk to you and try to explain what happened. If they throw me in jail, well, so be it," Matt insisted.

"We'll cross that bridge when we come to it," said Helen.

"When I came to the house and found the agent unconscious, I knew something was wrong. So I crept up to the window and saw Howard shouting at you," responded Matt. "I figured you'd be okay and he wouldn't do anything until he got what he was looking for, so I went to find the kids. It appeared you weren't going to give it to him any way soon."

"You're right about that, and I'm glad you got the kids," responded Helen.

"I shinnied up the tree on the side of the house, crawled through a window, and told the kids to keep quiet and hide. They thought it was all a game until the gun went off and scared them. By the time that happened, everything was all over," said Matt.

"You climbed a tree? No wonder your clothes look so ratty," said the woman.

"Helen, I've missed you. I had nothing to do with those guys, and didn't know them. When the cops told me you saw me near the coffee stand, I didn't know what they were talking about at first," Matt explained. "Then I remembered, the guy struck up a conversation, which I thought was odd. We only spoke for a couple of seconds, and I had forgotten about it. He looked familiar, but I didn't recognize where I saw him until the cops asked about him."

"Matt, I believe you. I've had time to think about what happened, and I jumped to conclusions. I have a tough time believing you had anything to do with that bunch. You're not the type," Helen remarked.

"What type is that?" remarked Matt.

"I know what's in your heart, Matt Walker, and you're a good man," Helen replied. "I should never have doubted you. There are times when whatever is seen can't be believed."

The couple's lips met for the first time since before Helen made the delivery to the reporter. The kiss was intense, warm, and passionate, unlike the peck on the cheek when they last separated.

"I believe all the excitement is getting the best of me. I need to lie down," Helen said. "I'm woozy."

"Do I have that affect on you?" asked Matt.

"I suppose so," remarked Helen.

"Here, lie on the couch and rest. You've been through a lot in the last few minutes. I'd be dizzy, too," said Matt.

Matt ran to get a cool, damp washcloth to place on her forehead, and returned holding a glass of water and Tylenol.

"I thought you might need these," he said as he swabbed her face and placed the damp towel on her forehead.

"That feels so good. Thanks," she said, downing the tablets with water. Her eyes closed out the world to keep it from spinning as she dozed off.

The Federal agents arrived and found Jenkins hogtied with duct tape. They hauled him off to jail for lock up with the other scoundrels. The last member of the group was still at bay and on the run.

FOURTEEN

Arraigned in Federal court and charged with the crime of embezzlement were Clark Ford, Gordon Compton, Eric Camp, and Howard Jenkins. Other crimes included in the indictment were fraud, extortion, attempted murder, conspiracy, and a list of other nefarious offenses. Evidence favored a conviction, with the defendants looking at their remaining natural life in an 8 by 12 cell. Helen was the primary witness to testify, the video the smoking gun.

Expected was a conviction on all counts after a jury heard and validated the combined evidence. Sealed would be the fate of the defendants, and the cell door welded shut to end their freedom. When considering the grief they caused, sympathy that may have existed for the accused evaporated.

With the exception of Jenkins, the other co-conspirators were spilling their guts, and divulging everything they knew about the whole shebang. All fingers point at Howard as the culprit. By volunteering information, the bunch hoped this would mean a shorter prison term. With a trial carried out and the group convicted, sentencing would be a roll of the dice.

The defendants had the option of waiving trial, assert complicity in the crimes and request leniency. If this didn't appeal to them, they needed to expect a lengthy court date.

Foraging through the evidence, and with Helen highlighting scenes from the video, the prosecution was walking tall. Confidence ran high the evidence would yield jail time. Once convicted, the feeling was a judge would impose harsh sentences for the heinous acts, therefore, the prosecution spurned a request for a plea agreement.

Three of the defendants came to their senses, caved-in to the futility of the circumstances and agreed to avoid a protracted battle. Accepting their misfortune, they yielded to terms proposed, and further consented to testify against Jenkins as the mastermind. Each held on to a sliver of hope that a reprieve at a minimum-security prison was possible. Time behind bars at this type facility wouldn't be as harsh. If released on good behavior, they could take comfort knowing they wouldn't die while incarcerated.

Howard Jenkins was the lone holdout, and he wouldn't budge. Breathing the same air as other fools for twenty-three hours a day wasn't in his playbook. Jenkins didn't plan to draw from a 401(k), Social Security, or even lock-up for the remainder of his life. His expectations were much loftier. He was gambling on walking away a free man.

* * * *

Helen relished her time with Mike and Sam after the newspaper broke the Beeson story. The unforgettable day she witnessed the five men in Jenkins office was now history and somehow she would one day happily put it behind her, but not yet. Apprehending the people responsible carried with it hope they would be put away for a lengthy period considering the severity of wrongdoing.

After the bad guys were in jail, the FBI relinquished its post at Helen's home. No longer considered a threat, Busby was thought out of the country and hiding in a foxhole. Life at the Faulkner's was leveling out and normalizing, each day a little smoother. The future appeared brighter as the corner turned, and living seemed good again.

Convalescing included cherished moments with her children in an orchard Helen had grown to love. She could only see this special place from a distance by looking through a window during home confinement. In the aftermath, she once again enjoyed the abundance of treasure and inhaled the marvels evident all around.

Sometimes, she walked between the trees with her eyes closed, breathing deeply the aromatic scent of the season. When returning to reality, pulled from storage were fond memories of the legacy her parents provided. When roaming the orchard was unthinkable, she dusted off and pulled these recollections to the forefront.

But at the moment, Helen sat on her bench in cutoffs and a blouse tied at the waist, barefoot, swinging her legs like a young girl as she watched Sam and Mike scurry among the trees. The children hung from branches and crawled among the limbs, and brought to mind monkeys scurrying around at the zoo. A slight breeze had picked up and felt good on her skin with the late afternoon sun high overhead.

"I thought I might find you here," Pete Drucker said, as he high-stepped through the grass walking toward Helen. "I hope you don't mind the intrusion."

"No. Heavens no, not at all," replied Helen. "Please forgive my appearance."

"You look great."

"This is where I come to reenergize," she said.

"Looks like a good place to be," replied the reporter.

"I just love it out here. I really enjoy simply watching the kids play, and I'm happy you came by. Come, sit on my bench. I'm always eager for company. You're welcome anytime."

"I can see why you like it here. This place is awesome," remarked Pete. "The view is breathtaking."

"Yes, I know," responded the woman.

"I wouldn't have guessed a place like this existed in the Hoosier state," Pete observed.

"Now you know my secret. It's closely guarded so don't tell anyone." Hesitating, Helen remarked, "While I was watching the kids play, I wondered what was going on at Beeson. I haven't talked to Eve recently, so I don't know what the mood is there."

"From what I hear it's on the upswing," responded Pete.

"I suspect that no one is too happy with me, being a whistleblower and all," added Helen.

"You might be surprised. I believe the vibes could be just the opposite. It took a lot of guts to stand up to those guys," Drucker remarked. "If it wasn't for you, all jobs would have been lost and the company gone under."

"I can't take all the credit."

"Believe me, if you hadn't come forth that company would have gone down the tubes," Pete acknowledged. "If that happened the repercussions would have been incalculable. So don't cut your fellow workers short."

"I guess I'll find out. I'm supposed to check-in before long and make arrangements to return to work," said Helen. "That's if I go back. I'm not so sure I want to return to that job. Not with everything that's happened, too many bad memories."

"I understand," Pete empathized. "Just give it time. You'll work it out and make the right decision."

"What have you heard about the guys in jail? Is it certain they'll go to prison?" asked Helen.

"Three of the four are singing like Canaries, and talking like you wouldn't believe. None of them will accept fault for any part of the crimes. Instead, they're pointing at Howard. It's like a broken record. They all say the same thing, everything's Howard's fault. He came up with the idea and planned the whole mess. Those guys are just not willing to accept culpability for anything."

"I guess that's easier, and sad," remarked Helen. "Greed got the best of them and they won't acknowledge it."

"Howard's not saying a word about anything, according to what I've been told, and that bothers everybody," said Pete. "He's being watched like a hawk, and they even have a snitch in the next cell. But he's still not talking but just growls. They're trying to figure out what he's got up his sleeve, and don't believe for a second he's going to take this lying down. That man is a crafty old buzzard, I'll hand him that."

"You don't have to tell me about Howard Jenkins," replied Helen. "I worked with him long enough to know how his mind works. He's slippery as an eel, and if he's not saying anything, you'd better watch out. There's something going on in that head of his."

"Not the others, they're telling everything, names, dates, how they got involved, and how Howard came up with the idea and set the wheels in motion," said Drucker. "Based on what I've been able to gather, I believe Howard sucked them in by painting a picture with so many dollar signs they couldn't turn down the proposition. So much money was involved that all of them were blinded, or simply didn't care who'd get hurt."

"They could have said no," said Helen.

"I'll agree. It's unfortunate, but it looks like they are all going to jail together," Pete said. "They have so much talent, and it's all going to waste."

"Those guys accomplished so much with the company to make it one of the largest in the world. Now the legacy left behind will be they're jailbirds," said Helen.

"Maybe something good will come out of all this. We never really know how things are going to turn out," Pete responded.

"How are you holding up now you're a big-time reporter?" asked Helen. "I've heard your name appeared in every newspaper in the country. That's quite an accomplishment. Next thing we know you'll be getting a Pulitzer."

Pete stood and bowed as he said, "Thank you. Thank you. I owe it all to you."

"Why don't you stay for dinner?" asked Helen. "We've got plenty. Here comes Matt now."

Matt was walking toward them. He had loosened his tie and the button on his collar, but carrying his jacket across his arm. He walked over to Helen and kissed her on the cheek.

"Welcome home," she said. "Are you hungry?"

"I've missed you today. Yes, I'm hungry. It's been a long day. Nothing seemed to go right," said Matt. "But look on the bright side. Tomorrow's a new day."

"Pete's staying for dinner, would you round up the kids so we can eat?" asked Helen. "Everything's about ready. I just need to set the table."

"Great! A friend to share a meal is always a welcome treat," replied Matt.

Matt took off to fetch the children as Helen gathered the belongings brought, and then she and Pete began to drift toward the house while they chatted. Although unmotivated to look through it, a magazine she carried slipped from her arm, and she bent to pick it up.

Zip! Thud!

Helen smashed headfirst and hit the ground hard. The stuff she held spilled out and scattered across the grass carpet.

"SNIPER! SNIPER! GET DOWN. GET DOWN," Pete shouted as he dropped and buried himself in the grass, snaking his way to Helen.

Drucker moved as close as he could to the woman to get a better look at her injury. Blood was oozing freely from her neck. With a handkerchief, he dabbed at the wound to find the point of origin hoping to stop the bleeding. The cloth soaked quickly as blood seemed to percolate from everywhere.

He was thankful the wound wasn't spurting or he couldn't contain it and she'd be dead before an ambulance arrived. Applying pressure, he attempted to stem the bleeding.

Drucker heard the sound of a sniper round cutting through the air enough times to last a lifetime while a reporter in the last War. In only a split second, the inexplicable echo could resonate to take a life.

Hearing the yell, sniper, Matt corralled the kids and fell flat. He pushed their heads snug into the grass.

Continuing pressure with one hand, Drucker attempted to impede the blood flow. With his free hand he flipped open his cell and poked 9-1-1 with his thumb.

A calm demeanor was difficult to muster, but Pete spoke slow and distinct, "There's been a sniper shooting, send an ambulance, and hurry, Helen's bleeding to death."

The dispatcher asked a million questions Drucker considered irritating, but all the while kept in mind he had to think clearly and remain calm. Hugging the ground, pressure remained on the stubborn wound which refused to stop bleeding. After a final question from the dispatcher, he called Joe Doyle.

"Helen's been shot," he shouted. "Come quick."

Recognizing the voice, the agent yelled, "Pete, where are you?"

"At the farm," Drucker called out.

"I'm on my way," replied Doyle.

Snapping the phone shut, he probed the terrain, and yelled, "Where's that damn ambulance?"

"Can I do anything?" Matt called out.

"No, just stay down and cover the kids," Drucker responded. "That sniper may still be out there. But, where's the ambulance?"

The reporter scanned the landscape, and combed the area carefully to locate the shooter's whereabouts.

"Matt, do you see him?" asked Pete.

Matt had his eyes peeled for movement, and answered, "No, I don't see anybody moving."

Before long, from a distance came a faint shrill. Yet an eternity passed as the beautiful cacophony came closer with each heartbeat. Along with the ambulance, law enforcement arrived in mass.

Police cordoned the perimeter as paramedics assessed Helen's injury. The emergency team knew instantly the blood loss was life threatening, and had to slow before transfer or the patient wouldn't make it alive to the hospital.

Paramedics labored ardently to curtail the bleeding while others worked to prepare her for transport. The woman lost a lot of blood, and would be dead if Drucker wasn't alert and took prompt action.

The air ambulance arrived and landed in a nearby field, with the patient soon carted to the chopper. Ascending smoothly, the aircraft headed toward the nearest trauma center. On board the patient's assessment continued for the never-ending journey.

The cops locked down and searched the area upon arrival, and roadblocks were thrown together, although too late. Whomever the shooter, he had vanished. A grassy knoll overshadowing the orchard yielded remnants of a presence. A rifle, along side a depression in the grass, gave up an outline of a body. From this post, the shooter observed Helen's every movement while waiting patiently for the perfect shot, and discharge the weapon at the precise moment.

Airports, bus stations, and a broadcast for every mode of transportation to watch, went out to find the shooter. Efforts ramped up to apprehend whoever gunned down Helen Faulkner.

* * * *

Matt, Sam, Michael, and Pete were sitting on edge as time crept slowly. Patiently they anticipated a report about the patient from someone, just anyone. Minutes turned to hours. Periodicals thumbed through to fill time, but with no success in absorbing the content. Repetitive footsteps carefully counted each crack in the floor as the minutes mounted. Prayers offered aloud were to entice the Almighty to spare the patient's life.

I wonder if the person assigned to tell us about Helen's condition was sidetracked, Pete considered, and forgot we're here.

"Maybe they've gone home till the next shift," Matt remarked.

Fears that Helen died and somebody failed to tell the family was in the back of their minds.

"I wonder what's taking so long," Matt mumbled.

Whoever coined the term, no news was good news, hadn't spent time waiting for someone with their life hanging by a thread. The room should be renamed The Torture Chamber, and the no news part was hell on earth when life or death was in the balance.

After hours passed, the FBI agent checked-in.

"What's the word?" the agent asked.

"Nothing," said Matt. "We haven't been told a thing. We hope she's still in surgery rather than the morgue but haven't been told."

"How's the search for the sniper?" asked Drucker.

The federal agent told of measures in use to find the shooter, and efforts were futile to this point.

"We'll catch him, it's just a matter of when," the agent remarked. "It's a good thing you were there, Pete. But how'd you know it was a sniper?"

"I've heard the sound of a sniper round too many times on assignment. Before allowed in a war zone, the military gives correspondents a course on how to react in the event of gunfire. That's in addition to a reminder to change your underwear," Pete remarked, as everyone laughed. He grimaced as he continued, "The sound is distinctive, and one you never forget."

All heads turned as a young man in surgical scrubs walked into the waiting room, a mask hung from his neck. Small in stature, he didn't appear old enough to be out of high school, much less medical school.

"Are you the family of Helen Faulkner?" asked the surgeon. His mannerisms were curt and professional, but showed an eagerness to cover all bases and pass on the condition of the patient.

Matt stood, offered his hand and said, "Hi, I'm Matt Walker, and these are her two children. These other folks are friends, Pete Drucker from the *Star,* and Joe Doyle with the FBI. So what's the story?"

After a polite handshake, the surgeon continued the discourse, "She's critical but resting comfortably in ICU. The bullet nicked an artery in her neck. Had it been a hair in the opposite direction she wouldn't be alive. When she first came in, she'd lost a lot of blood, and continued to lose it about as fast as we could replace it. It was a struggle to keep her alive.

"She was given 12 pints before the bleeding stopped, and was fortunate. It could have been much more. She's a fighter, that's for certain. Whoever was there to apply pressure to the wound saved her life. Otherwise, she wouldn't have made it.

"In twenty-four hours we'll know more about how she's doing. If she's better we'll move her to a room," remarked the doctor.

"When will we be allowed to see her?" asked Matt.

"You can go in two or three at a time, but don't stay long, and keep the noise down. She needs rest, as much as possible. Her body's had a lot of trauma. She's unconscious, but she may know you're in the room, so be careful and don't upset her. Twenty-four hours will make a big difference in her condition. Are there any questions?"

"What about long-term?" inquired Matt.

"Barring something unforeseen, she should have a full recovery, although she's going to be sore for quite a while. Anything else?" said the surgeon.

"Will there be any memory loss?" asked Pete.

"We're not sure. But we'll know more when she wakes up," replied the surgeon.

After nodding to the family, the doctor was gone in a flash.

FIFTEEN

Careful analysis of the sniper's lair yielded a wealth of data pertinent to the assassin. A rifle, a body indentation, and a single set of boot depressions fostered a lone gunman theory. Indelible fragments providing added pieces to the puzzle were boot size, and a rough calculation of height and weight. Expansion of the search uncovered a trail fleeing from the property. An elongated stride and deep impressions showed the escape was hurried.

A path routed the search to a stream meandering through the countryside and from there it was lost. Tracking dogs were dispatched to pin down where the person abandoned the water and reinstate the pursuit.

Patrolling the gravel byways, off the beaten path and to the rear of the Faulkner place, a sheriff's deputy came upon hunter's clothing discarded in a ditch. Awkward to distinguish while moving in a patrol car, the unusual fabric was stuffed in a storm drain with only a small portion protruding.

Catching the eye of the officer, he stopped and pulled the garment from the mud to get a better look at the material. Had the deputy been careless, or he wasn't vigilant and rushed, the object jutting from the culvert would have easily been overlooked.

The fabric was stuffed deep, and gave the officer the impression that whoever discarded it took special effort for it not to be found. The garment appeared new, although hunting season was months away.

Further inspection provided evidence of a vehicle parked along side the road in proximity to the discarded clothing. A fresh puddle of oil from the undercarriage was a sign it sat in the spot for some time. The location was secluded, within walking distance of the Faulkner place, and an unusual stopover for this time of year, even for local farmers.

The discoveries seemed relevant to the deputy as he contacted the dispatcher for instructions. Until an investigator arrived, he was directed to remain on post, preserve the setting, and keep intruders at bay.

From the short list of data collected, the FBI worked on a profile for an assassin and created a framework to identify the person responsible. Lawmen planned to use this as a tool to direct the search.

Huddling with a group of officers, the profiler offered a preliminary description of the shooter.

"The perpetrator is male, about six feet in height, and weighs about 190. He likely has a military training, and may have been a sniper with Special Forces. The man is left-handed. Most people would describe his appearance as average, and nothing out of the ordinary. He could easily be mistaken for your next-door neighbor.

"Nothing about him would stand out, therefore, he could easily blend into a crowd. He is a loner and takes special care to be inconspicuous and avoid attention, yet would kill without hesitation or remorse. This single trait makes him deadly."

On the gravel road, tire prints were identified as those from a later model Chevrolet pickup truck. The inside of the right front tire had a bald edge signifying the wheel was out of alignment.

With the profile provided, combined with the truck details, the cops had some direction of what to look for. The shooter was a crack shot, and if cornered would kill or die in the process.

The FBI solicited the military for secrets used in training snipers, and requested names of persons with similar backgrounds. Two hits were returned, but both had dropped off the grid upon discharge years earlier with no subsequent contact. The addresses of each man were faxed to the FBI together with accompanying pictures, and agents were dispatched to locate them.

* * * *

A trio waited patiently outside the ICU hoping for positive news. Every half-hour the threesome was permitted to sit quietly and monitor the patient. One-by-one Matt would lift Sam and Mike the height of the bed so they could plant a soft kiss on their mother's cheek. He never missed the opportunity to apply his lips tenderly, and hoped she would realize the sincerity.

As quietly as two small curious children could sit in a hospital room, the kids whispered, but yet were mesmerized by small screens emitting beeps and blips. Numbers and lines scrolled, the whoosh of oxygen escaped, and everything was taken in with silver dollar eyes.

A jagged stripe signaled a heartbeat as the line rose and fell rushing across the screen. The stream of nurses that ebbed and flowed kept them informed the numbers were within normal range.

When the allotted time came to a close, a kiss was again applied to say goodbye, and they were banished, till next time.

* * * *

The FBI dispatched separate teams to ferret out the two suspects. One of the names matched a description of a man living in Cincinnati, Ohio. His siblings reported their brother was deceased, killed in a head-on collision two years earlier.

The agents analyzed the reports of the crash, examined pictures and interviewed witnesses. They also perused the autopsy report and death certificate as assurance of his demise. After a careful analysis, the agents were convinced the man mangled in the car wasn't the person they were after. The description provided by the military was a perfect match, but unless he rose from the dead, he couldn't have pulled-off this job.

James C. Cooper, a/k/a Buck Cooper, was an alternate. Agents visited his last known address on Seventh Street in Owensboro, Kentucky. This well-hidden community was on the Southern bank of the Ohio River. A city no one would suspect had produced one-of-their-own as an assassin.

Neighbors around when Buck Cooper ran the streets remembered him. They told the agents he lived at the address his entire life before joining the military. These same neighbors offered that he was an only child and his mother passed-away years earlier.

People interviewed couldn't recall if he attended his mother's funeral, and were unaware of other living relatives. But they were certain the day he left for Service, he was never seen in the old neighborhood again.

The agents spoke with the attorney who Probated Buck's mother's estate. He couldn't recall if the man was at the funeral, but said Jim Cooper hadn't contacted him after her death. The attorney told the agents, "if Buck is found, have him get in touch with the law office. A small nest egg is still waiting after the estate was settled."

For the FBI, this was another dead-end.

* * * *

The children and Matt ate hurriedly in the hospital cafeteria before the clock struck the end for visiting. Once again, the three slipped into ICU to gaze upon the woman clutching to life. They looked on as her chest rose, fell, and examined the bandages on her neck. For the final visit of the day, small lips gently touched their mother's cheek, and then Matt took the weary children home. The nurse's station had his contact number if a change in her condition popped up.

For two small children, the day was long. Mike and Sam were grumpy, exhausted, and had begun to pick at each other, all normal responses for siblings. If the children remained at the hospital longer, they would have been detrimental to the patient and the medical unit.

Drucker was working overtime to help apprehend the killer. His stake in the incident had transitioned from being merely a journalist reporting the news to become part of the story. At the moment of the shooting, in conjunction with the surgeon's comments, Pete realized had he not been there to attend her wound she'd be dead. For him this was not just another news story, it had become a personal vendetta. He sensed a responsibility to facilitate the capture of the varmint who shot her.

He was fortunate the FBI provided him an inside track for regular updates, and once a column was published, it was snatched-up by the wire service. His commentary provided background for her efforts to single-handedly return life to an ailing company when she prevented the theft. The stories underscored the attempted murder after she reported the illegal activities. And, the articles told of her fight for life in an Indianapolis hospital with another effort to take her life.

Unanswered was the job to connect the dots to the men behind bars, although, Pete raised the question of who might benefit by her death. Each column hammered away and supplied essentials to the rescue of Beeson, teetering on the brink of disaster. Emphasis was placed on how her life had been jeopardized by reporting the crimes, and held her out as a hero, yet another victim of the criminal activities.

The article beside Buck Cooper's picture described his military occupation, and that the FBI wanted to question him. An appeal was included to notify law enforcement of his whereabouts, with a tip line established to receive calls.

* * * *

In a beguiling neighborhood of Indianapolis known as Broad Ripple, discovered was a deserted truck that matched the description of a vehicle sought in Helen Faulkner's shooting. Discarded in the parking lot of a restaurant catering to the late-night crowd, the restaurant's owner reported the mysterious pickup upon arriving to prepare for the evening trade.

Unfortunately, cameras were non-existent in the lot, therefore, unknown was when the truck was dumped. Scrubbed of fingerprints or other traces of the driver, the truck was as sterile as an operating room.

So far, the shooter had been careful. The truck was stolen, and had no conspicuous markings as hundreds of similar pickups rolling on the streets of the city. Although, the rifle was custom and untraceable, the Camos could be bought in any Army surplus store.

Authorities had little to work with except a generalized description of a shooter, and that the person most likely had a military background. But the FBI had no doubt that firing a weapon under the adverse conditions in the orchard with any expectation of striking a target took special skills.

The distance between shooter and victim was too great for simple target practice. With trees and other clutter in the path, the maneuver required honed expertise and sophisticated preparation, patience, and a sliver of luck. This described a sniper perfectly. Anticipating the person was former military was no stretch of the imagination, and a testament to his killing abilities. Disregarding the obstacles encountered, the person was within a millimeter of achieving his goal.

In addition to the FBI profile, the agency was unrelenting and persistent. The assassin would eventually make a mistake, and the Bureau planned to be there to catch him.

* * * *

A stranger hobbled across the macadam struggling to reach his destination. Sharp, piercing barbs spiked his leg with every stride, the throbbing worsened with each footfall. He teetered on the ball of his foot and ambulated like someone with a peg leg. This was a first, he'd never been injured on the job before. The mission and getaway weren't clean as he had meticulously designed, and he was seething.

His body had endured countless abuses crawling through the underbrush of tropical forests, and scampering over mountains in unspeakable countries. When combined with hundreds of other asphalt jungles he'd been in to eliminate dictators and drug lords, his body had seen untold abuse without incident. But this was a first for him to encounter an injury.

For reasons he didn't care to understand, and known only to the employer, he removed tyrants and would then cut and run without a hitch. But this time was different. In the rush to escape, hustling through the shallow creek bed he stepped in a crevice and twisted his ankle. Then the agony began.

His ankle had swollen and needed medical attention, and it had to heal before he returned to finish the job. And he would return to complete the assignment. When committed to a mission, he was drawn like a politician craving a TV camera. Each time he squeezed the trigger he felt a rush, and this alone was strong enough to draw him back to complete the contract.

From experience, he knew the target wasn't eliminated. He didn't need to read a newspaper for confirmation. On-the-job attention to detail told him the result.

That bitch flinched just as I fired, he thought in an attempt to justify what happened. I didn't have a clear shot, she moved.

The man was berating himself because of the shut out.

Dammit, I gambled and lost. I got in too big a hurry to get away. Son-nuv-va-bitch. Now I've got to go back and finish the damn job.

The shooter was agitated. Failure to remove a mark with one blow was intolerable and unacceptable in his vocabulary.

The drifter had borrowed another car to replace the pickup. He would keep it until something better came along or the job done. Finishing the assignment was a must or word might spread his service wasn't reliable. If that happened, his days for hire would be over and he may as well be dead.

He loved the adrenaline surge through his body each time he squeezed the trigger. No drug on earth could replace the sensation, and the pay wasn't bad either. But unemployment was not an option, not now. If he made the decision to quit, it would be on his terms.

James C. "Buck" Cooper became a gun for hire the day of discharge from the military. Trained for the role by the best military in the world, the job made perfect sense. The Army begged him to stay on, and gave him the song and dance about being patriotic. He was also offered a higher rank and other perks, but he wanted none of it.

Hands down, he was considered the best sniper to ever complete the program. Consistently during his time in the military, he received the highest marks and awards in the annual sniper competition from among all the Service branches.

But Buck wanted out. When time came to re-up, he had other ideas. Forget about the new grade and added benefits, working for the Army was lousy and he wanted to be his own boss and travel. He knew his skills were in demand and far more valuable outside the military than grunt wages.

He hated being told what to do by assholes that weren't very bright or couldn't think for themselves. All his superiors were good for was shouting orders he ignored. His preference was to work alone, under his own conditions, and do as he pleased. Self-employment fulfilled that dream.

Buck didn't have to look someone in the eye when he fired, therefore, had no qualms about killing. A target was not a person, they were an inconvenience, and someone no longer valuable to whomever paid the freight.

People hiring him had the money to play God and create death. What the target had done to piss them off or the reason for wanting them done-in wasn't his concern. Who was he to raise the question. Nothing mattered other than a cash transfer to Buck for a job he was well trained. Business, that's all it was just business, another day's work.

The day his military career was over, he vanished. Since then he was constantly on the move, country-to-country, town-to-town, and job-to-job. For most contracts, he was never in one spot long enough to unpack a bag, and always prepared to move at the drop of a dime.

Long ago Buck lost track of the string of bodies that trailed him, but never really kept count. Forgetting was much easier than to remember. Thinking about those he killed gave credibility to the notion these were everyday folk, or somebody loved them. But thinking of their deaths wouldn't resurrect a single soul, and discarding memories came easier with each squeeze of the trigger.

North on Interstate 65 to Lafayette was his current destination. This was a college town, an easy place to mingle and get lost in a crowd of students. Here he could find a place to sleep and a doctor to look at his ankle. While on the mend, he'd prepare to return and finish the job he botched. After registering at a hotel, his next stop was to find a hospital and have his foot examined.

Whoever hired him was anonymous, they always are. After receiving payment, and the target identified, how to orchestrate the endeavor was his design. Men that paid his fee asked only for results, and didn't want excuses. But Buck carefully planned every mission and approached each with caution.

For some reason this mission was urgent with a small window to complete the task, but he didn't care why. Whomever he was working for wanted this person gone, pronto.

SIXTEEN

Helen awoke sore, weak, and gazing into Matt's ocean blue eyes. Captivating when they first met, these compassionate eyes were more magnetic now that she had come to know his heart. While growing up she was told, *"Eyes are the windows to the soul."*

"Welcome back, stranger," Matt acknowledged. "Glad to see you're finally awake."

"Have I ever told you I love looking into your eyes?" remarked Helen. "They remind me so much of a big, deep blue ocean."

"Yes, many times," Matt replied. "But, how do you feel?"

"Well I ache all over. I feel like I'm drained, and my head hurts. I guess other than that, I'm fine. Why am I here?" Helen replied, "What happened? The last thing I remember is talking with Pete in the orchard."

Straightforward Matt offered. "You were shot."

Helen looked strangely at her housemate and was astonished by his matter-of-fact comment.

"How did it happen? Was it an accident?" she asked.

Matt hesitated before answering, and then said, "No, it was intentional. Apparently, someone was hired to kill you."

Helen was confused, a lump formed in her throat and became unable to speak. In addition to the ailments vocalized, she suddenly felt sick to her stomach. The revelation overloaded her senses, and slowly the magnitude of the message began to sink in. Tears formed in her eyes as she turned her head and looked toward the ceiling. Her expression blank, she stared in the distance and became oblivious to everything.

When she returned to reality, she remarked, "I don't understand. Why would anybody want to kill me? I'm a nobody."

"The shooter hasn't been caught, but the cops believe one of the guys involved in that Beeson scheme hired someone. They think Howard's behind the hit and that's why he's been so silent."

"Why would he do that? What they did is right on that disc. He can't refute that. All you have to do is watch it, and it's self-evident."

Matt paused and carefully collected his words, then remarked, "It's only good if you're around to testify. If you're dead, a defense lawyer would try to explain away the video and have it excluded from evidence. If that happens, the whole case falls apart."

"Oh my." The sudden revelation crystallized in Helen the severity of why this happened. She was silent and stared into space, and withdrawn while considering her mortality. With a determination Matt knew well, she suddenly blurted out, "Then I've just got to stay alive. Are the kids okay?"

"They're fine. They were never in danger," responded Matt.

"So what can we do?"

"Hello beautiful," said Pete Drucker as he strolled into ICU with Joe Doyle in tow.

"Well, the doctors want to move you out of Intensive Care now that you're better," said Matt. "I'll let Mr. Doyle explain the options of where the FBI will go from here."

"I'm glad you're awake and doing well," said Pete.

"I'm also pleased to see you're feeling better," remarked the FBI agent.

"I'm not so sure about the feeling better part. Only time will tell. What about it, Joe? What do we do now?"

"What have you been told? I don't want to bore you and repeat something you already know."

"Matt told me I've been shot and there's a contract out to kill me. That's all I know."

"We're certain it was a hired gun, although he's not been apprehended. We believe he'll try again. Without a good reason, a contract killer won't just walk away before a job's finished. This would give him a bad image. I don't believe he'll make an attempt in the hospital, though, but guards are outside your door just in case. They'll be with you until discharge. When you go home, with your permission, we'd like to place agents inside your home."

Helen became agitated and remarked, "You mean I'm going to be held prisoner, again?"

"The intent is to situate our people where they won't be seen. To draw him out, we want the shooter to believe you're unguarded."

"Whew. You guys are going to have to leave. I need to rest. All this talk about dying and being cooped up is making me dizzy."

"We'll come back later when you're feeling stronger," said Matt. "Get some rest."

"No, Matt. I want you to stay for a while, at least until I fall asleep. I've missed seeing you."

* * * *

The climate at Beeson changed from demoralized to upbeat with a thriving prognosis, once word spread like wildfire of recovering the missing cash. Employees soon felt that both a job and retirement, once teetering, were now secure. By comprehending the company was again on sound footing, everyone began to breathe easier.

The grapevine was rampant with rumors of Helen being shot as a result of the mess, and the hat was passed for flowers anticipating the patient needed cheering up. No one doubted that had she been negligent, the employees would be jobless.

Throughout the company, Get Well Cards appeared to garner signatures for humorous and cheerful greetings. Other than by name, most didn't know Helen Faulkner from a fly on the wall. But they understood she had put herself on the line, and that made her special in their eyes. They felt compelled to express some sentiment regardless of how small.

The Board of Directors replaced the Audit Committee, and the new team plowed through the accounts to investigate intricate details of the conspiracy to bilk the company. The group intended to strengthen internal controls, and other systems used to conduct daily operations, and forever alter these to prevent similar headaches in the future. Initiated were added checks and balances on cash transactions.

While attempting to tally the amount, Beeson's directors attached personal assets of the defendants to recover funds unable to be rectified. Making the company whole was essential, although for a company as large as Beeson, the unrecovered portion was trivial considering the magnitude of the theft. Beeson had turned the corner and the future appeared bright as job retention stabilized.

A celebration was in the works for Helen when she returned to the labor force. To honor her vigilance, a day was set aside with a big gala in the works. Beeson was grateful to the woman who saved its future.

* * * *

When Helen awoke, she was far from ICU. While asleep, she had a dream.

In the vision were images of her children when they were younger. And Jerry was there, as they again shared good times romping through the orchard. They were playful and laughed, while dashing through the trees chasing one another, and had a picnic with the kids under the trees. The couple played with Mike and Sam, and then placed them on a blanket to nap. While the children slept, the couple was intimate on the lush carpet of grass, and ecstasy from long past returned.

Before the dream concluded, she and Jerry were cuddling on her bench, and somehow turned into a fixture rapidly decomposing. After the children awoke, they ran through the trees and swung from the limbs as the couple laughed and looked on. Then abruptly the fantasy dissipated. Helen couldn't grasp its meaning, but she was blissful, as when she and Jerry were first married and the endorphins flowed freely. Intoxicated by the fantasy, she had no desire for the elation to fade.

In the illusion, the couple kissed and snuggled as if life was good between them. Jerry seemed to sense what she was experiencing, told her he always loved her, and the turmoil would work its way out.

Then he added, *"I'll see you soon."*

In her mind, Jerry had returned to life and they were together as she came around. Tingling all over with a recollection so vivid, she wanted to believe it genuine.

The dream made her feel warm and comfortable, and a flush surrounded her like a blanket. She recalled their honeymoon, how frequent they made love and the euphoria of the moment. Ignoring his faults, Helen deeply loved her husband. In spite of his drinking, the marriage held many good memories. But she knew in her heart, and for the children's sake, life was better now that he was no longer with them.

Had he lived, Mike and Sam would have gone through hell. Screaming, vomiting, cowing to constant insults, and continual disruption in the household would have been the norm. Drunkenness would bar him from holding employment long-term. And, he would have been sprawled out unemployed, unable to provide for a family.

Helen understood booze was a sickness that consumed him, and one he couldn't defeat. It devoured him, and alcohol became more essential than life.

Pressing the button Helen rang for the nurse. As she strolled into the room, Helen inquired, "May I have something for a headache?"

"Sure. I'll see what the doctor ordered," she responded. "How are you feeling?" the nurse asked as she went about looking at the machines recording Helen's vitals.

"If I could get rid of this incessant headache, I'd feel fine," replied Helen.

"Pretty bad, huh? I'll see what I can do," replied the nurse. "I'll be right back."

A fragrance filled the air as Helen caught a wisp of the unusual. She glanced around and realized the room was packed with floral arrangements. Baskets of blooms or potted plants filled every available crevice, along with one lonely Bonsai Tree to accentuate a table. Elaborate and elegant designs captured every shade of a rainbow.

Familiar flowers and exotic varieties Helen didn't know the names of surrounded her. The mix of aromas given off by the blossoms was exhilarating.

The nurse returned carrying an injection. "This will take care of your headache," she said.

"Thanks," said Helen as she rolled over to give the nurse access.

"Where did all these flowers come from?" Helen inquired. "I didn't think I knew this many people. Are you sure they're mine?"

"Oh, you're quite the heroine," replied the nurse. "Rumor has it there are tons of people who think a lot of you and wish you a quick recovery. In fact, there are more flowers than these strung down the hallway that won't fit in the room," said the nurse. "But wait until you see all the mail you've received, cards and letters from around the world. There's so much mail, it's being held by the mailroom in bags. We don't have room on the floor."

"Bags? Bags, did you say?"

"Yes, bags. There are at least two I'm aware of, and probably more since I first heard the cards began to arrive. You're quite the celebrity."

"You are kidding," Helen remarked, "aren't you?"

"I'm afraid not," replied the nurse.

"Oh my gosh."

Helen was overwhelmed. She didn't feel important, a hero, or anything special for that matter. She did the job she'd been hired to do, and felt anyone would have done the same.

"Is your headache any better?" inquired the nurse when she returned to the room.

"I'm feeling a little better."

"Are you getting hungry? We can order something to eat."

"Not now, maybe in a while. Have Matt and the kids been here?"

"We just called him. Most of the night he's been sitting with you over in that chair, and went home a short while ago to get some rest," replied the nurse. "That poor man, I don't see how he functions on such little sleep. He's a keeper, I'd hang on to him."

"Is he coming back?" asked Helen.

"He left his cell number and asked us to call as soon as you awoke," replied the nurse. "I believe he was going to bring your children in for a visit. How many kids do you have?"

"Two. A boy and a girl."

Whatever she was given for the headache began to take affect, and Helen became drowsy, gently closing her eyes in mid-sentence.

* * * *

At the hospital, Buck's leg was bandaged. X-Rays showed the joint wasn't fractured, but advised to put a hold on strenuous activities, stay off the foot, and keep the ankle elevated. Therapy ordered included cold compresses, and Motrin for swelling to relieve discomfort.

In the days that followed, the patient respected the doctor's orders and his mobility gradually returned. The swelling soon subsided and the pain became tolerable. It was time to get back to work and conclude the job he'd started. While off his feet, he'd been thinking about the best tactic to penetrate security around the woman.

As his recuperation progressed, he followed the articles in the newspaper and learned which hospital the patient occupied. Running accounts told of Helen's progress. Columns were filled with the ongoing saga in the life of Helen Faulkner, what she had done to catch the thieves, her family, and anything else possible to be printed.

He came face-to-face with old pictures of himself obtained from the military before discharge.

"I'm glad I don't look like that anymore. Damn I'm ugly," said Buck as he laughed. "Nobody would know me from those shots."

Buck watched for anything to suggest when the patient would go home. He had three options to finish the job.

He could hit her while still in the hospital. He knew this was risky and the cops probably would expect such an attack and have her heavily guarded.

The next choice was to take her out as she was being discharged. This could be done from a distance provided he could find out when, where, and how she was to be released. Also, a clear shot would be helpful.

His best option was to wait, hang back until she was home, and hope they would forget about him and lower the guard. In the meantime, he could design a plan, move in, take the shot, be in, out, and gone in a hurry. This was exactly what he wanted, and wouldn't create unnecessary complications. But the shot wouldn't take place in the orchard with all the clutter as before.

"This time I won't miss. It will be clean and quick. Old Buck has a reputation to uphold, you know," he declared to an audience of one.

* * * *

Discharged into the hands of the FBI after a lengthy confinement, as a safeguard Helen was whisked unannounced through a service entrance under intense security. Clearing a truck freight dock freed the lone patient for transport through large overhead doors. This provision avoided an attack from a lurking would-be killer, and provided safe passage. The Agency was unwilling to release her in the normal manner, aware the gunman had a long arm.

Lowering the overhead door on the service dock to mask the escape, a wheelchair rolled the patient to the exit. Summarily swept away, the release went without notice or fanfare with the event intending to be low key.

The solitary passenger escaped in a black, Government Issue SUV. For the ride through the countryside, the tinted windows averted locking a bead on its occupant.

A team of agents had meticulously coordinated efforts to maintain safety. The patient's testimony was essential to establish a foundation for the criminal activities perpetrated. These same acts would prove the catalyst to destroy the company.

Unable to discern what was stirring outdoors from a hospital bed, the passenger eagerly chatted with the agents. She was upbeat, thrilled to be free from the medical facility, and delighted with the view from the backseat.

As always, Helen treasured the open air and to be part of nature. Relying on others for a continuous monologue of what was happening didn't help her disposition. She was a country girl and had a desire to experience the goings-on of nature first hand, and found it arduous while trapped for a long stretch. When working, the ability to enjoy her orchard after hours was a reality. Hospital confinement sucked.

"Isn't the scenery exhilarating?" Helen expressed as she smiled broadly. Sprung by the capable hands of Federal agents, she felt fantastic knowing she was free again.

"Yes, ma'am, it's a beautiful day," the agent, riding shotgun, responded in a monotone, acquired from years of interrogating would-be criminals. While his eyes darted about searching, he displayed little emotion.

"The birds are chirping, and the sky is beautiful," remarked Helen. "I've never seen it so wonderful as it is today. The sun is shining, God is in the Heavens, and all's right with the world. What else can you ask for?"

"Yes, ma'am, I agree," the agent commented in the same banal intonation while his trained eyes foraged for threats.

Man, this woman is a regular Chatty Cathy. She's been locked-up way too long, thought the agent.

As expected, the drive from the hospital to the farm was without incident. Upbeat, and allowing no room for pessimism, Helen was free momentarily and had the intention of retaining a positive attitude in spite of being shot.

However short lived, she intended to absorb the beauty of the surroundings, too often taken for granted. While separated from humanity, during the time of reflection she contemplated the future, and launched on a steady, well-defined, course to adhere.

Life is a treasure and far too short, Helen decided. I'll live and enjoy the rest of my days in spite of the wicked intentions of a few. I'm not going to dwell on what will happen in the future or let it control me. I will not live in fear.

The excitement of being released overshadowed the persistent headache that plagued her. Doctors proposed these were a side affect from trauma of the gunshot they hoped would eventually subside. To Helen, the pain was annoying and becoming protracted. But, doctors were optimistic the intervals would shorten and eventually dissipate.

Arranged for her homecoming was a small celebration. Threatened with cutting out their tongues if the secret escaped, the agents delivered the patient as requested.

Matt, Michael, Samantha, the reporter, and the FBI agent waited. Multi-colored balloons floated about the house, and hanging over the dining room table was a WELCOME HOME banner.

Centered on the table was a chocolate fudge cake with chocolate fudge frosting, Helen's favorite. Across the top in large, bold white letters, was scrolled, WELCOME HOME MOM. When the car was spotted at the end of the driveway, a dozen candles were lighted that Helen was expected to blow out, and the driver rolled to a stop at the front steps as instructed.

The children insisted the partygoers wear hats, blow whistles, and yell, "surprise," to liven up the festivities as their mother stepped through the front door. The adults acquiesced, and for just a few moments, they returned to an earlier time, and became kids again.

The homecoming was a tearful event. Once the candles were extinguished Helen wrapped her arms around her children, and clutched them to her breast. Elephant tears streamed and she was reminded just how near the assassin came to preclude this celebration, or allow her to lay eyes on these beautiful little people in this lifetime.

After being clued-in a hired gun attempted to kill her, she pondered the aftermath had the event been accomplished. She reflected on how death passed her by, and gave thanks for what few additional moments she had remaining for her family. Life as she knew it could have ceased in a fraction of a second. Spared, she was now curious what the future held in store.

"Helen, I hate to break up the party, but we need to thrash out where the agents will be stationed around the house," remarked Joe Doyle.

With the reception over, FBI agents apprised Helen of the measures in place to keep her alive. Unrolling a diagram of the residence, key spots were marked where agents could best protect her.

"We're going to have three agents in the house at all times, a female and two males," said Doyle. "We feel it best if they roam from place to place. If you need someone, just call out, one will be close by. How does that sound?"

"I appreciate what you're doing, but I'm beginning to get the impression I'm a prisoner again. I don't like that at all."

Efforts describing how security would work continued along with the protocol needed to maintain her well-being.

"Windows will be covered as you go from room-to-room. It will be necessary to shy away from openings on the perimeter of the house," the agent continued.

All measures were unappealing to Helen and provided little comfort. She had been restricted at the hospital, but now felt further hampered with her movements. She wasn't eager to swap one form of captivity over another.

"Life's not living if you're pinned down and in constant fear," she scolded. "Is all this really necessary? Isn't there some other way?"

The news of added restrictions caused a headache to ensue. Quickly tiring of the gibberish, she told those present she was feeling faint, and meandered to her bedroom.

* * * *

In the days leading to Helen's discharge, Buck scrutinized the terrain around the Faulkner place. He assessed the possibility for another shooting and the correct angle. A farmhouse analysis increased his confidence a clean shot was possible.

With the rear of the property used for the unsuccessful first shot, the current assessment proved his original angle of attack correct. Again using the backside of the property, his plan was to only alter the location where he set up shop.

Central Indiana was prairie land, flat country, farm country, and urbanization of the Hoosier state had a slow evolution. Hills were shallow and the earth well suited for raising crops. But for a sniper to reach an elevation to secure a bead on a quarry, it was inefficient.

The laws of physics wouldn't allow a straight shot from a distance. The curvature of the earth and gravity created a natural drop on a trajectory.

The highest structure in this topography was a barn or a grain silo. To locate a place needed to make a shot twenty-five hundred meters from the target was problematic, yet feasible. From target to point of contact, a direct line of sight was essential. But to attain altitude and remove ground clutter from a great distance Buck had to improvise.

The angle for impact was calculated. For success, Buck ascertained his best opportunity would be from a grove of trees, with a Sycamore in the center rising thirty meters to the heavens. A slight rise beneath the woods provided additional height. Ascending to the apex and using a scope, a clear observation to the rear of the house was possible.

Buck deliberated on several old barns and grain bins. He soon realized these would be first on the list to be searched if the cops believed he existed, therefore, excluded from consideration.

High in the Sycamore a lightweight-ridged platform was secured as the base camp. For stability, the structure was anchored to thick tree limbs. The elevation chosen was a precise distance off ground level, where a pre-engineered six-foot square surface of polymer compounds was snapped together, and a synthetic fabric stretched across the surface to reduce heat absorption.

MREs, Meals Ready to Eat, and other provisions were hoisted for what was hoped to be a brief hiatus, although, preparations were made for a protracted perch. An escape rope extended from the platform to the base of the tree to provide a swift retreat. A quick jerk made the getaway operational.

Camouflage netting hung over limbs above the platform to render the site invisible from overhead, and provide a secure working arena. Once in position, the small 6 x 6 space would be home until the contract was satisfied.

Patience was the only ingredient needed to expose the woman in a window. A few seconds to lock the target, and the job would be over. He could then move on to the next job waiting.

A custom, bolt action, fifty-caliber sniper rifle with a polymer stock, strong yet lightweight, was used for construction of the weapon. The rifle had no optics signature, meaning the color blended to the surroundings. A single shot was all he would need.

Attached to the muzzle was a suppressor, a sixty-inch barrel provided stability for the round. A shell traveling one and a half miles to the point of impact would take 4.5 seconds. A scope with a non-glare lens brought objects on the opposite end close enough to touch. The weapon, when attached to a tripod for ease of maneuverability was secure to the platform. On getaway, everything would be cast-off.

To balance the sway at higher elevation, the rifle was secure on an instrument to compensate for wind velocity. When the air current exceeded 15 knots, he postponed the effort. With everything in place, the job now was all about waiting, patience and timing, all were essential to complete the task.

To be certain the mechanism did the job intended, and before taking delivery of the device, Buck calibrated the weapon to strike the center of a bull's-eye from the distance needed. With a carefully attuned instrument, confidence of its lethal ability was in his corner.

Preparations complete, a vehicle awaited under branches at the base of the Sycamore for a quick escape. Tire tracks erased, grease paint smeared over his white face to provide added cover, and Camos slipped on to blend with the elements. He was now on the job, dressed for success, and just another day at work. This was one game he would win.

* * * *

A Marine Corp specialist worked feverishly alongside the FBI to fashion a framework to outwit the assassin. The agency was attempting to anticipate how, and predict where and when the shot would take place, and how he would strike. A myriad of data about snipers provided the Federal agents was sobering. The fallout deadly without a solution found to counteract the attack.

Training of snipers included how to be invisible, the agents were advised. An intended target wouldn't be aware of a stalking, or an attacker was close by. Someone stumbling on a shooter wouldn't live to tell the tale. If the assassin's post was compromised, it was abandoned.

Scrutiny of the location on the grassy mound from the first shot provided the specialist with abnormalities that allowed Helen to continue breathing. The line of sight from shooter to the point of impact was obscure. With so much clutter, a small limb could have diverted the shell, or the intended victim may have moved abruptly. The list of possibilities was endless.

The military consultant speculated the shooter may have been in a hurry, overconfident, or could have decided an opportunity was diminishing. On a second shot, he would take no risk. In the trainer's eyes, the round that nicked Helen proved him an excellent marksman under murky conditions, and made him a bigger threat.

The military engrains in snipers to be imperceptible and strike a target dead center with each squeeze of the trigger. The Service trains only the best of the best. Failure to strike a mark wasn't uncommon if the shot was initially high-risk, or an unforeseen factor intervened. The FBI was told there was no such thing as a perfect shot, and the marksman was trained to adapt on the fly.

Where he would fire the next round was ambiguous, although the specialist believed the rear of the property was a distinct possibility. For reasons of his own, the killer was fond of that angle.

He could be a mile away or lying in a patch along the outskirts of the property waiting. But, the shooter wouldn't be visible unless he chose to show himself. The possibilities of what might happen were without end. The only means to beat this guy would be to give him a reason to fire. It would be at this moment he would be most vulnerable.

* * * *

Helen worked vigorously to develop a routine to co-exist with the agents. She made every attempt to accommodate the restrictions imposed. Doors and windows were constrained and safeguarded in each room she broached. Preparations had to be made for her to move within the confines of the house where she might be visible from outside.

A female officer was dressed as a housekeeper in the event someone knocked on the door for deliveries or a visitor came knocking. This could be the killer wanting information on what was stirring.

But in short order, the limitations to protect her took a toll hampering the familiarity she had with her home. She felt handcuffed, constrained like a prisoner in a cage, and this was exactly what she dreaded. The newness soon wore thin and the walls began to close in.

"How much longer can I stand being held captive? Every time I turn around a new face appears," she told one of the agents. "How much longer will this go on? I want to scream!"

SEVENTEEN

On his belly foraging with the scope, Buck combed the terrain. Patient, deliberate, and focused, his single interest was to locate the target. The objective was to take out the woman at the precise moment, not too soon, not too late, a gentle squeeze and he'd be done.

With one botched effort, Buck was compelled to hit the mark. He'd never missed a first shot before. Dredged up deep from within and converging on this moment was years of training. Instructions long forgotten were brought to surface and on full alert, his senses circumspect for anything that might alter the outcome. An obstructed view or unexpected motion created an opportunity for failure, but he couldn't let that happen, not this time. Patience and preparation were the remedies. Buck's reputation rested on the moment and he wouldn't allow another blunder.

From this vantage point was a clear line of sight, the same bearing as his first attempt but at a higher elevation and greater expanse. Training instilled in him, if it could be seen through a scope, he could take it out, and distance wasn't an issue.

In an effort to bolster confidence and influence the outcome, Buck reflected, I can shoot the balls off a gnat at a thousand paces. Ain't technology great?

Relying on the woman to appear at the rear of the property was a higher probability than from another angle. The initial survey of the property concluded she favored the trees. Occasionally she relaxed on the porch, but she preferred that orchard.

A student of behavior, Buck knew people were creatures of habit. Predictable, changeable for a short while, but in the end they always returned to a comfort zone. As many times as he gazed on her strolling through the trees he knew this was her comfort zone, and confident she would eventually return. When she did he would be expecting her arrival.

Heads bobbing through a lower window gave Buck the impression this was the kitchen, although unable to discern who was shifting about through the thick curtains. Upper windows similar in size were believed bedrooms, a smaller more central window the bath.

Lights flipped on, and then off. Toys could be seen through a slit in the curtains of one window, the other sealed.

A wooden deck extending across the back had a connecting path that lead toward the trees, and then precipitously ended. A man moved freely around the property, his car parked alongside the house. Buck had no interest in him.

This had to be a boyfriend, Buck surmised. I was told her husband's dead. This guy's a gofer.

Children played in the yard and around the trees from time-to-time. Delivery vehicles were in and out. He hadn't laid eyes on the woman, but Buck was convinced she was inside. He watched as the SUV pull away carrying the protection detail when she was dropped on the front steps.

Everything appeared normal. There were no signs to indicate the unusual, but Buck knew she was guarded. Otherwise, she would have already been to the orchard.

Being cooped-up gets old, Buck reasoned, and the guards will get sloppy. They always do.

As the days and nights stretched, the sniper slept little as his vigilance prevailed to capture events that happen. Daybreak flickered and confronted him. He squinted as first light blinked through the branches. After many of these, the days soon began to fuse. Keeping them separated was a challenge as each day became a repeat and merged with the last. Buck began to lose track.

The platform was draped with an obscure fabric the animals jumped and nibbled on, the thin membrane intended to simulate foliage and coalesce with the environment. Too quickly the camp surface turned brutally harsh and unforgiving, and a far cry from a mattress. Overall Buck's temporary home showed no comforts and was slowly becoming a detriment.

Exposed to sudden bursts of wind that shook the camp, roasting in oven temperatures at high noon, and vertigo were all taking a toll. Unexpected, effortless, haphazard motions of the stand dangling from a tree limb made him feel like he wanted to puke.

Night chills and dampness followed, and Buck was primed for the intended to show so he could get the hell out. His job was to shoot and leave, not be confronted with continuous bombardment by impediments. Flat for days on his belly doomed him to be too hot, too cold, unable to walk, straighten his legs, or exercise other than limited stretching.

This job should have been set up for a robot to handle, not somebody like me, he thought. Set the damn thing in place, point at a target and program firing instructions. Hey, that kind of contraption could be one hell of an invention. I wonder, could something like that be patented?

Regardless of the degree of training, no one becomes accustomed to prolonged intervals of trepidation. When protracted, monotony sets in and takes its toll, then mistakes occur. Screw-ups in this line of work are barred, but boredom crept in as Buck peered through the glass and the days continued to merge. He willed something to happen, just anything to break the tedium.

"What the hell is taking so long? Show your damn face, would you?" Buck mouthed.

Two seconds, just two seconds is all I need, Buck contemplated. Come on Buck, be patient, wait for the right moment. That time will come soon enough, and when it does there'll be a hole, dead center of her chest. She'll not be around any longer after I'm done, he reflected. I'm going to make damn sure this time.

Buck was prone for hours and moved only his eyes while scanning the terrain. An indoctrination and discipline regimen forces a body to exceed the normal boundaries of endurance, but everyone has limitations, and those limits are idiosyncratic.

Buck always thought this life was instilled in him, part of his genes. He did whatever necessary to finish a mission, but hesitant to admit the inevitable. He also had boundaries and after hanging in the tree forever, eager for this cat-and-mouse game to be over.

Regardless of how the cake was sliced, eating crappy food and sleeping on a surface hard as bricks caused the body to pay a price. Urinating and defecating from a six-foot square cramped for space platform that moved at-will one hundred feet off the ground, had grown old and the novelty long gone.

There was no contest, having sex, eating a charbroiled steak, or sipping vintage wine had this current circumstance beat all to hell. And right now, the job sucked. Insults to the body harden a physique, but monotony numbs the mind, and Buck had to keep nudging himself to stay alert. He remembered his instructor insisted that pleasures softened the body and made the mind weak. At the moment, he decided to live with a few less brain cells.

Isolated on his island in the sky, he envisioned himself with a calling. Regardless of the hardship, he had been trained to see the situation through to the end. But he was weary of the milieu, and wanted the assignment over, sooner rather than later.

Swinging in a tree like a chimpanzee was not part of training and he was unprepared for the affects of the assignment. He also hadn't anticipated the delay would be relentless and as long lasting. Unfortunately, he was at the mercy of a target that refused to present herself.

"I'm going to puke," Buck yelled an instant before heaving over the side of the platform.

Wiping his mouth with his sleeve he considered, this could be my last job. I'm tired of this goddamn shit. I have all the money I can use stashed away, and could live anywhere. A dollar goes a long way in South America. Besides, sleeping with a Muchacha is cheap, and nothing ties me here. The work may pay well, but I'm tired of cleaning up somebody else's mess. I'm getting too old for this shit and should have quit long ago.

A sudden gust of wind rattled the camp and brought him back to reality, rescuing him from disparaging himself.

"Dammit, I've got to stay focused or this'll never be over. If I'm not careful I'll miss a chance."

Glancing through the eyepiece, the shade covering the bathroom window had risen and caught his attention.

"Damn, I almost missed it," he said. "That's what happens when you get sloppy."

Through the small casement window, the shooter was looking squarely at the woman he was to take out. She was in his crosshairs in clear view, the safety off, sight on target as the index finger eased in position. He checked the wind velocity and adjusted the firing angle to align the shot. One shot and he planned to make certain the round found its mark.

"Maybe the cops thought I went away and would never come back. Boy, are those bastards in for a surprise. "

Suddenly he stopped dead. "Wait a minute," he said.

Buck was dead still, and carefully examined the subject at the end of the glass.

"That's a reflection," he said. "A reflection in a mirror, she's standing off to the side."

Initially fooled, he thought, dammit Buck, you can't even tell the difference between a live woman and a reflection. You've been in this tree too long. Be patient. She'll eventually come out in the open, he assured himself. And when she does, she's mine.

His finger backed away from the firing mechanism. Through the reflective surface he watched the woman. He was mesmerized by her appearance as she stood in her nightgown, diligently rolling each lock of blonde hair. He saw her coil the golden strands carefully around the rollers to form curls at the end of the long tresses. When finished, brusquely she turned and disappeared.

Too much time had passed since he'd spoken to anyone, much less a woman. He even forgot to bring a *Playboy* with him to pass the time, didn't think he would be camped out this long.

As quickly as she disappeared, she reappeared, now naked. With her nightgown gone, he could see just how lovely her body was.

"Pictures don't do her justice. She's fine looking," Buck remarked.

Until this moment, he hadn't given much thought to the job he was hired to do. Through the eyepiece he saw a beautiful creature, like one he had never seen before, and he felt a desire to touch her.

Her pale skin and gentle curves were seductive. The fluid extraction she made removing each roller seemed in slow motion. With each brushstroke she fawned over the long honey strands. Stroke, after stroke, she carefully manipulated the curls with her fingertips.

His eyes were fixated on breasts that rose and fell as she moved while lifting and lowering her arms. Up and down, side-to-side, picking up this and that, placing it on the counter, and then picking it up again. Buck was hard as a rock as his eyes drank in her beauty.

I love blondes. If I'd known she was this good-looking I wouldn't have taken the job, he thought. Goddamn, now I can't back out. I'll bet she'd be a good roll in the hay. Damn, she has nice tits.

Abruptly she turned and disappeared. Buck was perturbed that he could no longer see her but kept his eye fixed in place, waiting. Gawking through the lens, he watched for her to show again, probing for the target.

Spontaneously she reappeared clad in a plain white blouse. Buck mulled over how magnificent she was in the simplest of garments, and looked on as her curls bobbed when she stirred. Absorbed by her beauty, a hand came from nowhere, pulled the cord, and the show was over.

"I don't understand why anybody would want to get rid of such a beautiful woman. I know a lot of ugly ones that need done in," Buck said. "But, why kill one that's so damn pretty? What could she possibly have done to warrant being rubbed out? I'm not so sure I want to do this job. I don't like the idea of killing a woman, much less one with such nice tits."

Buck paused and was having second thoughts as he reconsidered the situation.

But if I don't do it, someone else will, so calm down and be patient, Buck. She'll be back. You'll get your chance. She'll come out into the open and you'll get a clear shot. Just chill out and stay cool. And quit thinking about how fine looking she is or you won't be able to focus. That kind of thinking will get you in trouble. There are lots of blondes in the world. Taking one out is not that big of a deal.

Buck hadn't been with a woman since his reprieve with the sprained ankle. The image at the end of the sight glass reminded him just how long.

Man, she's gorgeous and has a nice chest. She still has a good figure even after two kids, Buck thought, and blonde hair. I love blondes. And, damn, I love those tits. Women south of the border are okay, but I'd rather have a blonde with nice tits any day.

Come to think of it, that college student was blonde, Buck reflected. Man, she was feisty and wanted to roll all night. I almost couldn't keep up. And, damn, what she could do with her tongue.

It's too damn bad I have to take this one out. I didn't think about it before, but this will be the first woman I've done, he reflected. Shit, and she's blonde to boot. Shit! Shit! Shit! God-dam-mitt! "Buck, are you sure you want to take her out?" he asked, hesitated, and then replied, "Hell, yes. There's too damn much at stake. The world's full of blondes. Now stay alert, there'll always be another blonde around the corner."

Focus, he reminded himself, this isn't personal it's business. That's why I get the big bucks, and occasionally a blonde has to go.

His eye was pressed to the glass as he scanned and probed while the hours ticked off and nothing happened. Movement, the covering over a window went up slightly. The window lifted a bit, and through the diminutive gap, he could see a hazy view into the room.

He caught sight of the lower part of a body. The person wore jeans but he couldn't identify the form. The view was fuzzy and imperceptible, and he wouldn't take a chance and eliminate the wrong person.

"Dammit, open the window a little more," Buck mouthed. "Just a wee bit more is all I need and you'll be history."

There would be no second chance, no return trip no matter how nice her tits were. The shade dropped unexpectedly.

Damn, what's going on now? Open the window, he wanted to shout, and was irritated because he couldn't see his quarry.

Once the rifle was discharged, his plan was flawless. To escape without complications, the strategy allowed for no wiggle-room. Although he was using a silencer to mask the sound, it wouldn't make a difference. He knew that whoever was guarding her anticipated his presence and sensors were in place to pinpoint the location for a gunshot.

Those bastards will swarm all over these woods to find whatever they can to figure out who I am, Buck thought. Not in my lifetime, they won't. Not if I have anything to say about it.

As the day progressed with his eye attached to the small lens, he observed children run through the yard. The same man he saw earlier was hovering over them like a mother hen sheltering their every move. Buck turned his vigil back to the house to catch sight of the woman if she reappeared.

The sun was directly overhead, and his body warmed as sunlight filtered through the tree leaves. His eyelids drooped, caught himself nodding, and shook his head to stay awake. As he snapped out of the nod, he cursed under his breath. But with the sun's warmth and lack of activity, drowsiness soon won out. His lids became heavy and he couldn't hold them open, and dropped off to sleep.

* * * *

"How much longer am I going to be a prisoner?" Helen howled at Special Agent Doyle. "How do you know somebody is even out there? How do I know you aren't making this whole thing up? I have no intention of going through life fearing to breathe. That's no way to live."

"Helen, we're trying to keep you alive. Why would I make up a story like that? If you'd like to test my theory, poke your head out the door and you'd be dead in a few seconds."

"How do you know?" Helen questioned. "Are you sure he's even out there?"

"Have we seen him? No, but that's not uncommon for a professional sniper," said Doyle. "Do we think he's watching at this very minute? Yes, without a doubt."

"How are you so sure," asked Helen.

"A killer like this guy will wait forever if necessary. He's relentless and just won't give up easily," replied the agent. "I'm not trying to scare you, but in your case, if you stuck your head outside for thirty seconds, you won't be alive. Helen, I want something better for you. Remember, you've got to stay alive to testify against those guys and put them away for a long time.

That's why we're putting so much effort into this. Just keep in mind, one of them hired this guy and we've got to stop him."

"Well, I want it over," Helen demanded.

"I know you do, and we're trying to force his hand. We're enticing him with tidbits through the window using our agent," said Doyle. "From a distance this woman looks enough like you to be your twin. We don't believe he'll expect somebody to be taking your place."

"I suppose that's a good thing. I wouldn't expect that either," said Helen.

"We're playing on his primal instinct, hoping he's been isolated long enough he'll take the bait. This should affect his judgment enough to throw his game off," remarked Joe offhandedly. "The Bureau will not intentionally place you in harm's way."

"Game? Game? I can assure you this is not a game," yelled Helen. "If you think it is, then I don't want to play anymore."

Helen was irritated and tired of being held at bay without the ability to enjoy the things she had become accustomed. She'd been cloistered too long.

"I want my life back. I miss the orchard and my bench where the kids play and have fun. I can't do that if I'm a prisoner. I want the wind to blow through my hair, and smell the trees, and hear the birds chirping," Helen remarked. "If this is a game it's gone on far too long, and I want it over."

Joe realized his terminology was wrong and tried to rectify what was said. "Helen, I'm sorry. Please try to be reasonable," Joe pleaded. "We're trying to return your life to normal, but to do that we've got to keep you alive. I'd like to say I know what you're going through, but I can't. I've never been hunted by a killer," remarked the agent. "But the FBI has had success in ferreting out murderers. Now we're trying to do our job and keep you alive in the process."

"How many times has a person you've guarded been killed anyway? Can you tell me that, or is that classified?" Helen maligned.

"I agree our success rate hasn't been exemplary, but I'm asking that you give us a chance," said Doyle. "Unless you have an alternative we haven't thought of, please be patient a while longer so we can catch this guy. He's killed many times before and we need to get him off the streets. Hopefully, with a little encouragement this guy will make a mistake, and then we'll have him."

"Well, please hurry it up," petitioned Helen.

"The experts tell us he opted for the back of your house for reasons only he knows," replied Joe. "We believe it's because it's assessable, and gives him better visibility. The open yard allows for easy access. It's logical he'd use the same angle unless something would negate the possibility."

"I hope you know what you're doing and this won't last much longer. I'm going stir-crazy. You've got to get this over with," remarked Helen.

"Helen, I promise you, I'll do whatever is within my power to end this," promised the agent.

* * * *

Startled by a sudden burst of wind whipping the platform in different directions, Buck was jarred and realized he'd fallen asleep. He snatched up the scope to take a quick look around and ascertain if something had happened while he slept. He shook his head, knew he screwed up, and wondered what he missed. He scolded himself for not staying alert and vigilant, and questioned why he allowed himself to lose focus in the middle of the day, wondering how long he slept. Gazing at the sky and based on the sun's position, a best guess was he napped for hours.

So what have I missed for the last two hours? He thought. Dammit, I can't believe I did that.

He roamed through the back yard with the scope to find someone moving. The yard was barren. The man and children had disappeared. The bright orange ball hanging in the western sky was slowly drooping. The windows were closed and no one was moving about.

He turned his attention to the grove of trees to locate someone strolling in the orchard but nothing stirred. A sweep of the yard gave him the idea he was looking at a wasteland as wind whipped leaves and twigs and scattered them about. The air was heavy, it felt of rain as the wait continued.

Did I miss an opportunity while I slept? Damn, I hope not, Buck thought.

He relaxed a bit. There was nothing he could do until the woman showed.

* * * *

An FBI agent pulled Joe Doyle aside and whispered, "The request for the CIA to divert a satellite over the area to pick up a heat signature has been denied. The search we have going on isn't a high enough priority. Too many fires are being put out in the rest of the world."

"Well, I'm not surprised. I was expecting that answer," responded Doyle. "It was a long shot anyway. Has the request for a fly over by a drone been considered?"

"Same answer. It was also rejected," replied the agent. "According to the guys upstairs, they are limited on assets, and the ones they have are tied up."

"Then I guess we'll have to catch this guy the old fashioned way through good old police work. We've just got to out-think him."

EIGHTEEN

In the crest of a giant Sycamore the vigil persisted. The watchful eye of the gunman witnessed lights flicking with the approach of darkness. Slowly sliding the scope from window to window, the marksman hoped to catch sight of the woman for a clear shot when her head emerged. Unexpectedly a window lifted several inches.

Probably to let in the night air, Buck considered.

The bathroom light came on and through the mirror Buck saw the woman moving about preparing for bed. She was applying lotion to her skin, and he watched as if she was in slow motion casually rubbing cream on her face.

She kneaded her shoulders and arms with moisturizer, saving the torso till last. Lotion covered her skin as Buck held his breath anticipating every move.

Applying cream to her chest, gently she stroked each breast as he watched. His desire rampant, she manipulated and caressed each nipple. Imagination in high gear, he was prone and rock hard, and Buck had to roll on his side to reduce the agony.

"Man, what would I do if I had her in bed? Damn, I love those tits."

Buck's imagination was wild, but as soon as the woman slipped from view and the light went out, his longings dispersed.

The scope followed the woman to the adjacent room where he caught sight of bare legs between a narrow window opening. Slipping a finger on the trigger, he hesitated, realizing this wasn't a high percentage shot. He couldn't see her face, wasn't certain this was the target, and wouldn't chance a misfire. The one shot had to be precise.

The bedroom lamp went out. A much dimmer light provided enough illumination for the executioner to still peer around the room. From out of nowhere, a hand appeared to raise the window. Without warning, the prey he waited so patient for was in his crosshair, sitting on the edge of the bed.

The assassin's finger eased in place, he checked calibration and wind direction, and gently squeezed. Counting off the seconds, he watched as the object tumbled to the floor with the impact of the single shot aimed at the heart.

With no time to dally, the woods would be flooded with cops within ten minutes. The rifleman intended to be gone in four. Foreseeing this moment, advance preparations were extensive and in a flurry thrust into motion.

One swift jerk released the escape line. Buck latched on, swung out, and shimmied to the ground abandoning camp. Rushing to a pile of brush, he tugged at the limbs exposing a four-wheeler. A twist of the key and the engine of the Honda began a low purr.

Stripping, clothes worn for days fell to the ground. Plastic bags attached to the vehicle provided damp towels to wipe off the grime. In a hurry, he pulled on jeans and a shirt, sneakers came from another bag.

Straddling the Honda, Buck pointed it across an open field. Clouds hid the moonlight and he ran low and slow as he felt his way on a memorized course. Four minutes had ticked off, he was right on schedule.

Miles away a truck was tucked away to transform him into a local farmer and carry him out of the area. The plan gave him adequate time to be completely out of the fray.

* * * *

With the flash of the projectile, the FBI sprung into action. Until the sniper sighted the victim, providing freedom from the continued menace was impossible. Offering him a target he couldn't refuse was the agreed solution to eliminate the danger and set up the shooter for capture.

Although expected, Helen was startled as the shell whistled through the window. Anticipating how an event will play out before it occurs conjures up a myriad of what ifs.

What happens if the agent taking her place falls oddly and her action doesn't appear realistic? What if the assassin realizes the setting is bogus? What happens if there is no shooter or he doesn't fire?

The whiz from the bullet brought reality to the forefront. Shaken by this consciousness, a dawning came over the woman that had she not followed instructions she'd now be dead.

Remorse for rebuking the agent overcame her as tears of gratitude poured forth, and she made a mental note to thank agent Doyle.

The female agent that played the role for Helen was safely in another room. From the outside looking in, it appeared she was on the bed. An image projected on a screen appeared palpable in dim light and through an open window. The fall was practiced repeatedly to get it down pat. Anticipating the flash, counting the seconds, and the whistle of the round spinning through the window, the agent's fall relayed to the marksman his prowess and believability of the kill. This precluded a second shot if this was his intention, although, the military advised he would attempt just one, one perfect shot.

In anticipation of a weapon discharge, lawmen prepared to nab the sharpshooter when he surfaced. Cops moved in darkness to block roads and stop and search the few vehicles out, but no one unusual materialized.

* * * *

Over rough terrain, Buck bounced on the four-wheeler across fields and into a creek. He followed until it widened into a larger stream where tied off in the underbrush was a canoe. Dismounting the Honda, he trudged knee deep through the dark waters, stabilized the boat, straddled the gunwale, and rolled in. The four-wheeler idled quietly as Buck got situated.

Punching the gearshift with the canoe paddle, the machine advanced slowly through the murky water. After attaching a silencer to a Beretta from his belt, Buck carefully squeezed four times. A whoosh of air escaping was heard as the balloon tires cycled through the water. Water filled the chambers while the vehicle was propelling forward and descended below the surface. The engine began to gurgle as it became silent and slipped to the bottom of the lake, its usefulness fulfilled.

Paddling the narrow body of water to a waiting vehicle, midstream Buck heard multiple explosions that lit-up the night sky like a Christmas tree. One of the blast locations the sharpshooter called home while passing time stretched out on his belly for so many long days and nights. The others were diversions. Planted earlier, incendiary devices were timed to detonate when cops arrived at the woods. The white-hot flames enveloped the grove and destroyed traceable evidence.

* * * *

Awaiting discharge of the weapon by the gunman, the kitchen at the Faulkner place was abuzz as a makeshift war room. To isolate and catch the shooter, agent Doyle and other officers gathered to coordinate efforts. Information from all sources flowed freely through this central point for anything concerning the killer.

Stretched across a table centered in the room, in plain view was an aerial map. Search plans and strategies originated from here and it acted as a communications hub. Strategically placed, pushpins were at precise points to indicate roadblocks. Also highlighted were roads, landmarks and contours, with waterways prominent. Torched areas were circled, and the location where the shot originated, accented.

Renovated in recent years, modernization of the kitchen pulled it into the current century. Enlarged, it accommodated a hefty number of bodies in anticipation of an expanding family. Folks tend to congregate in a galley, and this household was no exception. But the flood of people strained the room beyond its capacity, and the space was chaotic.

FBI officials and other branches of law enforcement working the detail filtered through the room as they milled about. As time elapsed, discontent weighed in with the lack of progress to locate the sharpshooter. Ideas thrown about speculated on where he went, but these were all conjecture.

The team struggled with a consensus of where he vanished without arriving at a solution. The map was studied, possibilities thrashed about, but until daylight the lawmen couldn't nail down anything concrete.

The location where the sniper fired the shot was simple to nail down. And by probing through the torched remains, a team could locate smoldering evidence of his presence. But with daylight signaling on the horizon, a fresh assessment would yield additional clues.

Between the bodies packed in the room, pancakes and mounds of bacon and sausages disappeared as quickly as Helen and Matt cooked them while officers lined up. Coffee flowed freely to drive off the chill, the caffeine providing a jolt for those working long hours and running on fumes.

Wedged between the clutter was Pete Drucker representing the newspaper, and assured of the exclusive. Gunning down Helen to preclude her testimony was a topic for print, but he was also angered. The crooks wouldn't leave her alone, and he was concerned which of the scoundrels sanctioned the hit. Unfortunately, this wasn't the first time they tried to kill, and may not be the last.

Entrusted with the story of the theft at Beeson, and present when she was wounded holding her life in his hands, he felt a vested interest in her welfare. Identifying with the Faulkner clan upon his initial meeting with Helen, after she was shot he vowed to assist in the capture of whomever committed the heinous act.

As an observer he milled about taking notes, listened to discourse, and like everyone else, was waiting for first light.

"How's it going?" Helen inquired while flipping pancakes and keeping one eye on the map. "Found anything yet?"

"Roadblocks have been up all night and so far nobody has been through the checkpoints that we don't recognize," replied Doyle. "After daybreak we'll broaden the search and be able to track him better. We know where he was, just not sure where he went. He could still be in the area lying in a foxhole until the pressure is off. I don't believe that's the case, but it's possible. If I were in his shoes I'd be long gone."

"Sounds like he's going to be hard to find," remarked Matt.

"I'll have to give him credit, he was smart when he set off those explosions trying to throw us off his trail. If we weren't prepared to catch the echo when the shell was fired, it would have been tricky to get a fix on where it came from."

"Do you think you'll be able to find him," asked Helen, "or is he going to make certain that I'm dead before he leaves, and comes back tonight to finish the job?"

"We're told there's no reason for him to hang around unless he knows he failed. His chances of being caught are too great. Another attempt would require excruciating precision to detail, more than previous," Doyle remarked. "His timing would have to be impeccable."

"What makes you say that?" asked Helen.

"He's lost the element of surprise. Unless there's something we don't know about, he couldn't pull off a third attempt. I believe you're home free and he's on his way out of the country."

"I hope you're right," said Helen.

"But, we'll continue around-the-clock protection through the trial. When we planned this, we didn't intend to leave any doubt in his mind you're dead. He's not coming back. What we need to do now is catch him."

"You're not sounding hopeful, Joe," said Helen. "Will you be able to find him?"

"Honestly, I don't know. We're going to use everything we have, but there're no guarantees," replied the FBI agent. "This guy is smart and knows exactly what he's doing. If he didn't, he wouldn't have evaded the law and been on the loose as long as he has."

The sun started to rise and a radio squawked to report search efforts. A curt, rapid, crackling voice came over the airwaves.

"We've found a trail across a field. It looks fresh and disappears into a stream," the voice hissed. "The tires look like he's on a four wheeler. We'll follow the stream to see if we can find where he went and report later."

"That's how he was able to disappear so fast," added Doyle.

The lawmen in the war room hurriedly gathered round the map, a line extended from where he fired to the stream marking an escape route.

"If he fired from here," an agent pointed, "it would make sense for him to go that direction. It's almost in a direct line. The creek flows into the lake and that's probably where he went."

"If he got out somewhere before he reached the lake, he may have doubled back?" another officer suggested.

"Possible, but it's not probable with all the men stationed in the area. Besides, where would he go?" Looking broadly at the map, Doyle continued, "There's no place to hide, it's locked down. His plan was to use the lake all along. Dammit, we should have seen that. No wonder our roadblocks were useless. Let's direct efforts to the stream and lake. If he has a boat stashed somewhere he could make a clean getaway."

"That makes sense," remarked an agent.

"Tell the men to keep this in mind as they search around the water," Doyle stressed. "Watch out for someplace he may have gotten out of the water or it looks like he backtracked. I have a hunch he's across the lake and has a vehicle somewhere. Let's send men to check every house on the other side of the lake."

Quickly gathering their belongings, the officers thanked Helen for the hospitality and moved out leaving a mound of trash behind. Conversation in a once bustling kitchen within seconds turned uncommonly quiet. Matt and Helen began to pick up the mess but felt orphaned now that the gaggle had disappeared.

Awake throughout the night with the rest of the crowd, the couple listened to the banter of the lawmen working the case. Suddenly, they became cognizant of exhaustion and decided to finish the job after some sleep. Besides, the heads of two children would be bobbing awake soon and require the couple to be on full alert.

With all that had happened, Helen had forgotten about the headaches, and been free of them for some time. This perception gave her hope that what the doctors said about the headaches dissipating was an accurate assessment.

The kitchen now vacant, Matt and Helen imagined sources of information would dry up. Bodies once cramming the room and bouncing ideas around were gone. So until someone came forward, specifics of the efforts would be foreign. Weariness had taken over and presently they could care less, and just wanted to sleep.

* * * *

Buck was driving west on I-70, planning to hop a plane from St. Louis bound for L.A. There he would catch the first flight to South America and then play it by ear.

After all the days and nights hanging from a tree, he was exhausted. But he couldn't allow himself to sleep until safely in the air. He wanted a greater distance from central Indiana before getting too comfortable by closing his eyes. Every cop would be on alert, and he wasn't in the mood to provide an excuse to be detained.

Traveling the speed limit, he would continue to be a nobody and keep a low profile. The driver's license he carried indicated he was Charles Renfrew from Topeka. If pulled over the car was a loaner, and he was returning from a business trip. If that didn't satisfy the officer, he would shoot him.

He recalled the previous night and how everything fell into place just like a well-oiled machine. A smile crossed his face in congratulation for precision of the design and how furtive the operation and escape had come off. He made his kill and got away under the cops' noses.

After paddling across the small lake, he reached the opposite shore to a waiting pickup. Several carefully placed shots sank the canoe. Very few remnants left behind to explain his disappearance was the goal as he left the area.

With a carefully planned and uneventful trip from the Faulkner place and the truck deposited in the parking lot of a Holiday Inn, he picked the car he was currently driving. If successful, he would be safely out of the country before the end of the day.

He had fulfilled the contract and felt entitled to some needed time off. Still kicking himself for missing his mark the first time, he was satisfied with the redemption, but hated to eliminate a blonde.

"Damn, she was pretty. I'll never shoot another blonde again," he vowed.

* * * *

The manager of the Holiday Inn on North Michigan Road, reported to local police an abandoned vehicle was on the premises. Enhancement of the video footage gave them a photo of James C. 'Buck' Cooper.

Although grainy, facial recognition software confirmed his identity, the abandoned truck proved the one sought in the execution by tire tracks matching those taken where it had been stored on the lake.

"You're getting sloppy," remarked Doyle when he reviewed the photo. "I would never have expected a picture of this guy. He's been good at evading us so far and I wouldn't have expected to tie him to the area."

"He must have missed this camera or didn't see it pointed at him," replied a colleague.

"We knew he was a sharpshooter and can now place him in the vicinity and tie him to the truck. If he's not already gone, let's turn up the heat and catch him before he leaves the country," remarked Doyle. "He'll likely catch a plane. So let's plaster his picture in every airport within a day's drive. Come on, guys, let's catch him," said Doyle.

Those words ratcheted up the efforts of nationwide law enforcement and placed them on high alert. An all-out effort was launched to snare the assassin.

NINETEEN

Laughing with arms outstretched and head thrown back, Helen twirled through the endless rows of trees. She had a sense of how Julie Andrews's character, Maria, felt strolling through the Alps in the movie, *The Sound of Music*. With the children at her side, she was fulfilled with a return to the orchard once again.

Feeling like a young girl, she was free and no longer emotionally shackled inside her home. The place she loved most had returned.

Doubts of how much freedom she would be afforded before Howard's trial annoyed her. But his conviction would provide a huge step in the right direction to keep him off the streets.

Legal wrangling, appeals and other shenanigans could stretch out for years, but at least he would be behind bars. And all this from a man she admired once, yet, witnessed his cavalier confession to a list of crimes. So until the trial was over, and he was behind bars permanently, she wasn't safe.

Samantha and Michael mimicked their mother as they spun around with her. Together they all laughed and shrieked, relishing liberation from the confines of a makeshift prison.

Helen wasn't sure she ever wanted to return indoors to what had become a dungeon. Upon regaining freedom, the idea of going back to her private cell wasn't appealing. If she had her way, she would linger here forever. She loved the old farm, and as she grew older came to realize the family legacy was what attracted and drew her to the place like a magnet.

Her love for the land, and all the trappings that came with it, had intensified as an adult. She enjoyed the simply pleasure of stretching out on her bench, and taking pleasure while gazing at Michael and Samantha romp through life.

Much had happened in such a short span, more than she could have anticipated before drumming up the resolve to expose the deception. As a person of conviction and a conscience, she couldn't allow a crime to go unpunished, hide under a basket without consequences, or at least try to stop it.

With evil chipping away at the core of the company, she wouldn't stand by and allow fellow workers to be ruined by a group of egomaniacs without striving to incapacitate them. Dredging up the resolve, taking a stand, and stripping away at the façade to expose the crimes took guts, more than she realized she possessed.

Finding courage to go head-to-toe with people in charge surprised even her, and was a move neither commonplace nor politically correct. Yet, this was an action the executives hadn't anticipated, and when she reacted, they panicked. In the process, she jeopardized her safety and made her family vulnerable.

Unforeseen was the retribution and long arm of someone in the group intent on having her exterminated. But, thanks to people working feverishly to keep her breathing, at present she was alive to bring the villains to justice.

"Look. Mommy fell down," cried Michael. "Let's fall down with her."

"Maybe she's just asleep," said the girl. "Let's go see."

The two children ran over and knelt beside their mother, tugging to rouse her with their small hands. She was spread-out on the grass under trees heavy with fruit with limbs that sagged.

"Mommy! Mommy, wake up," the children called out. They shook and tried to get her up to play again. Unable to conjure a reaction, Michael told Sam, "You stay here. I'm going to get Matt. He'll know what to do." Darting off, he ran as fast as his feet would carry him, the entire time wishing the distance to the house would shorten. The child knew his mother didn't look well.

The protective detail stationed at the farm insisted she remain in the house, but Helen refused to follow the advice. She reminded them agent Doyle said danger of the shooter returning was behind them. Whether they liked it or not, she planned to revive and squander as much time in the orchard as possible.

The only alternative for the agents was to walk the tree line keeping an eye open for anything that may be harmful. Once she fell, guns were drawn as the agents anticipated another incident from a shooter, although, the sound of a weapon discharging wasn't apparent.

* * * *

While waiting, an ambulance never reaches its destination soon enough. For those hanging around, it's as if the wheels are anchored in concrete and unable to gain traction.

The Faulkners lingered and listened for the high-pitched whine. Matt gave his friend a perfunctory examination searching for signs of a gunshot. The FBI agents had performed a similar exam when finding her on the grass. Neither assessment revealed an obvious injury.

Matt first thought the sniper returned to complete his mission. A bullet wound was the only injury he could give consideration to because of the earlier attack. Without medical training or a noticeable blood flow, his only option was to quash the fears of the children and kill time until the paramedics arrived.

Kneeling beside their mother, Michael and Samantha hovered over her outstretched body, held her hands, and cried while begging her to wake up. Through tears, they wanted her to get up to play and have fun.

Without understanding the extent of her injury, Matt feared moving her with concern of causing additional harm. He did what he knew by wiping her brow with a damp cloth, and placing it on her forehead to comfort her. She liked that, he knew. Her skin color wasn't normal and he hoped a blush would return to her ashen complexion.

"Dammit, where in hell is that ambulance?" Matt cursed. "What's taking them so long? Did those guys get lost, and having trouble finding the way here?"

He felt helpless and imagined the worst as he pondered what could have happened. Suppositions rushed through his mind as the small group listened for a shrill noise from a distance.

Did somebody attempt to kill her again and finish the job this time? Matt considered. There's no evidence of a shooting, what other injury would she receive? Poison's a possibility. But she hasn't been anywhere, so how would that be doable?

When idle, the mind tends to run amuck. Remaining lucid was a challenge.

* * * *

Matt prayed silently for Helen as he followed the ambulance with its lights flashing, as it pealed a warning and barreled toward the emergency room. He hoped that Helen had passed out from too much excitement, and prayed she would awaken upon reaching the hospital and they could then turn around and go home.

But, his gut transmitted sinister vibes and signaled something ominous in the works. His suspicion was whatever instigated the circumstance, it could be more menacing and too great a battle to overcome. He wished this instinct was wrong and the whole ordeal would turn out to be much of nothing.

Arriving at the ER, and with the patient in good hands, Matt sequestered the children to the waiting area. There they lingered to anticipate a looming diagnosis he hoped would simply be unpleasant, rather than catastrophic.

Regrettably separated from their mother, the children appeared sedated as they halfheartedly watched the Cartoon Network until their eyes became heavy and drifted off to sleep.

With the children's heads on his lap, Matt called Pete and Joe to advise them of Helen's blackout and report she was at the hospital. An unusual alliance had developed between this group in the short interval they became acquainted. Matt believed the others would expect a call concerning the incident. This was especially true if the episode had anything to do with another attempt on her life.

Michael and Samantha awoke hungry, thirsty, and bewildered by all the goings-on. They wanted to take their mother home, return to familiar surroundings and the fun packed moments in paradise.

The day was closing fast, and the waiting room filling with relatives of other patients. Various moods were prevalent, ranging from somber or crying, to refusing to accept something more sinister. Folks attempted to use armchairs for beds, while others sprawled across the floor. But each hoped the relative carted-off would walk through the swinging doors and be raised like Lazarus.

Michael and Samantha didn't expect a miracle, their request was simple. They just wanted to talk to their mother and return to the sanctuary of the orchard they grew so fond.

When the children awoke the newspaper reporter and the FBI agent were in the waiting room. Familiar with the two men, the children readily accepted them as family as each man took a child by the hand and strolled to the cafeteria.

Matt had to move around to get blood flowing through his legs, and rid his limbs of the pins and needles sensation sitting in the same position for such a lengthy period. He also needed adult conversation, something other than cartoons and coloring books, and welcomed the two men lending a hand even if short-lived.

While the children snacked in the cafeteria, Matt eagerly passed on the little information he had about Helen's condition. He explained the assessment in process should ascertain the reason for the black out.

"They're doing so many tests I can't remember what they are," admitted Matt. "But they seem intent to find the root of the problem. The plan is to keep her sedated until the tests are complete."

"That's probably a good idea," added Pete.

"I'm taking the children home to sleep. After lining up a sitter, I'll return to spend the night. By the time I get back maybe somebody will have answers."

"If there's something you need, please let us know," responded Pete. "I'll be praying for her."

"Yeah, same here," replied Doyle. "We think Helen is quite a gal and have grown fond of her."

Before the support group broke-up Matt asked, "Anything new on the shooter?"

"We followed the trail across the lake, and later found an abandoned truck at a hotel on the north side," replied the agent.

"Sounds like you're making some progress," replied Matt.

"And we were lucky to get a picture of the guy, and have sent it to all the airports. The only option now is to wait until something pops and chase what few leads we have. Unless we somehow get a break, I'm afraid the trail is cold. I wish I could provide you with something encouraging."

"Thanks for your honesty. I'm glad this incident didn't have anything to do with a shooter. That was my first thought when the kids ran to get me," said Matt. "Now we have a new battle to fight and I don't get a good feeling about the outcome."

"I'm hoping we catch the bastard before the guys in jail find out Helen's alive," reported Doyle. "If he's not caught, I fear someone else will be sent to get her. Next time they could be successful. Being a major witness, if she doesn't testify they'll walk."

* * * *

Helen roused from the coma with her head pounding. Groggy and bleary eyed, the surroundings were blurry and her eyes refused to focus. Unable to distinguish what was happening, she was disoriented and confused by all the paraphernalia surrounding her.

Lights were dim, machines beeped, and an indiscriminative whirling and whooshing seemed all around.

I'm inside a space ship and abducted by aliens. They're holding me against my will, she thought.

Perplexity and strange noises clouded her judgment. Helen thought the surroundings were odd and couldn't differentiate anything.

Am I tied down? How did I get here? What are they doing to me? Are they running experiments? I'm not letting those little pointy-heads know I'm awake, she vowed. I'll keep my eyes shut, that'll fool them. What have they done with the kids? Are they hidden in another room? What are they doing to them? Why would anybody want to capture me? I know, they want the money.

Delirium had taken over as the throbbing intensified. The constant drum in her skull replaced every form of rational thinking. She thrashed and moaned while rubbing her temples in an effort to alleviate the torture.

"Hi, beautiful."

An alien spoke. She was fearful and glared at the stranger through eyes that were glazed over, as she struggled to make out the life form beside her.

"Who are you?" she said harshly and stared at the trespasser. The voice seemed familiar, but she was having difficulty making out the alien's features through the fog. Suddenly she recognized the voice. "Matt? Matt is that you, or is this another trick? I know that voice, I just can't see. My head is killing me. Please get me some aspirin."

"I'll get the nurse," his voice trailed off on his way out the room.

Returning, Helen bombarded him with questions, "Where am I? What am I doing here? When I woke up, I thought I was in a space ship, floating around somewhere. Everything's so strange and sounds funny. I can't see clearly, and god my head hurts."

On cue, the nurse crossed the threshold to give Helen some relief. Matt parked on the bed and picked up her hand, and tried to renew a closeness lost before his friend collapsed. As the painkiller kicked-in, the curtain of fog and haze began to lift.

"We've got to quit meeting like this," Matt remarked. "All this time you're spending in a hospital room isn't good for my ego. Are you trying to get out of marrying me?"

"What am I doing in a hospital?"

"You don't remember?" asked Matt. "You blacked out in the orchard while playing with the kids. I wondered if it was because you had been cooped up for so long."

"I don't remember any of it. Where are the kids, by the way?" asked Helen. "Everything's such a blur. How long have I been here?"

"The kids are home. Susan's staying with them," Matt remarked. "She plans to be there until you get home."

Susan Davis was a teen who lived down the road from the Faulkner place and kept the children as the need arose. They could call her on a moment's notice and helped many times.

"You've been here about three days," Matt continued. "Doctors have run a bunch of tests to find out why you blacked out, but so far they haven't told me anything."

"Can't they figure out what the problem is? Why would I just pass out?"

* * * *

The automobile that carried its lone inhabitant ascended the ramp to the bridge without a glitch. It was early in the morning but the sun overhead appeared as a ball of fire providing a glow over the city. Heat and humidity had already begun to rise and the day was promising to be a scorcher.

The driver had no interest in architectural lines of the cityscape or the temperature. On a mission, he was intent on crossing the bridge but on constant alert for anyone showing an unnatural interest in him.

He swapped vehicles again. The sedan he drove had some age on it, but otherwise unremarkable and the engine ran well. Shunning attention was intentional, for this was his way of life, and helped him melt comfortably into humanity.

For him a car shouldn't be flashy or someone might take notice. Besides, it would be cleaned and dumped soon.

He wore the same clothing from the night before, but had slipped a jacket on to cover the many tattoos down his arm from his days in the Army. He carried no luggage and wore a baseball cap and sunglasses. A common, nameless face in a crowd, who would pass-by without notice and blend nicely with every other ordinary face.

Stopping at the checkpoint in center-bridge, he showed a passport to the border guard. When waved through, he continued the remaining length into Windsor, Canada, the nearest exit in the U.S. from Indiana.

His original escape route changed on a whim. While driving west he detoured, and turned north onto Interstate 69. This direction pointed him toward Michigan, then Detroit, and across the bridge into Canada. He was now home free and could catch the first flight to Brazil.

I love Brazil. On the beaches, those chicks run around with nothing on. I can't wait to get back there. Buck decided he could relax and thought, I'm going to take some time off, maybe retire. I've got enough money to last forever.

But Buck knew he would become restless and the urge would return. He would get an itch again to seek out the rush he received when he pursued human prey. The thrill of the chase, and the elation received with each squeeze of the trigger caused him to know there would be another. He was an addict, nothing came close to that sensation.

* * * *

A man in a long white coat sauntered into the room and greeted the couple. With a forced smile, his exterior was amiable but he seemed preoccupied.

Drugs were flowing freely in Helen, and the throbbing had ceased temporarily. With the headaches subdued, her spirits were elevated.

The couple had been chatting and laughing and for the moment the adversity in the orchard was forgotten and in the past. They were catching up on current events about the family.

This was a good day, an about face from when first brought out of the coma. Helen and Matt were taking days one at a time, cherishing the good ones.

"How are you, doctor? greeted Helen. This was her first day to smile. "Did those tests tell you anything?" she asked offhandedly. "Discover anything important?" she said flippantly.

Doctor Kline acknowledged the patient, smiled, hesitated, and then remarked, "I'm afraid I have some bad news."

Helen glared blankly at the physician and felt a chill run down her spine. A hard knot formed in her stomach. Unsure of what he was about to say, his tone carried an ominous warning. She caught the bad news part of the comment, but wondered just how terrible this news could be?

Somebody's already tried to kill me, twice. I recovered from that and I'm feeling fine, Helen thought. I simply want someone to cure my headaches. Will I have to keep taking all those drugs?

Is that what he's going to tell me? If I don't, will another blackout be looming and I'll wind up back in the hospital? Just how awful could the news possibly be?

"We believe you have what's known as an Astrocytoma."

Stone faced, Helen stared at the doctor quietly for a few seconds. Baffled by what he said, she remarked, "Can you tell me what that means in plain English, please."

"An Astrocytoma is a high-grade tumor on the brain. The MRI shows it is rather large, and has tentacles spreading like fingers that are overtaking it. The headaches are a result of the mass growing larger and creating pressure. It is wedged between the cerebrum, that's the largest part of you brain, and the cranial cavity, or the outer shell." The doctor mimicked what he was telling them by making a fist. With his opposite hand, he spread his fingers and rolled them over the top of his hand, surrounding it.

"I said, we believe," continued Doctor Kline, "because to get an accurate diagnosis we must do a biopsy."

"That doesn't sound good. What will that entail?" asked Matt.

"The biopsy will allow us to grade the tumor. Brain tumors are generally slow growing, graded either 1 or 2, or these could be a higher grade 3 or 4, which grow rapidly. It may be benign, of course, but a mass this large has a greater potential of being malignant. The biopsy will allow us to determine how fast it is progressing, and then we can recommend treatment. If you decide not to do the biopsy, we really are guessing and won't know how fast its growing or how to manage it."

"How will the procedure be performed? Can this be done with a blood test?" asked Helen.

"Our only option is to drill a small hole in your cranium. We'll insert a long needle in the opening to extract cells. These will be examined under a microscope and provide us the information needed. We'll learn what kind of cells they are, and how fast they're growing. And we'll also be able to figure out the treatment needed to shrink it."

"This sounds painful," remarked Helen.

"Not really. You'll be given a local anesthetic, and except for some pressure, you won't feel much," remarked the doctor. "In fact, you'll be awake for the entire procedure."

"Are these tests absolutely necessary?" said Helen. "There's no other way?"

"Without these tests, we're flying blind. Any treatment we attempt would be guesswork. We know the tumor is large. What we don't know is how fast it's growing, and this can't be determined without a biopsy. To diagnose and treat your condition, we must have cells from that tumor."

"What do you think, Matt?" asked Helen. "Can you live with someone that has another hole in her head?"

"What's one more hole? That's the least of my concerns," replied Matt. "Do we really have much choice? The way it sounds, you've got to do the procedure or you'll never know what's going on inside that head of yours. And, from what the doctor just said, he won't be able to tailor your treatment."

"Even though the tumor is large, without a biopsy we'd be guessing at whatever we did, and never understand how to care for your condition," replied Doctor Kline.

"Just how long will it take to get the results back? She's got to get rid of these headaches or she'll never rest," remarked Matt. "They are relentless, and continued far too long. She never knows when they'll flare up."

"Because of the size of the tumor and where it's located, I'll put a rush on the results and push for a fast turn-around. We'll try to get an answer just as quickly as possible."

"Okay, doctor," Helen announced. "Let's get this over with. I want to go home, so drill your hole and get the tissue. When are you planning to do it?"

"We'll schedule the procedure for first thing in the morning. You'll have a small bandage, but there's no reason you should remain in the hospital. When it's over, you'll be out and home to your family before the end of the day. After the report is in, I'll have my office call and schedule an appointment to go over the results."

"That sounds like a plan," replied Helen. "At least we're moving forward."

"I understand you've been having these headaches for quite some time," questioned the doctor. "Do you remember anything that might have contributed to the problem? Have you had an injury of some type? Hit your head on something lately? Been in a car crash that would cause a head injury?"

"No car crashes that I recall," replied Helen. "I did take a tumble down the stairs at work and bang my head against the wall. When that happened, I spent some time here in the hospital. Those records are here on file. It wasn't long ago the fall occurred."

"It's good to know those are available. I'll take a look at the file," offered the doctor. "The pictures could provide a clue to the root of the problem. In the meantime let's get the procedure done."

The following morning surgery was performed, and by early afternoon, Matt and Helen were on the way home. The children were thrilled to see their mother. Except for the occasional visit, they had been separated and anxious to see her. Although Matt provided them with updates, seeing her was icing on the cake.

With help from the sitter, the children arranged a small party for her arrival. Rushing through the door, Helen couldn't hold back her enthusiasm and smothered the children with hugs and kisses. "I'm so happy to see you guys. I've missed you so much," she said.

From the turmoil experienced, small arms wrapped around their mother's legs and held tight as she hurried through the door. The children feared she might disappear again.

Kissing her they declared, "Oh, Mommy, Mommy. We're so glad you're home."

TWENTY

Helen was sitting on a powder keg, uncertain of what the biopsy might prove. Initially, she and Matt didn't discuss the ordeal and tried to act nonchalant. But each was going through a private hell from a prognosis front and center.

Working on their psyche, every moment the unknown became increasingly ominous. The tension mounted and intensified as each day passed. An illusive outcome was looming that would solidify the future. Both were apprehensive about what awaited but couldn't get a handle on the culprit.

Helen awoke mornings to drums pounding. Devouring painkillers, she struggled to dull the ache and make the throbbing bearable. The banging returned throughout the day, and the tedious ritual of downing additional medication turned full circle to alleviate the discomfort.

Slowly she became aware her strength waned easily, and was readily fatigued. Tying words together to complete a sentence became taxing on occasion. Previously her memory was sharp as she recalled events effortlessly. Summoning yesterday was now fuzzy as her short-term memory began to wane.

Her vision would blur, focus muddle, and recognizing objects became difficult. And then in a snap her sight returned to normal. This happened on several occasions before, but she gave those incidents little significance. The symptoms were becoming more prominent as other characteristics became increasingly obvious and persistent.

"Matt. We need to talk," Helen pleaded after the couple read a story to the children and tucked them in bed.

She explained the increased weariness, the dizziness, and the lack of ability to focus.

"Am I putting too much emphasis on what's going on as a result of what the doctor told us?" she inquired. "Or have the signs been there all along and I ignored them because they were subtle. Either way, I feel the tumor is getting bigger."

As she spoke of the condition, she let her guard down and tears streaked her cheeks. Placing an arm around her, Matt pulled her close and kissed her forehead.

"Has the doctor's office called?" he asked. "It's been a day or two longer than I thought it would have taken."

Through red eyes, a runny nose, snivels, and tears dripping from her chin, she replied, "I was going to call his office in the morning to find out what's going on. I can't figure out what's taking so long either. If this is a rush job, I'd hate to think how long a normal turn around is. Inasmuch as we've been told nothing, I don't get a good feel for what they've found. It's like we're waiting for the next shoe to drop."

Matt reached over, picked up her hand, and responded, "Helen, I love you regardless of what happens or how sick you become. Somehow, we'll get through this. Let's just take it day-by-day." He leaned over, gently raised her chin, and kissed her tenderly. "Like I've told you before, we've got to look at each day as a gift."

"Matt, I don't want you to think you have to stay here just because I'm sick and you're feeling sorry for me," remarked Helen.

"I'm not here because I feel sorry for you," Matt replied.

"Well, whatever this turns out to be, there's just too much uncertainty," she continued. "We have no future as a couple. We're not married and you have no obligations to stay here. There's no good reason for you to hang around. Why don't you go back to your apartment and get on with your life. Find a woman who will give you a little joy, and a houseful of kids. I can't offer you that."

"If I wanted another woman I'd look for one," replied Matt. "But I don't."

"Why be stuck here with someone who's sick," added Helen. "I feel like I'm slowly becoming an invalid and there's no assurance of how long this will last, it may be forever."

"Is that really what you want?" Matt asked.

"I can't see you spending the rest of your life here with me and two kids under these circumstances. Maybe it's time you moved on."

"Helen, I'm not here because of feeling sorry for you or any other reason. I'm here because I love you. Just because we've found out you're sick doesn't change anything. I'd marry you in a minute if you'd just say the word."

"Matt, you're asking for more than you can bargain for."

"Helen, you don't understand. My whole life I've been searching for a person like you. Now that you've finally been found you're trying to push me away, and just because of some illness the doctor might be able to fix."

"I'm not so sure it can be cured," she responded.

"That doesn't matter. Toothless, bald, one-legged or whatever condition your body's in, it's what's in your heart that's important. And Helen, you have the biggest heart of anyone I know, and that's why I love you so. I'll take you any way I can."

"Oh, Matt," Helen remarked with tears dribbling.

"Yes, I've told you repeatedly I love you. You should know that by now. The first moment we met, I knew you were the one. When I looked into your eyes, I thought I had died and gone to heaven. I couldn't believe I finally stumbled onto the woman of my dreams. But, if you tell me you don't love me and want me to leave, I'll go. I won't like it, but I'll go. Otherwise, I'm here for the duration. For richer or poorer, in sickness or health, till death do us part, married or not, I'll still be here for you."

Crying freely, Helen clutched Matt and kissed him fervently, "Matthew Walker, thank you. I needed to hear that. Of course, I love you and want to always be near you. But, I'm afraid you're bargaining with the devil."

Matt lifted her chin, smiled tenderly, and said, "One day at a time. That's all we can do."

* * * *

Helen was restless. With sleep fractured, she tossed and turned although her bloodstream was filled with painkillers. She was sick with concerns about the tumor increasing in size, sick of waking each morning feeling like her head was in the center of a kettledrum, and sick of thoughts about the future absent her children. What would be in store for the family if a malignancy couldn't be beaten?

She was also weary of agonizing over Matt being stuck with her illness and two kids. These were the only people that brought joy to her life, yet he remained committed to someone slowly becoming an invalid with no stake in the outcome.

Lying in bed awake, waiting for sleep that wouldn't come, she shoved the covers aside, rolled over and her feet hit the floor. Meandering through the hall to the children's quarters, she felt a need to look in on them. Standing at the doorway to her son's room, she watched as he slept and dredged up distant memories.

Toddling across the room, she sat on the edge of the bed. His face turned away from her, she placed a hand on his back to feel the warmth of his body and the rhythmic, steady beat of his heart. She saw his hair was messed, and his mouth slightly open and askew as he continued in deep slumber. Brushing hair out of his face, she lightly placed a kiss on his cheek. Recalling the day he was born, she had delivered a beautiful eight pounds, six ounces baby boy with hair as white as fresh snow.

She was reminded of the joy experienced while alone with him nursing, and recalled how he changed before her eyes. The fun enjoyed playing with him as he grew, walks through the orchard, and how he took to his sister as her protector when she came along.

Kissing him again, she muttered in his ear, "Sleep, my sweet prince. May God be with you always."

She then strolled the short distance to her daughter's room.

In the dim light, she could make out the outline of the small child curled under the covers. She walked over, leaned down, and kissed her as she carefully moved strands of long blonde hair behind her ear. She sat on the bed with the memory of the girl's childhood. Clinging to her brother came natural, and she wondered if they would remain close as adults. Lightly rubbing her back, she kissed her and murmured, "Sleep little princess. May God always be at your side."

Helen's head was beginning to throb as she downed additional pills to soothe the agony she felt coming on. She hoped drowsiness would overtake her soon, but wanted to look in on Matt before treading back to bed. She pushed opened his bedroom door and he was sound asleep. Strolling to the side of his bed, she leaned over and kissed him on the cheek.

Helen whispered, "Matt, you're the most wonderfully unselfish person I've ever met. Your kindness seems endless. You're a rock and my foundation for I couldn't have made it through this nightmare without you here. You are my Guardian Angel. Thanks for everything. I do love you so."

* * * *

The following morning Helen placed a call to the Oncologist, and an appointment was set for the afternoon to review the report so anxiously awaited. Fretful, Helen and Matt arrived early. As they ambled through the entry, they were ushered into a small room.

The space was bland, the walls beige, the furniture a matching shade accented in white. Cabinets were filled with a variety of medical supplies. An examination table centered in the room was draped with a disposable sheath. With chairs positioned against the wall, a stool for the doctor to roll around on stood in the corner. Certificates of medical achievements hung on the wall beside a light-box to view photographic negatives. These were the typical trappings of an exam room.

Few words were verbalized as the couple shuffled uncomfortably while they waited. Ideas had been thrashed about, and tears shed leading up to this day as contingencies of the verdict debated.

The net was surfed and information gleaned from medical journals to become educated on a prognosis. But, none of the options appealed to them. The couple hoped something new, but untried, was known by the doctor to exist, perhaps an alternative management for the condition. At this stage, the severity and grade of the tumor was speculative, based on data located. Every sliver of knowledge that could be uncovered was sought out to better understand the disease. But without early detection, the chances for a curing a tumor were slim.

The couple was in denial and not ready to grip its severity. No one wants to believe something dreadful could happen to them. Things like this occur to someone else.

Although terribly sick, Helen didn't believe the tumor was life threatening. She was convinced a cure was just around the corner, prayed for a miracle, a therapy, or anything the doctor would come up with to make it go away. Besides, it hadn't been that long ago she first met Matt, and fresh enough they had talked of a future together.

Was God punishing me for something? Helen wondered. This whole thing may be a mistake. Maybe the pictures got mixed-up and those aren't really mine.

Helen was trying to rationalize this as a hoax. Although, in her heart she knew what the doctor told her was true and the symptoms she experienced were real.

Garnered from research, she could identify with most characteristics of the disease. Along with the severe headaches, she felt sick to her stomach with frequent vomiting, had slurred speech, wasn't as laid back as usual and became easily irritated. Brain tumors can cause seizures and strokes, although she hadn't experienced these, yet, and felt relief in that respect. The problems stemmed from an increase in pressure and swelling in the surrounding tissue as the mass enlarged.

She became educated to the obscure fact that the actual cause of tumors was unknown. Whether these were genetic, or attributable to the environment was unclear.

At this stage, whatever triggered the thing wasn't important. Isolating a cause wouldn't make the problem disappear. Whatever happens in the future doesn't matter. It's the present, the here and now that's important. Her children and Matt are the only people affected, and she had to make the best of the conditions for their well-being.

"Hello," Doctor Kline said as he strolled through the door. "How are you feeling this afternoon, Helen?" His voice was upbeat, but his expression haggard and demeanor somber. In his left hand, he held a letter-size manila folder with notes about the medical tests. On this visit, he would jot down added comments inside the folder.

He also carried a larger sheath containing negatives, pictures of Helen's brain scan. Before sitting, he removed the celluloid sheets and shoved them under the clips on the light-box. The multitude of black and white images overwhelmed Helen, and she thought it would take someone with a lot of smarts to unravel these.

"Today is an okay day," replied Helen. "I've seen worse. How are you, Doctor Kline?" She interrupted before he could answer, and said, "What have you found out?" Small talk was minimal. Her intention was to remain focused on the issue. She wasn't there for a social visit.

The doctor began an immediate explanation of the report, and responded, "Unfortunately the biopsy did not provide us with good news."

These words captured Helen and Matt's attention instantly as they adjusted their posture, and sat upright with eyes locked on the doctor. Their hearing perked up to catch each phrase the physician relayed, and Matt eased his hand over to hold Helen's.

The doctor stood and pointed to the black and white images displayed as his commentary continued. "You can see here, the tumor has spread across the frontal lobe and rapidly expanding."

The couple watched as the tip of a pen floated across a large white splotch on the pictures. The negatives illustrated Helen's condition from numerous angles.

"The biopsy indicates the tumor is a Glioblastoma Multiforme, or a grade 4 tumor."

Helen recognized the jargon instantly. "That's serious. Are you sure?"

"Yes, we're certain," replied Dr. Kline.

"As large as it appears, is there any way to make it shrink? What's the possibility for surgery?" Helen's questions seemed to flow freely.

"With a tumor this large our options are few. Because it's so large, surgery isn't recommended. A surgical procedure would remove too much brain matter, and most likely affect your motor skills or bodily functions due to the location. As you can see here, the fingers are pronounced and too elongated to eradicate. We couldn't successfully remove all of it and trying to do so may cause more harm. Some portions of the tumor we couldn't reach and remnants would remain behind."

"Do you have an idea of what caused this?" asked Matt.

"Brain tumors are poorly understood. There is a distinct possibility the fall you had earlier may have triggered the growth. I've looked at the report made when you were in the hospital before. The tumor is in the same area of the brain where the injury occurred," the doctor said as he traced the outline on the film. "A growth wasn't obvious when pictures were made at the time you fell. Based on the timeline, if that prompted the tumor, it has developed very fast."

"What about Chemotherapy? Will that help?" asked Helen.

"Normally, we suggest Radiation be administered as a first choice to shrink a tumor. Chemotherapy would be a second therapy. But due to the vastness and its position, we see no long-term benefit from either Radiation or Chemotherapy."

"What are you telling me, doctor?" asked Helen. "Do you mean there's no way to shrink this thing?"

The physician hesitated, looked at the floor, and remarked, "None that will be effective."

"So you're telling me there is no treatment," responded the patient. "What happens next?"

"We could try Radiation, and then Chemo. These may help for a while. But, the treatments may also drastically affect your quality of life."

"When you say long-term, how much time are you talking about? What do you mean, exactly?"

The physician looked pale, stammered, and said "The size and location of the tumor leads us to believe you have about three months to live, maybe as much as nine months at the present rate of growth."

Helen stared at the doctor when his words came out and she was speechless. Her remaining time on earth was reduced to a timeframe of a few months, and her mind was in a struggle to accept the inevitable. Running through her head was the effect this would have on her children.

I don't feel like I'm dying, Helen thought. Sure, I have a few headaches and some other aches and pains, but who doesn't? But, how am I supposed to feel when somebody says that you'll be dead in one hundred and twenty days. That's one fourth of a year. I won't see Christmas with the kids.

Tears flowed as the words hit home. Matt placed his arm around Helen, squeezed her hand and kissed it.

"What can I expect if I have the Radiation and Chemo, doctor?" asked Helen.

"Optimistically, those treatments may give you a few extra months, maybe as much as a year. There are no guarantees," responded the doctor.

"What happens if I don't have the treatment," Helen asked.

"In its present state, as the tumor continues to amplify, you'll experience other symptoms associated with the disease, weakness, loss of bodily functions, and you could have a stroke. Your overall health will continue to decline and should do so in proportion to the tumor's growth. Presently, it seems out of control, although, Radiation and Chemo could put the brakes on and slow it a bit. We really don't know. For the long run, the prognosis doesn't look good. I'm sorry. I wish I had better news."

* * * *

Helen was numb. How was she supposed to react when someone says you'll be dead in a few months? She stared at the wall but saw nothing. She was devastated by what the doctor had told her, and thought about Michael and Samantha.

What will happen to them? Helen wondered. They've already lost their father, and now their mother will be gone. Where will they go? Who will care for them, and wipe their runny noses or bandage their knees when they fall and are scratched up? Who will be there when they graduate from college or get married? Dammit, I won't be around to see any of that. Life is so unfair.

Should I ask Matt to be both father and mother? Taking on that kind of responsibility is too much to ask of anybody, but my options are limited. What other choice do I have?

Overwhelmed by the doctor's comments, Helen was a lifeless statue, unable to move. She was absorbed in thought, concerned with how the children will be affected and what has to be done to protect them.

I've got a lot of decisions to make soon while I can still think, and have the ability to make choices or understand what I'm doing. There will come a time when I won't be able to do any of that. Who'll make them for me then? I need to do something to protect Mike and Sam. But what's that? Maybe the Radiation and Chemo would be a good idea. Those treatments may buy me a few more months.

Her thoughts rambled for she was troubled. Realizing something had to be in place for the children after she was gone, she had to face the disease head-on before it handled her, regardless of Radiation or Chemotherapy.

At this moment, she recalled the comment Jerry made in the dream, *"I'll see you soon."*

TWENTY-ONE

On the way home, Helen was stoic and rode in silence. No comments were made about the doctor's account or depiction of what would be forthcoming. Matt tried to strike up a conversation and spark a discussion about anything, but Helen was in a world of silence, and gazed out the window as the landscape flew by.

When she arrived home and stumbled through the door, she called to her children to take them in her arms and hold them. As they scrambled down the stairs, she hugged and held them tight, snug against her breast. A realization this may be one of the last few times she would have enough strength to embrace them hit home. She squeezed them so tight Michael complained, "Stop, mom. You're choking me."

"I'm sorry," she said smothering both with kisses. "I love you guys so much. I just want you to know it."

"Love you, too, mom," the children managed to get out through an abundance of tangled arms and kisses.

Catching his breath, Michael asked, "What did that stupid doctor tell you?"

"It's not important, I'll tell you later. How about let's go to the orchard. Do you want to?"

She ambled leisurely to her favorite spot while the children ran ahead. Helen watched as they played in the tall grass between the trees lined in long rows. Looking on, she smiled as they scurried about and crawled over branches, each chasing the other through the dense foliage.

I wonder who they'll resemble when they're older. Will Michael be tall? His father was. Will his hair remain blond, I hope so. That hair color looks good on him. I wonder if he'll take after his dad. That wouldn't be such a bad thing. Jerry was nice-looking, and I imagine Michael will be handsome. He's a good-looking boy now. I hope he doesn't inherit his father's craving for alcohol. That would be a disaster. But, if he continues to watch out for his younger sister like he does now that would be a blessing.

Sam will be a beautiful young woman when she grows up. She'll be a knock out with her long blonde hair, and eyes as blue as the sky. The boys will chase her, she'll flirt and drive them crazy, and then won't give them the time of day. Knowing Samantha, I believe she'll be picky and wait for just the right one. She's fairly self-reliant. I have no doubt she'll be confident and independent. She already is, and knows exactly what she wants, and then goes after it. Surely, her nose will be like mine instead of her father's. His had a small knot on the bridge.

"Hey, may I join you?" asked Matt.

Helen was in a trance but snapped to reality when Matt spoke. She felt queasy and could tell a headache was coming on.

"Hey yourself," she said.

"Have you said anything to the kids?"

"Not yet. I've got to do some thinking first and decide what it is I want them to know, at least initially. I don't want to tell them more than they can handle."

"Maybe you should agree to go ahead with the treatment the doctor suggested. You might live a lot longer than what the doctor told you. He doesn't know everything. Have you considered getting a second opinion?"

"I've thought about both of those possibilities. I just need a little while to consider the options and decide what would be best for the kids. You haven't told me how you feel about all this. Did what the doctor say scare you off? You know," Helen paused to carefully consider the words she was about to use. "As I told you the other day, you don't have to stick around for what I'll be going through. This will be a huge burden for anybody to take on. Things will get a lot worse and I'll understand if you don't want to hang around."

Matt turned to look at Helen. He gazed deep into her eyes and hesitated before responding, "Just where would I go? I told you before that I love you, and want to spend the rest of my life here with you, even if it's only a short while. It doesn't matter to me if you're sick. I love you because you're who you are, not the condition your body's in, or how long you'll live. You're a good person Helen, and you don't give yourself enough credit. So, you're not chasing me off that easily. I'll take whatever I can get whether it's for a day, a week, or a hundred years, I don't care. Whatever that doctor said doesn't change anything for me. Besides, someone has to be here for Michael and Samantha."

"Matthew Walker, where did you come from? You're almost too good to be true. How would you feel about adopting Michael and Samantha?" Helen blurted out instinctively.

Matt hesitated, looked at Helen and thought about what she'd asked. He then glanced to where the children were playing, dropped his head and paused, deep in contemplation. After several seconds, he looked at Helen and replied, "I would consider it an honor to be their father, and I'm flattered. I feel humble that you asked, but I'm not so sure I'm up to the task. How do you think the kids would feel?"

"Michael and Samantha already love you as if you were their father. I'm sure they would be keen on the idea. Let's ask them." Helen yelled out, "Hey, kids, come over here." The children sprinted to the bench where the couple was sitting, and their mother asked, "How would you guys like for Matt to be your new father?"

"Yeah, yippee," the children shrieked, jumping up and down as they cheered, then scurried off through the trees once again.

"I'm glad they've got all that energy, a lot more than I do," remarked Helen. "I'm beginning to feel a little tired, and my head is starting to spin. I've got to lie down. I'll call the estate planner first thing in the morning to get the ball rolling on the adoption."

* * * *

During a meeting with the expert, Helen explained the health issues the doctor had informed her about. Over the next week Helen was inundated with drafts and redrafts of documents prepared for her demise and the children's future. Guardianship, Adoption, Will, Trust, the papers mounted and the pages seemed endless.

She wanted these completed in a hurry before her memory began to fade and thoughts became muddled. With the documents finalized, Matt took Helen to pen her signature on the forms.

Now this was behind her, life and the future of the children were solely in the hands of Matthew Walker.

In the mornings, Helen awoke to drums pounding, complemented by vertigo and vomiting. As the days progressed, the affliction escalated in proportion to a decline in stamina. Matt attended her needs throughout each ordeal to be certain she had proper care.

Painkillers helped to some extent, but even these were declining in effectiveness, although a cool washcloth provided comfort. Throwing up, he wiped her face, cleaned her after being soiled, and helped her bathe and dress. Her motor activities were slowly being robbed of simple functions, yet Matt made existing bearable. With an escalation of the condition, the rituals of one day stretched out a slight bit longer than the previous. Matt sensed the mass was expanding and wondered how long Helen's body could endure the constant abuse.

After providing for her children and possessions, she could now acquiesce to the remainder of life and whatever insults her body would take, regardless of how short the time. Each day she felt more fragile and anemic. She sensed the tumor growing and just as sure it was taking over her whole being with control diminishing.

On days of feeling stronger, she would stroll to the orchard to sit, look around, think and pray. Praying was something she did a lot lately with plenty of time on hand for that now. While the illness hastened to progress and destroy her body, she wanted her soul ready for the hereafter.

Throughout life, she attended Mass each Sunday. With faltering health she could no longer go to church services, therefore, a minister brought the Eucharist to her home. Anointed, she knew her soul was ready for the next life. The faith she received as a child and anchored her in life was helping her transition over rough times to become her bedrock. There was no reason she knew that this same devotion shouldn't accompany her into death.

Why has God chosen to cut my life short, she questioned. Although she wasn't angry, she thought, I just wish I could be around longer and see the kids grow up. I'm going to miss them so much.

"May I sit?" asked Matt.

"For the price of a kiss," Helen demanded.

"I think that can be arranged," and leaned over to pucker up. "My, it's beautiful out here this time of day."

"It's lovely here any time," Helen affirmed.

"Have you decided against the Chemo?" asked Matt.

"I don't see there'd be any benefit. There's no reason to prolong the inevitable. I can tell this thing is getting bigger, fast, and there's no reason to give you and the kids false hope."

"You might live a while longer," replied Matt.

"My health will not improve with additional treatments. It's just not going to happen. All medicine can do now is help to curb the pain and even that is becoming iffy. The few good days I have left I want to enjoy the children without complications of added treatments that will be useless."

"Helen, will you marry me?"

"Matt, you know I love you, but why would you want to marry me now? My health is failing," Helen remarked. "A marriage to me would be a sham and in name only. We wouldn't have a real marriage, and I couldn't be a wife to you."

"I've loved you from the first moment I laid eyes on you in the coffee shop," Matt said. "I don't love you any less just because you're sick. Please marry me and be my wife, even if it is for just a short while."

Helen paused and thought about her first marriage. She remembered the abuse and the drunken, violent behavior of her husband, and realized Matt was nothing like him. She now understood this was what held her back all this time.

She had already placed the children and her life in his hands. She thought about how much she loved him and also believed he'd been sent by a higher power, then replied, "Okay, Matt, I'll marry you. That's something else I should have done long ago. Make the arrangements." Helen had yielded.

"And thank you. Thank you for all the little things you do," remarked Helen. "Loving me, taking care of the kids, cleaning up when I'm sick, cooking, and keeping the house in order. All the things I can't even think about doing. You never ask for anything in return. Your quiet strength is the pillar I lean on for support, and I don't have any idea what we would have done if you hadn't been here. So all I can do is to say thanks, and I love you."

* * * *

Cheerfully the sun rose, birds were chirping, and no clouds spoiled the sky, but Helen awoke in a stupor, confined to her bed. Lack of energy, nausea, and headaches plagued her when she awoke, and then fell back asleep until early afternoon.

Between attending to the patient and watching the children run through the yard, Matt juggled chores as he worked around the house to keep things functioning. Because of the illness, he had taken some long overdue time off to attend to Helen and the children.

When Helen awoke, again she asked to go to her bench in the orchard.

"Are you strong enough for that," Matt asked.

"This may be the last time I get to see all the beauty. Please take me there, and let me sit for a while," pleaded Helen.

"Would you want me to stay with you for a while?" he asked.

"No, just let me sit alone, quietly. You can come back later to get me," replied the woman.

"It's supposed to rain," said Matt.

"A little rain won't hurt. I'll take my umbrella," replied Helen.

The woman was content sitting on the bench, watching the wind whip through the trees and toss leaves through the breeze, as fruit fell all around her from branches overhead. She gave thanks for the good life she had, yet still couldn't figure out why God had chosen to cut it short.

"I finally got you alone," a voice from the past resonated.

Helen looked up at the man and asked, "Do I know you?"

"You should bitch," replied the man. "You ruined my life and now I'm going to destroy yours."

"I'm dying," replied Helen. "There's nothing you can do to me that's not going to happen anyway."

"But, I'm going to get the satisfaction of watching you die," the man responded.

Helen's eyes couldn't focus, but unafraid she asked, "How do you know me?"

"You're the bitch that stole our money," the voice replied.

Helen concentrated and attempted to identify the voice but couldn't place it. "I'm sorry, I don't know who you are or what you're talking about."

"Don't play dumb with me. You know damn well the cops have been hunting me all over the world, but I came back to finish the job those guys in jail couldn't do," came the response.

"I don't know who you are or have a clue what you're talking about, but if you plan to hurt me I'll be dead soon anyway, so save yourself the trouble," Helen responded.

"I want to see you die for all the agony you put us through."

"I don't know what you're talking about," replied the woman.

"I could be living large with all the money you took from me. Now you're going to pay," the man said as he removed a pistol from his pocket and pointed it at Helen.

BAM, BAM.

TWENTY-TWO

Affixed to the crest of Helen's casket was a crucifix the priest tendered to Michael and Samantha at the conclusion of the service. Stirred by the episode, Matt was dawdling in the fog of events that raced swiftly after she passed.

Helen arranged the interment while she remained lucid and possessed acumen for sound choices. Selection of a funeral director and accoutrements, together with a gravesite carefully approved, she was prepared for life's ending.

For her final rest she designated a small knoll overlooking the orchard. This was a small slice of earth cherished since childhood, and here she would share the natural beauty forever with the sun and stars.

Living a modest life, she planned a simple ceremony, discouraging an elaborate affair. With the announcement of her demise, fame turned an uncomplicated occasion into an elaborate event as throngs of mourners streamed in to bid farewell.

During the service, Matt was in a trance while memories of good times with his friend flooded over him. In his mind, she was alive and vibrant as if watching a rerun of a home movie. In his reminiscence, she was healthy as he recalled their first meeting at the coffee shop, together with scores of interludes holding hands and rambling beneath the trees.

A foot in the orchard was a journey to heaven, or what the human mind could envision was a state of perpetual bliss. Offered was the fusion of peace and tranquility with one simple step. The power invoked from this unpretentious postage stamp of earth ensnared a soul and possessed it as if passing through a portal.

As the service ended, well-wishers gathered at graveside and funneled past the wooden box for a final touch. Kisses on the hand, and then conveyed to the box containing Helen's lifeless body, was the final show of respect. Mourners dabbed at dampened faces to forestall a semblance of rocks below a waterfall, but this didn't work.

After the final prayer, admirers hung around, milled about, talked, laughed, and made plans with forgotten friends to remain in touch. Many unseen in decades, the empty promises to stay connected were certain to be broken. As the event faded, life would return to normal and thoughts of Helen would soon pale, but fondly recalled if a certain event jogged a memory.

Matt and the children were statues, stone-faced and detached. His arms were around Sam and Mike to console them holding them close to his heart, fearing they might somehow vanish. He needed the warmth of the small bodies as assurance they were with him. Weeping, the arms of Sam and Mike also encircled their newest parent, and ambivalent yet terrified of their destiny.

Oblivious to the chatter carried on, Matt's face was drawn, ashen, and weary. He aged in the few short days once the activities were set in place and scooted past. The hours ran together as if in a stupor and he functioned on coffee and adrenaline.

The director explained to Matt how graveside services would be conducted and brought to a conclusion. Plain expressions that held little meaning at the time, therefore, pigeonholed as unforeseen on the horizon.

But the schedule fell in place as promised, yet Matt remained stationary, seemingly unable to move. Reality had to check in while the family remained in a stupor over the event. They were unprepared to say farewell although a man tugged at Matt's shirtsleeve to remind him the moment for goodbye was upon them.

Cut short, Helen was too young to die although her life wasn't wasted. As the struggles and hardships she endured turn to ashes, planted were seeds of excellence to flourish.

Surviving an abusive marriage, she gave life to two beautiful children, and her vigilance secured thousands of jobs. Tenacious for the truth, she was a formidable adversary with an unrelenting determination to catch the men destroying her employer. She was hell bent on removing the criminals from society for the damages they inflicted. Facing these obstacles undeterred took guts, determination, and a sense of purpose, a perfect description for a hero.

Helen lived with a positive attitude and a smile. Rather than faultfinding or dredging up evil from a person's soul, she searched out goodness along life's path. Her interest in the less fortunate was obvious, often without concern for her own safety.

Endeavors that occurred in her few short years were like cream rising to the top. Traits she possessed set her apart and made her admirable. With a show of unwavering love for her neighbor, Matt was certain God would address her warmly when she cashed in her ticket at the Pearly Gates.

Again, a hand firmly placed on his shoulder told Matt it was time to go. The inevitable had arrived. Ignoring the pigeonhole wasn't a possibility any longer.

* * * *

After Helen's diagnosis of the advanced stage of cancer the future appeared dubious because of her impending demise, therefore, the court permitted a recording of her deposition. Testimony electronically captured would validate removal of the disc from Howard Jenkins's office. The DVDs and deposition would be key evidence and the primary focus for a conviction.

With death looming, factual statements from Helen authenticated the discs, and substantiated how they originated and came into her possession. Her commentary regarding the conversations of the men would give credibility and first-hand support when presented to a jury.

Tying the cause of the tumor to her fall, the prosecutor intended to humanize the damage inflicted by the perpetrators. Men in a position of authority possessing a responsibility to protect the company had failed in their duty. The evidence offered to the jury should seal the fate of the criminals. Once convicted by testimony from the grave, Clark Ford, Gordon Compton, Eric Camp, and Howard Jenkins would pass their remaining days behind bars.

The Canadian Mounties alerted the FBI to a man crossing the border wanted for questioning in the Beeson theft. Locating him in Indiana, agents caught him shadowing the Faulkner property. And when Helen became vulnerable sitting in the orchard, the man approached and pulled a revolver from his pocket. When the agent detected the man had a gun, he fired his weapon. Leonard Busby was dead, slain by the FBI.

* * * *

Within days following Busby's attack, Matt strolled into Helen's bedroom to be certain she wasn't soiled or lying in vomit. Her breathing had slowed from its usual rhythm, but her temperature was slightly elevated.

As night approached, rain began to fall, lightly in the beginning, and increased in intensity bearing down on the shingled roof with a deafening rumble. Thunder rolled through the heavens and bolts of lightning brightened the sky. Through the windows the vivid flashes illuminated the old farmhouse. The clatter awoke Matt and he rolled over, looked out the window, and switched on the local radio station to determine if a tornado was passing through the area.

"Just an electrical storm," crackled the voice of the newscaster.

Matt strolled through the hallway to look in on the children, yet the storm hadn't awakened them. He pulled the blankets over them they kicked off, and left the door to their rooms ajar.

Meandering to Helen's room, he sensed she hadn't stirred. Her covers were unruffled and she hadn't moved from earlier in the evening. He leaned over, touched her face and found the body cold and clammy to touch, lifeless, and her breathing had ceased. Her skin felt plastic and unnatural when he placed his fingers to her neck and found no pulse. Tears welled up as he realized Helen's body finally gave out. Never again would they share the bench in the orchard.

Sitting on the side of her bed Matt bawled uncontrollably as teardrops flowed. The person he loved more than himself had died. He leaned over, kissed her on the cheek and said, "I love you, and may God be with you always."

Epilogue

The days crept following the funeral. Melancholy saturated the simplest activities. The sun rose and set but completing the basics became a chore. Matt sensed a break was essential and accompanied Michael and Samantha on an outing for a reading of Helen's last Will. He envisioned her words might pull the children from the doldrums.

Helen and Matt hadn't discussed exposing the children to the reading of the legal documents, but Matt deemed it important that someone besides him communicate her words. In time, the children might value what she prepared for their future. He realized at this early age they wouldn't comprehend the rudiments contained within the document, but confident they ultimately may appreciate a mother's wisdom. This was a formality for him. When she consummated the pages he was present and knew the content.

After a reading of their mother's wishes was concluded, a few simple questions were asked, Michael and Samantha thanked the man, and the group rose to leave.

"Matt," said the specialist. "After Helen signed the documents, she asked me to give these to you and the children after the funeral."

Handed to Michael, Samantha, and Matt were three sealed envelopes. Scrawled across the face of each was the name of its owner in Helen's undeniable handwriting.

"Were you aware these existed?" he asked.

Excited, Matt exclaimed, "No, I didn't have a clue. Thank you so much." To Mike and Sam, he said, "Let's go home kids and we'll read these tonight."

In anticipation of words from their mother, the journey was unusually quiet. With the surprise from Helen, the mood of the group had shifted to be more promising.

Arriving at the farm, the children hurried through the few chores they had, ever mindful of the messages that awaited them for perusal before bedtime. As the day wound down, they pestered Matt about the envelopes and asked to open them.

"Yeah, I want to read mine first," insisted Samantha.

The children cuddled up on the couch preparing to hear soothing words from their mother. Slicing open the envelope, Matt removed Samantha's letter and began to read it aloud. Upon seeing Helen's gentle script, Matt reflected on when she could have composed the letters, and struck by the beautiful scroll of her hand. He had seen this tender scrawl many times, recognized it well, and felt a tug at his heart.

* * * *

To Samantha, my darling baby girl,

Samantha, you were a second child, but never second in my heart. The day you were born, I was so thankful and felt gratified to accept a beautiful and healthy baby to call my daughter. Words do not exist that can express the happiness you've brought to life, emotions transcend language. As a child you have always been tender, loving, and with an undeniably sweet temperament. A room is brighter with you in it. Hold on to this charm as an adult and your rewards will be abundant.

I've told you many times, but this letter is to confirm my love for you. A mother's love is immeasurable and my affection will endure long after I've gone. I won't be here to experience those special occasions you will encounter. God called me to Heaven so my body would no longer be sick. But my spirit, and that of your father's, will be present to share those special moments.

Matt is your new father and will be your protector now that I am gone. You probably already know this, but he is a good person. Thoughtful and kind, he will make a wonderful dad. He will need your support so help him as much as you can. Boys don't know much about housekeeping or a lot of other things.

You are a lovely young girl, and I'm certain one day you will be a beautiful woman. Make choices carefully. You may not be in charge of the path God has in store for you, above all in love, but don't allow your heart to overshadow reason and common sense. If you choose to marry, my spirit will be with you on your wedding day. I hope you feel me beside you.

In a few short years, you will have many questions while becoming a woman. Don't be embarrassed or afraid to ask your new dad anything. He will help you with the answers.

Remember, I will be watching over you. If you want to talk, come to the orchard. My spirit will be there waiting. Love you and will miss you always.

Until forever, your mother,
Helen Faulkner

* * * *

Matt handed the letter to Sam. She held it in her small hands, and looked upon it as if a gem.

"I'll treasure this forever," she remarked.

"Let's do mine now," said Michael as he handed his letter to Matt.

Matt opened the envelope, handed it back to Michael, and remarked, "Why don't you try reading your own letter?"

The boy looked at Matt oddly, took the piece of paper and began to speak slowly, stumbling over the words.

* * * *

To my wonderful son Michael,

Knowing you, I'm sure you let your sister read her letter first. That makes you special. As you become older, continue to be her protector and watch out for Samantha. Little sisters will always need an older brother even though she may tell you she doesn't.

Before you were born, I never realized that the feelings for another could run so deep. As a new mom, having a new baby fascinated me. But at the same time, I was fearful. Afraid of hurting you if I held you too tight, although, I loved you dearly. Feeding you was the best part of my day. I had you to myself and could gaze into your sweet face and watch you change before my eyes.

When you looked up at me with plump, rosy cheeks that filled out with each passing day, your eyes seemed to twinkle. Your expressions were in constant flux, and that same transformation amazes me still, as I write this letter and watch you grow taller and closer to becoming an adult.

Before too many years, you'll be a man. Unfortunately, I won't be around to share those special moments in your future. God has other plans. I've gone to heaven so my body wouldn't be sick, and once again I'll see your father.

For the short time you've been my son I've been blessed. You have brought so much joy to my life that without you and Sam it would have been empty.

I'm sure you'll find the perfect girl and have lots of babies someday, at least I hope so. I also hope you'll remember me and understand that I loved you more than my own life.

Matt is your new dad, and he will look out for you now that I am gone. Be a good son for he is a good man, thoughtful, kind, and will make a wonderful father. He promised he would take you fishing.

If you ever want to talk, come to the orchard. My spirit will be there waiting. I love you.

Until forever, your mother,
Helen Faulkner

* * * *

Concluding the letter, Michael sat in silence and looked vacantly at the paper, wishing his mother was with them.

"Let's read your letter now, Matt," Samantha said.

"Call him dad. He's our daddy now," responded Michael.

"I think it's time for you kids to be in bed. We'll read mine later."

After a little grumbling, the children scurried off carrying their letters. Once Michael and Samantha were asleep, Matt fingered his letter as he sat on the couch and pondered if he was ready for the words inside. He had to be alone when he read Helen's final message. The wounds of her passing were still fresh and as raw as if he'd fallen and skinned his knee on the sidewalk.

He longed to see her smile, her beautiful face, her delicious blue eyes, and remembered how she always smelled of Lilacs. Now when he came into the house there was emptiness. A void existed because she was no longer there eager to greet him. When he awoke, there was a vacancy he couldn't fill. He caught himself looking for her throughout the day, and missed the attention they gave each other before bedtime. This left a gapping hole in the fabric of his soul.

Would the hurt ever get any easier or go away? he wondered.

His hands shook, and tears flowed in rivulets as he looked at the envelope from Helen.

Am I ready to read this? he wondered. Should I read it?

Trembling in anticipation, questions filled him for he was insecure of whether he was up to the task.

Tomorrow. No, I'll wait until tomorrow, he rationalized. She loved the sunrise. I'll go and read it in the orchard.

* * * *

Early the following morning, Matt strolled into Michael and Samantha bedrooms to check on them. Both children were sleeping peacefully. The morning had a chill in the air as he pulled the covers up over them, and then meandered to the kitchen. Coffee was dripping in a pot in no time, and he filled his cup to the brim. In the crisp morning air, with the envelope from Helen clutched tightly in his grip, and feeling like a kid with a new toy, he found his way to her bench.

This had to be done while he was alone, before the children arose. Otherwise, he feared, he would never finish it without them watching him fall apart.

Sitting on the bench they shared on many occasions, he glanced at the envelope with his name scrolled across its face and pulled out the neatly folded sheets. Along with the papers, a card fell out with words and a group of numbers inscribed. Laying it aside, he began to read the letter.

* * * *

My Dearest Matt,

Trying to put into words how I feel about you has always been difficult. I've told you many times I love you, and wanted us to always be together. But, these words are deficient in revealing how deep from within my being these sympathies stem. I love you are three simple words, but they cannot do justice to the true meaning of the phrase.

I realized almost too late how you completed my life. Never had I experienced true happiness until you came along. Your touch set my soul ablaze, a fire that was unquenchable and provided the embers to ignite a flame of desire within my heart.

Life isn't a chance encounter. Our first meeting was no accident. You were an angel sent to fill the emptiness in my heart.

Unfortunately, a long togetherness wasn't meant for us, God had other ideas. But in this world, you were my knight in shining armor, my hero, and the rock that I could always lean on. Michael, Samantha, and you filled my days with happiness and made them complete.

You are the most wonderfully unselfish person I have ever met. Without you at my side, I can only imagine how our family would have functioned through all the turmoil during the short time we've known each other. Thank you for being my foundation.

In just a few short years, the children have had an arduous task of hanging on to parents. First their father dies, now me, so Michael and Samantha are in your care. I carried them into this world, but it is your duty to see them bloom. It is up to you to carry the torch for their well-being and put them on a path to success, one you are uniquely equipped to handle with ease.

A future without a mother will be difficult with your patience tested often. Whether the family endures is up to you. Attitude will be the cohesiveness that holds the family together. Please be firm but gentle.

Someday, perhaps, another woman will come along to spark your attention. I know you want a soul mate and partner by your side so you won't be alone. When this happens, you have my blessings. As I've told the children, choose wisely, and pray to make the best choice. The woman will not only be your wife, but also Mike and Sam's new mother. Therefore, she must be up to the task.

I will miss seeing the children become adults with all the good things life offers. But my spirit will be there for those special moments. Thanks to Beeson, funds are set aside to use as you see fit for necessities and the children's education. You will use it wisely I'm certain. The enclosed card has the bank information and passwords to gain access.

I'm sure you're reading this letter sitting on our bench. That's what I would expect so return often. Remember that I will always be here waiting. When you need a friend, come to the orchard. I'll love you for eternity,

Your friend, companion,
and adoring wife,
Helen Faulkner

THE END

Writing fiction for a broad audience is a tricky assignment. As this story developed, the concept was to provide a narrative which appeals to the avid readers seeking a good ending. I hope I've succeeded in this endeavor, and you enjoyed the book and had as much fun reading it as I did writing it.

Thanks for supporting my passion,
dlhayden

About the author:

dlhayden is married and lives in the Indianapolis, Indiana area. *The Orchard* is his second effort at writing fiction as a novelist. *The Smell Test,* published in 2005, was his first. A yet unnamed book is in the works. His e-mail address is dhayden@AAMZPublishing.com.

Connect Online:

My blog: http://dlhayden.wordpress.com
Facebook: http://facebook.com/dlhayden9368
Twitter: http://twitter.com/dlhayden9368

http://www.AAMZPublishing.com

www.ingramcontent.com/pod-product-compliance
Lightning Source LLC
Chambersburg PA
CBHW051239260626

47162CB00002B/516